THEY WERE
THE RAILROAD BUILDERS ...

GLENN GILCHRIST—A Harvard-educated engineer, he believed in doing whatever it took to get the job done—even if that meant putting his own neck in danger.

JOSHUA HOOD—Chief scout and meat hunter for the railroad, he knew the plains as well as any white man. But even he could be caught off guard by a beautiful woman . . .

MEGAN O'CONNELL—She'd followed the railroad west, looking for a better life. Now the men wanted her to stay behind—but nobody could give Megan orders . . .

CAPTAIN MEDGAR TANEY—Commandant of Fort Kearney. His orders were to protect the railroad from the Indians—no matter how many he had to slaughter to do it.

THE CASEMENT BROTHERS—Two men whose drive and ambition belied their lack of stature. The railroad was their ticket to untold wealth, and they meant to collect every red cent they could.

LIAM O'CONNELL—Leaving Boston behind, he traveled west with his sister, searching for adventure. He found more than he bargained for—in the form of an enemy's bullet.

GENERAL DODGE—He'd made a treaty with the Sioux to let the railroad pass over their lands. Now he had to convince his own people to keep the peace . . .

RACHEL FOREMAN—She'd faced her share of dangers during the trek westward. They'd all be worth it—if she came out of it with the man she wanted.

LADDY SULLIVAN—Seventeen years old, and just off the boat from Ireland, he'd never seen an Indian before. Next thing he knew he was in the middle of a massacre . . .

LT. EDWARD WOLLINS—He was an officer and a gentleman—and ready to challenge any man alive to prove his honor.

*   *   *

Turn to the back for an exciting look at book three
in the *Rails West!* saga . . .
WYOMING TERRITORY,
which continues the inspiring tale of the mighty builders
of the nation's railroads!

The *Rails West!* series from Jove

RAILS WEST!
NEBRASKA CROSSING

RAILS WEST!
Nebraska Crossing

FRANKLIN CARTER

JOVE BOOKS, NEW YORK

If you purchased this book without a cover, you should be aware that this book is stolen property. It was reported as "unsold and destroyed" to the publisher, and neither the author nor the publisher has received any payment for this "stripped book."

NEBRASKA CROSSING

A Jove Book / published by arrangement with
the author

PRINTING HISTORY
Jove edition / October 1993

All rights reserved.
Copyright © 1993 by Jove Publications, Inc.
This book may not be reproduced in whole
or in part, by mimeograph or any other means,
without permission. For information address:
The Berkley Publishing Group,
200 Madison Avenue, New York, New York 10016.

ISBN: 0-515-11205-4

A JOVE BOOK®
Jove Books are published by The Berkley Publishing Group,
200 Madison Avenue, New York, New York 10016.
JOVE and the "J" design are trademarks belonging to Jove Publications, Inc.

PRINTED IN THE UNITED STATES OF AMERICA

10 9 8 7 6 5 4 3 2 1

CHAPTER
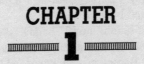
1

Indians! Real Indians. Wild Indians. Laddy Sullivan's eyes went wide, and he began to tremble. With excitement more than fear, but aye, there was fear there too. Never mind what was said about a truce having been arranged with the savages. These were the first true, fierce, wild and free Indians Laddy Sullivan—it was really Laechmon Shay Sullivan, but that was a case of the name being larger than the lad and who needed that—ever saw, and he was as fascinated now as a wee hen peering into a snake's narrow eyes. Danger or no, the fascination of it was hypnotic. And immobilizing. Laddy was frozen where he stood, unable to move or to pull his eyes away. Indians! Real ones. Sweet Jesus, Mary and Joseph!

It was difficult to see from so great a distance, but he did not believe the Indians were painted. Did they not paint themselves, then, as he'd been told? They were armed, though. They weren't so terrible far off that he couldn't see that. The Indians rode small, potbellied ponies, and they carried lances and bows held casually in their hands or laid light and balanced across their laps on the ponies' . . . the ponies' . . . it took him a moment to call the unfamiliar word to mind . . . the ponies' withers, that was it, withers. Laddy was but three months off the boat, and there was much he had yet to learn. The subject of wild Indians was but one of many in which his education proved lacking.

1

"D'you see 'em, Barney, do ye?" he whispered.

"I see 'em, boy," Barney said in a tight, grim voice. "I see the sons o' red bitches."

"Should we be runnin' now?" Laddy asked with a bit of a catch in his throat. For in truth there was no place they might run to for safety. Barney was stickman and Laddy his helper, and the two of them were out a good three hundred yards ahead of the nearest other pair in the advance survey party. There were eighteen men in this crew and a thousand more behind them. But the remaining sixteen of this particular crew were too far off to count on for help. And the thousand and more others that made up the grading and support and construction gangs of the grand Union Pacific Railroad? Why, they were a hundred miles or more back. Much help they would be if these wild Indians proved hostile. Laddy's throat was dry and scratchy, and there was a blockage that kept him from being able to swallow.

The Indians moved toward them in plain sight. A quarter mile away or more still. But too close. Much too close. They rode loose and easy atop their stocky ponies, weapons carried low, the bunch of them—there must have been a dozen warriors . . . no, fifteen; Laddy counted and there were definitely fifteen of them coming slow and steady across the dry, wildflower-studded grass—strung out in no particular formation that Laddy could detect.

"Whatever you do, kid, don't run. Don't set them off."

Barney's advice seemed silly in the extreme, but Laddy accepted it. He more or less had to. He was sure if he tried to run he would find himself unable to, was sure his muscles would refuse his commands whatever he might will himself to do, and it seemed preferable at the moment to stand and do nothing than to try to move and not be capable of doing it.

He could hear hoofbeats even though the Indians were still quite distant, and that surprised him. Then he realized the horse he could hear was behind him. And it was no Indian who rode it, for Laddy could hear the creak of leather and tink of chain that said it was an American horse with all the loud accoutrements that implied. Indians, he'd been told, rode their ponies with only a pad and perhaps a rawhide thong for equipage. In another few minutes he should be able to see for himself the truth of that claim. If he should live so long. Sweat beaded cold and greasy on his forehead, and there was a taste of bile at the back of his tongue.

"It looks like we'll have company for lunch," a voice came from the direction of the saddle sounds. Immediately Laddy felt better, for he recognized the voice. It was Assistant Chief Surveyor Mr. Glenn Gilchrist who'd ridden out to join them here and to stand beside them to meet the wild Indians.

Mr. Gilchrist's presence released Laddy from the frozen thrall fear had imposed on him, and he was again able to move. And to breathe. He turned and gratefully looked up at this tall boss with a highborn gentleman's fine manners but with eyes that were kind and gentle. It was Mr. Gilchrist who'd given Laddy this job, ignoring the liabilities of youth and inexperience and trusting Laddy to give an honest day's work in exchange for an honest day's pay. Laddy was only seventeen and small for his age, his people on the wee side to start with and his particular growth not helped by the failure of the potato crop back home. No other had been willing to take on a lad who was so undeniably slight of stature and lacking of experience. But Mr. Gilchrist had. Mr. Gilchrist believed in him. Laddy felt a particular affinity, therefore, to Mr. Gilchrist. A particular sort of trust. He stood now with considerably less fear as Mr. Gilchrist reined his handsome yellow horse to a halt and watched the approach of the Indians.

"Is it a fight we'll be havin', Mr. Gilchrist, sir?" Laddy asked.

"Not at all," the fine gentleman assured him. "We are under a truce with the Sioux now, remember? They are welcome in our camp. We'll feed them and talk a little while, and then they'll go on about their hunting or whatever business it is they have here. We've nothing to fear from them, nor they from us."

Laddy shivered. "It isn't them bein' scared of us that I'm thinkin' about, sir. Killin' is their business. That's what I was told. Killin' railroaders 'specially."

"We've lost men to Indian attacks in the past, Laddy, that's true enough. Entirely too many. That's why Mr. Hood and General Dodge met with the Sioux leaders. They parted friends. The Sioux will no longer make war on our people. And we in our turn will make them welcome in our camps." Mr. Gilchrist smiled. "The general feels it is much better to feed the Indians than to fight them. I agree. A few barrels of food are more easily replaced than the lives of good men."

"Are wild savages t' be trusted, Mr. Gilchrist, sir?"

"Mr. Hood says their word is good. I suppose he should know. He used to live with one of the tribes. It wasn't the Sioux he lived with, but he knows them. And he knows the sign language all the Plains tribes use. He says we can take these people at their word. Their fear is that they can't trust us. That is what we have to prove here today. Mind you make them welcome."

"Yes, sir. But you'll forgive me if I'm hopin' Mr. Hood knows what he's saying." Laddy knew who Mr. Hood was. That would be Mr. Joshua Hood, a leather- and buckskin-clad frontiersman who appeared as wild as any Indian and who was in charge of the railroad's scouts and meat hunters. All the lads on the line idolized Mr. Hood and his scouts as dashing, devil-may-care dandies. Dash in, aye, and twist the devil's tail. But when it came to solid, sensible judgment, then even a lad like Laddy would know that it was Mr. Gilchrist's word to be sworn to and not that of the more volatile Mr. Hood. And it was Mr. Hood who said these wild Indians were to be trusted.

Laddy gave Mr. Gilchrist a close look and was reassured to see that the gentleman was leaving his fine, brass-framed rifle in its leather keeper, and he wasn't paying any mind to the revolver that rested at his waist either. Mr. Gilchrist was trusting implicitly to the word of Mr. Hood. And that even though there was talk among some of the lads that Mr. Gilchrist and Mr. Hood were rivals for the affections of a certain lady.

Laddy had seen that certain lady and had to concede that she would be spoil well worth the contest. She'd come to Laddy's attention because she was the sister of the strapping American Irishman who among Mr. Joshua Hood's scouts was Laddy's particular idol, Liam O'Connell, late of Boston and now of the great and open plains of vast Nebraska. Liam had been wounded in a fight with Indians—a battle undertaken before Mr. Hood's treaty mission in the company of Union Pacific Chief Engineer Grenville Dodge—and it was to his sister's care that he was taken. It was when Laddy came round to give Liam a word of comfort that he first saw Liam's sister, Megan O'Connell. And no wonder a gentleman as fine as Mr. Gilchrist or a frontiersman as passionate as Mr. Hood would wish to court her. Megan was tall for a woman, with flaming red hair and a bold carriage about her. She had beauty, wit and courage. A man—or a boy—could see that quick enough. If things had been just

the least bit different, why, Laddy himself might have . . .
Ah, but things were only as they were. There was no point
to deluding himself about that, Laddy acknowledged now.
Better to think about wild Indians than the charms of Megan
O'Connell. Laddy was more apt to be accepted as a man
grown by standing firm in the face of these Indians than
by making a fool of himself chasing after Liam's big sister,
Megan.

"They look friendly enough," Barney said.

"Aye," Laddy agreed. "I'm seein' no paint. That's good,
ain't it?"

"They're just coming in to have a free lunch," Mr. Gilchrist
assured his crewmen, "like Mr. Hood and the general promised they could. Can you see those skin containers slung
behind them?"

"Aye."

"They carry their fighting duds in there. Mr. Hood asked
one to open his bag and show me. He had stoppered horn
vials of paint and a hat made of skin and feathers and ermine
tails, and he had a breastplate made of small bones and porcupine quills strung on sinew and some sort of talisman thing
in a pouch that he handled with special care and wouldn't
talk about. Mr. Hood said that could be something as simple
as a twist of grass, but whatever it was, it was very special,
very magical to the bearer, probably something suggested
to him in a trance or a vision. Anyway, if those men were
planning to attack us, their war bags would be empty now
and they would be wearing their paint."

"That's good t' know. I be thanking you."

"You're welcome, Laddy."

The Indians were closer now. The leaders of the group
were less than a hundred yards away, still riding forward
at a slow and steady gait. Their bows, Laddy could see

now, were unstrung. He found that particularly interesting because he hadn't known bows could be unstrung once they were made and did not understand why anyone would want to unstring them. He asked Mr. Gilchrist.

"The strings wear out rather quickly. They last longer— the bows do too—if they aren't under tension all the time."

"I should've figured that out, shouldn't I? I mean, it makes sense. I should've seen it."

Mr. Gilchrist smiled. "Then I should have seen it for myself too, but I didn't. Just like you, Laddy, I had to ask. That's how we all have to learn things. There's no shame in not knowing something, only in not bothering to learn."

Laddy grinned and was feeling quite comfortable now, in spite of everything, as he stood so close to Mr. Gilchrist while they waited for the Sioux warriors to reach them.

The Sioux were a sight. Lord, they were. They rode tall and proud, heads high and shoulders square, bending to no man. They were dark of body, dark of hair, dark of eye. Most of them wore little more than breechcloths, with perhaps a few ornaments woven into their braids or some necklaces and arm bands or other such adornments on their bodies.

Laddy would have expected them all to be as lean as wolfhounds, but they were not. Several of the men were quite roly-poly, and many of the rest were fairly flabby, their bellies bouncing with the movement of the ponies.

They were close enough now that Laddy could begin to observe them fairly well, one of them picking his nose while another chattered—nervously? It almost looked like it; could wild Indians be nervous about meeting white men? How odd to think that. A third Indian raised himself off his pony's back so he could scratch himself before settling back onto the grass-filled cloth pad that he was using for a saddle.

Now that they were coming closer, these wild Sioux warriors seemed . . . human. Less threatening, certainly, than Laddy would have believed possible.

Laddy turned his head to see if the others in the survey party were preparing for the arrival of their guests.

The road they were staking for the graders to prepare and the tie layers to build was out on the open grass. To the south less than half a mile was the barely visible dark foliage that marked the brushy, sporadically tree-lined course of the Platte River. Where the stakes were now being placed, the road would curve slightly to avoid a line of low ridges and turkey-foot coulees that broke up the flat prairie toward the north. The land here was not nearly so flat and table smooth as it appeared to be, and no one knew that better than the surveyors, whose job it was to maintain a nearly constant grade as the railroad right-of-way slowly, inexorably climbed ever higher, as it moved ever westward.

Laddy gave the terrain a brief glance and then looked overhead to the bright, buttermilk sky. A hawk wheeled and soared far above the earth, and closer, to the north, a pair of squawking thrushes burst into the air.

He looked back at the Sioux. The leader of the band was not more than sixty yards distant now. For some reason he had drawn rein and was peering with some alarm to his left, into the coulee from which the thrushes had risen a moment earlier. The warrior stiffened and wheeled, his jaw falling open and his head tipping back.

"What . . . ?"

Laddy never had time to finish his question.

There was a crash of noise from the mouth of the coulee, not thunder, more like a long rattle of dry sticks breaking.

Pale wisps lifted into the air, soft and white like tendrils of morning mist drifting over the River Shannon. But it couldn't be mist. This was midday and the country terrible dry.

There was the crackle of sudden sound, and then the leader of the Sioux swayed back, righted himself for an instant and then toppled face-forward to earth. The Indian hit the ground headfirst and made no move to catch himself or lessen the impact of his fall. Laddy took a step forward, thinking to see if the Indian was all right.

"What the . . . !"

"Get down, Mr. Gilchrist, take cover," Barney, an army veteran with a dozen fierce battles behind him, bellowed in quick reaction.

"But what . . . ?"

Another volley of fire burst from the mouth of the coulee, and four more Sioux were dropped from their ponies.

Before the survivors had time to gather their wits, a solid phalanx of blue-clad troopers on blood bay horses burst into view, and a bugle's brittle call danced on the dust-filled air.

Laddy stared in horror as the soldiers charged through the stunned Sioux, revolvers barking, gunsmoke swirling, sharp cries punctuating the ugly speech of the guns.

He saw one Indian shake his head and turn to face an oncoming soldier. The Indian's mouth worked as he said something Laddy was much too far away to hear, and he lifted a medallion from where it was suspended against his bare chest, turning it so the soldier could see. Or perhaps in the belief that the thing, whatever it was, would shield him from harm. Laddy would never know the Indian's intent. The soldier leveled his revolver and shot the Indian in the chest, his bullet striking roughly the same spot where the medallion had recently lain. The Indian fell, and his pony scampered wildly away.

Another Sioux spun to meet with a lance point the charge of the soldiers' revolvers. Bullets from at least three different guns thudded into his body, and he disappeared in the hoof-churned dust beneath the soldiers' horses.

The few remaining Indians broke and ran, with no chance to offer resistance. The formation of soldiers scattered as well into myriad small chases and smaller combats.

Laddy saw two troopers ride close behind a fat Indian and take turns shooting into his back until the Sioux finally dropped.

A young warrior—could he even be considered a warrior? Laddy was not sure; the Indian looked no older than fourteen if that—clung tight to the side of his frightened, rearing pony while all the others either died or raced away for safety, leaving this one youth behind, unable for the moment to control his mount.

Most of the soldiers charged past him, and for a moment Laddy thought the boy might escape.

Then a handful of stragglers coming out of the coulee saw him and spurred their horses at him.

The boy was cut off from his own kind, and there was nothing in any direction to offer hope. Except perhaps in one. He sawed at his pony's mouth and slammed his fist between the animal's ears to force its feet back to earth, then whirled toward Laddy and Barney and Mr. Gilchrist and the rest of the survey crew. This was where safety had been promised, and this was where he ran.

Shouting soldiers, steel and brass gleaming in the sunlight, raced after the copper-skinned boy.

They rode close behind the youngster, revolvers cocked and leveled.

"No, damn it, don't," Mr. Gilchrist shouted.

"Jesus, Mary an' Joseph," Laddy mumbled, intending it to be a prayer.

The boy was close enough now that Laddy could see the terror in his eyes. And the hope as he hauled back on his rein to slide his pony to a halt only a few paces in front of Laddy.

"Quick," Laddy shouted. "Over here."

Two of the soldiers reined away at the last instant. A third stopped, so close his horse's shoulder collided with the flank of the Indian boy's pony, jostling the boy and nearly unseating him.

"Here," Laddy repeated. "Quickly."

The Sioux boy's mouth opened.

The soldier behind him extended his fist, a cocked revolver in it, and gestured with the muzzle of the gun as if to prod the Sioux in the back of the head. But instead of poking him with the gun the trooper fired. A sheet of flame spread round the boy's head in a curious, halo-like effect, and the front of his face twisted and took on a new and ugly shape as a crimson spray briefly filled the air between him and Laddy.

The boy was flung down, rag-limp and lifeless, virtually at Laddy's feet, and the whooping, grinning soldier spun away to search for other prey.

Laddy was stunned. And sickened. Wisps of smoke rose from the back of the dead boy's head, and the stink of singed and burning hair filled Laddy's nostrils.

It was too much. Simply too much. His vision blurred and darkened. He was on his knees, throwing up into the grass. He dimly knew that, could taste the acid and feel the sharpness of it on his teeth. He could hear Mr. Gilchrist's voice reaching him through the mists of his tenuous hold on consciousness, but he could not understand what Mr. Gilchrist was trying to say to him.

Then the mists closed in and claimed him, and he could neither hear nor feel any more.

It was . . . simply . . . too, too much.

CHAPTER
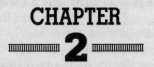
2

Glenn Gilchrist stood close by the two fallen youngsters. The one would recover soon enough. The other would never have that chance. Glenn was trembling with mingled fury and frustration. Before him on the dry, rolling plain he could see little now but dust and grass, blue sky and delicate cloud. And dark, blood-soaked bodies. So many bodies. And a few riderless horses wandering aimlessly to and fro. The live Indians—if any so remained—had disappeared from view and with them the pursuing soldiers.

Why? Glenn asked soundlessly. Why? This fight today—no, call it what it was—this slaughter today was without purpose, without cause, certainly without provocation. So . . . why?

He heard a groan and looked down. The boy Laddy's eyes were open now. Barney knelt over him, offering a canteen that likely contained a beverage considerably stronger than the river water that could be drawn from the barrel.

"Here, boy." Barney held the canteen to Laddy's lips and spilled some of the clear liquid into his mouth. Laddy swallowed, sputtered and came bolt upright in response.

"What . . . ?"

Barney glanced in Gilchrist's directions and declined to answer the half-uttered question. "Have another?"

Laddy nodded, big-eyed, and took another swallow, this one smaller and cautiously tried. He blinked rapidly and coughed. The color was returning to his thin cheeks, Glenn saw, and he was soon able to sit up without Barney's support.

"I'm sorry, Mr. Gilchrist, I . . ."

"It's all right, Laddy. You're fine now."

The boy looked again at the dead Indian who lay so close beside him. The Sioux youngster lay facedown. Probably that was a blessing. Laddy looked closely at him and shuddered but this time was able to regain his composure. After a moment he shook his head, reached out to Barney for a hand up and came somewhat shakily to his feet. "I won't let you down again, Mr. Gilchrist."

"You've let no one down, Laddy."

Out on the prairie Glenn could see movement now and then, troopers moving slowly across the grass as their pursuits were ended and they began drifting back to the scene of their treachery. They moved in ones and twos and threes now, with no order or formation. They seemed tired but still excited. They were animated and still eager, invigorated by the killing. It was, Glenn thought, much the same sort of excitement generated by a pigeon harvest, during one of those near-annual slaughters when the vast swarms of passenger pigeons would pass through a town. No danger existed, nor was there uncertainty as to the outcome whenever men dashed out to shoot or net or even club the tens of thousands of roosting, helpless birds. Danger, no, but there was a blood lust that took over men's impulses. Glenn had felt the pull of it himself once, its lure tainted by a belly-deep sense of sick, guilty revulsion that repelled him even while he continued to club score upon score of the fragile, defenseless creatures to death. Funny, he remembered now, how he had been unable to enjoy a single one of the pigeon pies afterward, no matter now succulent it appeared or how inviting its scent.

This slaughter of unsuspecting Sioux seemed remarkably similar to him now. Equally senseless. No, more so. At least the men who clubbed those birds did so in the knowledge that they were harvesting food. Here on this plain there had not even been that for an excuse. Here the killing was done solely for the sake of killing. And it was human beings this time, living men, who were the victims of the treachery.

"Laddy."

"Aye, sir?"

"Walk back to the wagons, son. Tell them we're all right and that they're to join us here. Make sure they bring whatever tools we have along. I suppose it will be up to us to bury the dead."

"The Indians, Mr. Gilchrist?"

"I see no other dead, Laddy."

"Aye, sir."

"I don't suppose any of them would particularly appreciate having a Christian burial, but we will do what we know how and hope they accept the intent if not the meaning of the ceremony."

"Aye, sir." The boy, a trifle wobbly at first but quickly growing stronger with the activity and purpose as Glenn had hoped and intended, began hiking back toward the wagons and the other members of the survey crew.

Out on the prairie the soldiers continued to gather. Most of the troopers, obviously proud of themselves, had dismounted and were lighting fires to boil coffee. A trio of proud soldiers remained horseback—a bugler, the guidon carrier and an officer in a fancy plumed hat. As Glenn watched, this coterie of popinjays started toward him. It took them only a few minutes to draw near.

The officer stopped his horse—all the mounts were similarly colored, rich red-brown bodies with dark points at mane, tail and lower legs—and looked down with apparent satisfaction at the corpse that so recently had been a teenage boy.

"One of my boys got the bastard in the nick of time, I see," the officer observed.

Glenn glared at him.

"What is that look about, mister? My men saved your life here. If you can't give them a cheer for that, man, at least grant them the credit due for their saving the lives of your men. This fellow here and the one yonder. I was watching, you know. I saw the whole thing."

"So did I, damn you, and there was no cause—"

"I submit, sir, that as a civilian you have no knowledge of the situation that—"

"Damn you, Lieutenant, we were in no danger here, and you—"

"Don't you cuss me, mister. Don't you *dare* cuss me, not ever."

The officer stepped down from his saddle, his suddenly furious expression infused with the dark red flush of his anger. Glenn handed his reins to Barney and stepped forward to meet the lieutenant midway.

"Don't you *ever* cuss me," the officer snarled nastily.

"I'll do as I damn please," Glenn declared. "As for what you did here today, I'll see you in irons. You murdered these Indians and you put my men at risk. We had a truce with these people. General Dodge and Mr. Hood reached a treaty agreement with the Sioux not three days ago. Now you've broken it, damn you. Now they will never trust us again."

The officer snorted. "You were going to trust the word of some stinking savages? Mister, you need our protection more than you realize. Why, these Indians would have killed you and every one of your men if we hadn't been here today."

"If you hadn't been here today, we would have given them something to eat and gotten our day's work done. Now God only knows what is going to happen."

"I'll tell you what is going to happen, mister. You are going to go on living, that's what is going to happen. Like it or not, realize it or not, you and your people are alive now because of me and my men. And that's the truth."

"Damn you," Glenn repeated.

The officer stiffened. He braced himself rigidly to attention and barked, "You were warned, sir. I am Edward Hale Wollins, first lieutenant, K Troop, Fort Kearney, Nebraska Territory. I have the honor, sir, to challenge you." The young idiot—for so Glenn took him to be—stared straight ahead, his eyes unfocused and his chin pulled so tight against his neck that wrinkled bands of flesh formed like wattles beneath his jaw. He needed a shave, Glenn saw, and a pimple that needed bursting made an angry red exclamation at the corner of his mouth. Glenn guessed Lieutenant Wollins's age at something in the very early twenties. He appeared young and inexperienced. And acted . . . young and inexperienced.

"A duel, Lieutenant? You are seriously challenging me to a duel?"

"I have that honor, sir."

Glenn folded his arms and gave Wollins a pitying look. "First you and your people murder a bunch of peaceful Indians. Now you want to murder me for not appreciating you for murdering them. Lieutenant, has it occurred to you that you are making an ass of yourself here? Well, think about it. Because you are."

"I am not . . . Will you accept my challenge, sir?"

"No, Lieutenant, I will not."

"But you must. If you are a gentleman, sir, you cannot refuse a challenge."

"If you say so," Glenn said agreeably.

"Does that mean you accept?"

"No, but I suppose it means I'm not a gentleman. At least not by your definition. This may surprise you, Lieutenant, but it really doesn't bother me very much what you think about me. What does bother me is that you attacked a band of peaceful Sioux without provocation."

"I don't . . . Darn it, sir, you really have to accept my challenge."

"Actually I don't."

"No?"

"No," Glenn assured him, even though Gilchrist had neither knowledge of nor interest in the ancient *code duelo,* beyond knowing that such a stupidity did exist, or anyway used to.

"But what am I . . . I mean, what . . . ?"

"Ask your commanding officer when you get back to Kearney. He'll tell you all about it. Of course he will also have to remind you that dueling is illegal nowadays. You've committed an illegal act by issuing the challenge. I suppose you could lose your commission because of it." Glenn had heard that somewhere. He had no idea if it was true or not. It was not exactly the sort of information he had ever had need of before now.

The officer blinked. His stance wilted until he was standing almost like a normal human being and less like a brightly painted tin soldier. "Is that right?"

"Oh, I think so, yes."

"Damn."

"Really," Glenn said with mock sympathy. "Now tell me the truth, Wollins. Why did you attack those Indians?"

"Why? Because that's what we are here for. To protect the railroad, and other whites too of course, from murdering savages."

"I see. So you commit murder in order to prevent murder, is that it?"

"You are trying to confuse me, sir."

"Not at all, Lieutenant. I'm certainly not trying to confuse you, and if I am doing so, then I apologize."

"That's better."

"Good. But, um, you didn't answer my question, Lieutenant. How is it that one murder is acceptable while another would not be?"

"Murder has nothing to do with this, sir. I was acting under the direct orders of Captain Medgar Taney, commanding officer of the garrison at Fort Kearney."

"And this Captain Taney ordered you to commit murder, Lieutenant? I find that rather difficult to believe."

"You know he gave no such order, sir. And you are trying to bait me now. I am on to you, sir. Captain Taney has been hounded by your General Dodge—who I remind you, sir, resigned his commission; he is no longer on active duty—and by Mr. Durant. Those civilian gentlemen have been begging the army for protection from marauding Indian bands. Well, sir, now they've gotten it. Captain Taney has agreed to provide that protection. The captain has pledged to sweep Nebraska free of all hostiles, sir. By the time we are done, sir, there will not be a living hostile this side of Fort Laramie. That is what the captain has declared, sir. I've heard him make that statement himself, as recently as four nights ago in the officers mess."

"And is your performance here today an example of what we can expect when it comes to determining which Indians are hostiles and which may be regarded as friendly?"

"Sir, Captain Taney says any Indian not within the bounds of an established agency reservation is to be regarded as hostile and, well, eliminated."

"I can see by this dead boy at my feet that your order

includes the murder of children, Lieutenant, but does it include women as well?"

"I . . . I'm not certain of that, sir. That subject has not come up."

"Don't you think it better be discussed, Wollins? What if these men had had their women with them today? Would you still have attacked?"

"I . . . Sir, I am only following orders."

"The fact that an order has been given, Lieutenant, does not turn wrong into right. Think about that."

Wollins looked troubled. And this time he had no answer. This time his eyes did not meet Glenn's.

"Go back to your men, Wollins," Glenn said, his voice and his expression more saddened than angry now.

"Sir."

"Yes, Wollins?"

"About that challenge, sir . . ."

"Sorry, Lieutenant. I still won't accept it."

"No, sir, what I wanted to say is that, well, I would like to withdraw my challenge. With your permission, that is."

"You have my permission to withdraw, Wollins."

"Yes, sir. Thank you, sir." Wollins came to attention once more, but this time he saluted then executed a smart about-face and returned to his horse, which his bugler had been holding. He mounted and rode away at a brisk trot, bugler and guidon close behind.

Glenn Gilchrist and Barney stood in the sun, surrounded by the drone of flies drawn to the fresh blood nearby, waiting for the men and wagons to arrive so they could begin the ugly task of burying men the troopers had so lightheartedly shot down and left sprawled on the prairie.

This was, Glenn thought, a rude end for a truce so earnestly undertaken.

CHAPTER

3

It had been a long day and wasn't close to being over yet, and Megan O'Connell was tired. Hot, tired, cranky and fed up. It really hadn't been a good day, that was the problem.

Once again end-of-track was moving forward, and if she expected to maintain her business, she had no choice but to move with it. That was understandable. She had known it to begin with. But she certainly didn't have to like it. Particularly on moving day.

Her feet hurt, her head ached, her hands and wrists stung like they were on fire. Perspiration—on a man it would have been sweat, but ladies never sweat—stained her dress under her arms and on her sides, and tickling trickles of it made her squirm and shiver when the droplets ran down between her breasts. Worst of all she had an itch that she didn't dare scratch, and it was driving her mad.

Trying to ignore the distractions, she continued doggedly on with her packing. Tin mugs by the score—there was a very good reason why she had abandoned the use of glass and crockery shortly after turning her old restaurant into this much more profitable mobile saloon—tumbled into a crate and were covered with a layer of sawdust to protect them against the worst of the inevitable bumps and bangs of travel. Sawdust, she'd discovered, was the perfect packing material. Not only did it protect her things while in transit, but also

once the boxes were unpacked at the other end, the sawdust
served again as flooring.

But that was only after one got there.

Megan stood, a sharp pain cutting through her lower back
as she did so, and ran a hand across her forehead. "Vic."

"Yes, ma'am?"

"This box is ready."

"Yes, ma'am." Victor Boyette, a sweet boy if not a particularly bright one, hurried over with his tack hammer and
bag of small wire nails. As Megan and her assistant, Rachel
Foreman, finished filling a crate, Vic would nail it shut and
carry it outside to the wagon.

Rachel was short and pretty, blond in contrast to Megan's
striking red-haired good looks. Rachel had lost her only
child and was widowed as well during the disastrous spring
flooding back in Omaha. Her own life was spared only
when Megan's brother, Liam, rescued her from the torrent.
Since then a romance of sorts, or at least an understanding,
had developed between Rachel and Liam, and Rachel had
become a fixture at Megan's side, working as a waitress
in the workingman's cafe Megan opened and now as a
barmaid and, most lately, a blackjack dealer of quickly
growing ability.

Megan allowed herself a moment's respite as Vic nailed
the crate lid in place and carried the bulky object out.

"How are you coming there, Rachel?"

"I won't be much longer. I can't hurry too much, though.
I don't want to spill any." Rachel was pouring oil out of the
lamps, tipping it into a funnel and returning the lamp oil to a
two-gallon tin so the brass-and-pewter lamps could be safely
transported. The globes had already been packed separately
and with care, the delicate glass protected in more of the
ubiquitous sawdust.

There were times, like today, when Megan thought saw-dust almost as necessary to the running of a saloon as liquor. The stuff was used to pack almost everything they carried, including the valuable bottled goods. While most of her liquid products came in kegs or barrels, the best of the potables, including the top grades of whiskey and all her brandies, were in bottles—fragile and highly breakable bottles. Those had been the very first things to be packed and loaded onto the wagon. For two reasons: to assure they were packed early, before there was any chance they could run out of sawdust, and, less obvious, to make sure the crates containing those expensive products would be buried under a mountain of other goods while they were in transit. The bottled goods would be unavailable to any casual pilferers they might encounter on the journey forward to the newest hell-on-wheels encampment. Wherever it might prove to be this time.

While Vic was outside the huge tent that housed the saloon and there was only Rachel there to see, Megan took the opportunity to scratch herself—thoroughly and gratefully. She sighed loudly.

"Sometimes it just makes you wanta spit, don't it, this having to playact at being perfect all the time?" Rachel said, correctly guessing at the cause of Megan's sigh.

Megan laughed—and immediately felt much better for it. She opened her mouth and would have continued the banter with Rachel except Vic chose that moment to lumber back inside the saloon tent, and the ladies had to revert to unwanted seriousness. Megan gave Rachel a quick wink and went back to her packing.

An hour or so later the last of the crates was closed and loaded onto the big freight wagon that Megan had inher-ited from old Walt Guthrie, her employee—and friend—

who'd been murdered by one of Ike Norman's henchmen
when all poor Walt was trying to do was protect Megan's
interests. To Megan's astonishment, Walt had left everything he possessed to her. Not that the estate amounted
to much in monetary terms, mostly this wagon, a camping
outfit and a team of slow and aging draft horses. Still,
the fact that Walt had thought so highly of her touched
Megan.

"All we have left, ma'am, is these tables an' the tent
itself," Vic said. "You want me to start knockin' the tables
apart now?"

"Yes, Vic, please."

Vic put his tack hammer and nails in the wagon and came
back inside with a short-handled maul. He turned the first of
the collapsible gaming tables onto its side and began tapping
out the pegs that held the leg sections in place. The bar itself
was only a few planks laid over upended beer barrels, and
the makeshift backbar was an arrangement of small kegs
and short planks that provided a sort of improvised shelv-
ing where mugs and bottles could be set. The only "sink"
Megan owned was an oak bucket, and she knew better than
to buy a mirror. She had learned that in a rough-and-ready
establishment like this it was folly to bother even with such
civilized niceties as cuspidors. The railroad gangs insisted on
using the floor anyway, so there was no point asking them
to behave as gents. Megan had long since swapped off her
pretty brass spittoons in favor of more tin mugs and some
fresh decks of cards.

Vic finished the first of the tables and carried the pieces
outside to add to the wagon load.

"Am I too late for a last drink?"

The voice came from behind Megan. She recognized it
instantly. And in spite of herself she felt a quickening of

her breath and a flutter of excitement low in her belly.

"Joshua? I thought you were out visiting in the Indian camps."

She turned to greet the tall, lean, buckskin-clad frontiersman who was the antithesis of everything she knew she wanted in a man, yet who aroused her senses to such heady extremes in spite of that.

She felt a catch in her throat as Joshua Hood, chief of scouts for the Union Pacific, came near with his loose, lanky, horseman's gait. Joshua was uneducated. And very rough. He could not read or write more than his own name. Perhaps not even that much. But . . . but he had the bluest, deepest eyes Megan had ever seen. And he was bold and strong and honest.

Sometimes too bold and honest.

He reached for her, his arm sliding around her waist in an attempt to draw her to him.

Deftly Megan turned, sliding out of his embrace with a cluck of her tongue and a shake of her head. Glenn Gilchrist was far and away the better match for any sensible girl to make. And both Glenn and Joshua were interested in her. Lord knew they both made that clear enough. Megan had as good as told Glenn that she would become his. Someday. Sort of.

But Joshua had an undeniable effect upon her too. And a strong effect at that. Much too strong to toy with. Too strong to trust herself with, even though she probably could trust him. Probably. But then that was at least a part of Joshua Hood's appeal, wasn't it? He was bold. He was rough. And somewhere there very likely was an end to his patience and to his forbearance. It was the attraction of the moth to the flame. So exciting a game it was to flutter on the fringes of disaster. To tempt the fates and see if you could come just that least bit closer to the light without succumbing to the flame.

"What, no kiss to greet me?" Joshua protested, but not angrily, his voice light and teasing and gay.

"A kiss no, but congratulations yes."

Joshua beamed. "You heard about it then?"

"Heard about it? There was talk of practically nothing else for the past two days, ever since word first came. Joshua Hood and General Dodge, General Dodge and Joshua Hood. I declare the men have talked of naught else. They are so happy there will be no more Indian fights that they've been celebrating until . . ." She smiled. "Well, let me put it this way. They've been celebrating until my profits these past few days have been positively obscene. I should be ashamed of myself. Except of course I am not. If I'd known a peace treaty with the Sioux would do so much for me, Joshua, I would have recommended one a long time ago."

It was his turn to laugh. "In that case, Megan, I'm doubly glad we made the agreement." After only a few seconds, though, he sobered. He took her by the shoulders, this time not to embrace her but to gain her undivided attention.

"Is something wrong, Joshua?"

"I don't know, Megan. I hope not. But that's what I came here to see you about." He blushed slightly and dropped his eyes from hers. "Well, it ain't the only reason. I expect you know that. I mean, I'd wanta see you anyhow. But I especial wanted t' see you today. I mean, when I heard the camp was breaking up and moving along."

"There is something wrong," Megan said.

"Now, I don't know that there is. Not for sure, see. But after me and General Dodge left Spotted Bull's camp, the general and his party headed for Omaha to report back to the stockholders."

"Yes, that's how we all heard about the treaty. Everyone was so happy when they came through here spreading that wonderful news."

"Right, well, after we left Spotted Bull, me and some of my boys came back by way of Fort Kearney. Figured the army oughta know about what us and the Sioux agreed to, you see."

"That's sensible, certainly."

"That's what I thought, Megan, but after talking to that . . . well, I can't tell you what I think of the fella they got in charge over there at that fort. Wouldn't be right t' use language like that where a lady could hear."

"That being said, Joshua, I think your meaning is clear enough without any elaboration," Megan said.

"Yeah, well, I met the man. Told him where we'd been an' what all we'd said an' done when we was setting in council with the Sioux. And he—his name is Taney, and he's still only a captain, though I take it he's been in the army since two days after dirt was discovered—he said he don't believe our treaty will hold up. Said he's been hearing some bands of the Sioux are arming themselves and are fixing to break the steel snake's back this summer. Said him and his troops have been preparing to put a wall of rifles an' bayonets between them and the railroad an' kill every Sioux in Nebraska if that's what it takes to get the rails safely through Sioux country."

"But if you already have a treaty with this Spotted Bull . . . doesn't that solve everything?" Megan asked.

"Well it does, Megan, an' it don't. That's what most of us whites can't seem t' get through our heads. Indian tribes ain't like white nations. I mean, we call them nations an' so we think they're like what we'd call countries. You know, there's Sioux and Cheyenne an' Arapaho an' such, and then there's also Americans an' English and French an' all them. Except when you make a deal with a Sioux, you ain't really making a deal with all the Sioux. Just with that one fella and maybe his family an' close pals. If you make a deal with the president of the United States, then the whole darn government stands behind whatever it was he said. Not every American, mind, but the government does. Well, with Indians it ain't like that. There is no one government for anybody t' deal with an' no president . . ."

"But a chief . . ."

"I know what you're thinking, Megan, but to an Indian a chief isn't no better than anybody else, an' he sure can't tell anybody else what they're to do. A chief is a leader, sure, but he only leads whoever feels like following him right then. Maybe today they'll follow along. Tomorrow they might take a nap instead. Besides, even for a strong leader like Spotted Bull, when you make your treaty with him, at the best you've made a treaty with, well, like with a town. It's like the king of England comes over here an' makes a treaty with the mayor of Omaha. The mayor, he can get the folks in Omaha to go along with that treaty, but their deal don't mean nothing to the people in Boston or, like, in New Orleans. You see what I'm telling you?"

"I . . . think so. Yes."

"The thing is, Megan, if this Captain Taney is right an' he's been hearing things from bands other than Spotted Bull's, then we still could be having Indian troubles along the right-o'-way this summer after all. I wanted you t' know that."

"Are you really all that worried, Joshua?"

"Enough so that I want you t' . . . I dunno . . . go back an' visit with your sister a spell. Just until we know how things are gonna shake out about this. You . . . you got to, Megan.

I'll let you know when it's safe for you t' come out again. I'll come back an' get you myself an' help you move. But for right now you got to go back. Until we get this thing worked out once an' for all."

Megan frowned at him. The idea of going back to Omaha now, back to her dear but timid sister Aileen . . . no. Absolutely not. Never.

"Don't look at me like that, Megan."

"Then don't try to be giving me orders, Mr. Hood. You have no right to do that. No man does. Especially not crazy orders like that. You have no authority to tell me what to do. And I wouldn't do what you tell me even if you did have the right. I'm my own person, Joshua. I'll not be ordered about. Not by anyone."

"But I'm only trying to—"

"I know what you are trying to do, Joshua. I appreciate your intention, but I reject your conclusion. Is that clear?"

"Clear enough, Miss O'Connell." He dropped his hands from her shoulders. Megan felt a chill replace the warmth his touch had given her. He turned to leave.

"Joshua."

"Yes?" He stopped but did not look back.

"Thank you."

"For ordering you around?"

"No, for caring. For that, Joshua, I truly do thank you."

He nodded and then, still without turning back to look at her again, marched out of the virtually empty saloon tent to disappear in the busy street traffic. Megan felt a brief pang— regret? perhaps—and returned her attention to the needs of the moment. As soon as the tables were loaded, the tent had to be struck and folded and muscled onto the trailer— oh, the tent was a heavy, awkward, ungainly horror once it was collapsed—so they would be ready to leave at first light tomorrow. No one Megan had spoken with knew where they were going. West. Follow the rails, and when there were no more rails, stop and rebuild. That was enough for them to know, because wherever the tracks ended, the construction gangs began.

But, oh, she would be glad to have things set up and running again. If only because then she could rest again. Lord, but she did despise moving.

"Vic."

"Yes, ma'am?"

"See if you can find Rachel, please. It will take all of us to get this miserable tent down."

"Yes, ma'am."

CHAPTER
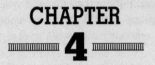
4

Joshua allowed the smiling, nodding Negro to guide him to a choice table and hold the chair while the chief of scouts was seated. Joshua was enjoying this. Not being fawned over, particularly, but simply being able to sit down to a meal for once, being able to eat at leisure without curious Sioux staring at him, without straitlaced army officers picking apart his manners, without need for haste and without any cause to wonder just what strange creature might be a part of the evening's menu. So ordinary a thing as a plain and everyday supper had become of late a rare and special treat, and this evening Joshua Hood fully intended to enjoy his opportunity to partake of one. To lessen the chance of being interrupted, Joshua had chosen this evening to eat in the mess tent—so termed even though it was more an elegant restaurant that happened to be mobile than it was either tent or mess—reserved for the upper echelons of the Union Pacific management. His wild and happy-go-lucky scouts and hunters would never think to look for him here.

"And what would be your pleasure tonight, Mr. Hood, suh?"

"What d'you recommend, Henry?"

"The antelope steaks look nice. They fresh today. I can get cook to cut you one nice an' thick."

"That sounds good."

"And the trimmin's?"

"Whatever you have, Henry."

"Fine, Mr. Hood. All the trimmin's, then. An' a nice big steak. You want coffee while you wait, suh?"

"And a drink, I think. Whiskey first, then the coffee."

"Comin' right up, Mr. Hood."

Joshua extended his long legs and crossed his boots at the ankles, leaning back in the chair and closing his eyes for a moment. Lord, he felt like he'd been on the move every minute for the past week. He felt . . . He frowned a little as, thinking about it, he realized he pretty much had been on the move for the past *several* weeks. Constantly moving, constantly on edge, constantly under strain or scrutiny of one sort or another. Perhaps it was no great wonder that he felt so drained and weary now that he was finally able to let down his guard.

Henry brought him a whiskey served in a brandy snifter. Joshua tossed it back, enjoying the heat of it in his belly, and reached for the cup of steaming coffee that had been brought along with the liquor.

It felt mighty good being able to relax now. If only Megan were here . . .

Megan. Thinking about her, about her beauty, her charm, her fire, was something that sustained Joshua during those moments when things seemed at their worst.

Megan O'Connell. He smiled quietly to himself. Megan herself didn't yet know that one day she would be his. But she would be. Joshua knew this was certain, as certain as where the sun would rise come the morrow, as certain as the inexhaustibility of the great buffalo herds, as certain as the fact that the Union Pacific *would* persevere to conquer prairie and mountain alike.

It was just that Megan herself did not yet recognize this inevitability. Not any more than that fancy schoolboy Glenn Gilchrist did.

Well, they would find out. Both of them. And when they did . . .

"Mr. Hood?"

Joshua opened his eyes—had he been napping for a moment there? surely not—to see Willard Valle standing beside his table. Valle, a slender young man who hid a sharp intellect behind a shy and sometimes bumbling facade, bobbed his head and nervously pushed his spectacles higher onto the bridge of his nose. Valle was private secretary and man-of-all-needs to General Jack Casement, who with his brother Dan was the U.P.'s construction contractor. "Mr. Hood?" he repeated.

"Yes, Will."

"The general sends his compliments, Mr. Hood, and wonders would you mind preparing a report for him."

"A report, Will?"

"Yes, sir. The general would like your impressions, Mr. Hood. About the sense of things in the Sioux encampment. Not so much what was said and done there—all of that is a matter of record—but what you sensed. You know. The feel of things among the Indians."

"I see."

"And, um, if you wouldn't mind, the general is interested as well in what you, um, sensed among the officers at Fort Kearney."

Joshua lifted an eyebrow. It wasn't like his visit to the army post had been a secret or anything. But it hadn't been announced either. How Jack Casement heard about it practically before Joshua got back . . . well, no one had ever accused either of the Casement brothers of stupidity. Both of those pint-sized firebrands were men who stayed ahead of things.

"I can't think of any reason why I shouldn't tell the general whatever he wants to know, Will. Where and when would he like me to call on him?"

"If it would be all right with you, Mr. Hood, it can be done in writing. The general has to go forward tonight to meet with his brother at rail's end, then before first light tomorrow he has to be on a special heading back to Omaha. He'll meet there with General Dodge and Mr. Durant. He'd like to pick your report up when the special passes through in the morning."

Joshua frowned. And sighed. A written report was not something he was prepared to come up with at a moment's notice.

Will Valle smiled. "You needn't worry, Mr. Hood. General Casement knows you aren't, um, overmuch fond of paperwork. He suggested you speak your piece just as if you were telling it to him in person. I can write it down for him as quick as you can tell it."

"No, go on with you."

"Oh, not whole words, Mr. Hood. Nobody could do that. But I can take it down with a sort of speedwriting. Shorthand, some call it. It doesn't look like much, but I can read it back later and transcribe it so it makes sense. I'll write it down for the general and make a copy for him to take to Mr. Durant. Would that be all right with you?"

"I reckon that sounds fair," Joshua agreed. At least with a copy going to Thomas Durant no one could accuse him of playing loose with his employers. Not that there was any friction between General Casement and Durant. None that Joshua knew of, anyway. But the structure of the railroad's management was so complex that Joshua didn't even try to keep it all straight. Thomas Durant, for instance, was vice president of the Union Pacific Railroad and was to all intents and purposes its principal manager and motivator too. But it was said Durant was also president of some other corporations that did business with the railroad and therefore was personally profiting from the business he managed on behalf of the Union Pacific shareholders. Not only by way of his construction contract with the Casements but in a whole interlocking chain of companies and corporations that supplied the railroad with iron and spikes, food and timber, advertisements and . . . Joshua didn't know what all might be involved. Furthermore he didn't want to have to think about all of that. It was enough that he could do his best for the Union Pacific as a whole and never mind the details of who would profit or how.

"I'll be glad t' help any way I can, Will," was all he said on the subject.

"The general's train will be pulling out in twenty minutes or so. I'll tell him he can expect your report to be ready when he comes back through in the morning."

"Sounds good," Joshua said.

"Enjoy your supper, Mr. Hood. I'll come back after the general's train leaves, and we can find a quiet spot where we can sit down while I record whatever you want to say."

Joshua smiled. "Y'know, Will, I ain't never done anything like this before."

"I don't think you'll find it too burdensome, Mr. Hood," Valle said, standing to excuse himself. He nodded and before turning away said, "I'll be back in a half hour or so, Mr. Hood."

Valle was, in fact, back within ten minutes. Joshua's antelope steak with all the appropriate trimmings was just being served when the young man came hurrying in.

"That was quick, Will. I—"

"No time to talk now, Mr. Hood. Come quickly."

"What the—"

"There's been a massacre, Mr. Hood. Somewhere out forward with one of the survey parties. The general wants you to join him on the train, Mr. Hood. Right now."

Joshua felt his gut knot and churn at this most unexpected news. He shoved his chair back and rose to his feet, dropping his napkin onto the untasted meal before him.

"Henry."

"Yes, Mr. Hood suh?"

"You know Miss O'Connell, don't you?"

"Yes, suh, I do."

"Get word to her, please. Tell her she mustn't take her wagon forward now. She must go back to Omaha. She simply must. Tell her . . . Oh, hell, I don't know. Tell her I said so. Tell her I'm begging her to go back. Tell her whatever you have to, Henry, but make sure she goes back to Omaha and not ahead to end-o'-track. You hear?"

"I hear, Mr. Hood. I do what I can."

"Will, you tell her the same—"

"Not me, Mr. Hood. The general wants me on that train tonight too."

"Then, Henry, it's up to you. Make sure Miss O'Connell and her baggage go back to Omaha tomorrow morning."

"I try, Mr. Hood," Henry said uncertainly.

By then, though, both Joshua and Willard Valle had left the mess tent at a pace that was just short of being a run.

Henry shook his head and, with a shrug of his shoulders, picked up the virtually untouched plate of succulent antelope steak and carried the meal back into the kitchen.

CHAPTER

5

Megan woke to the news. Massacre. The word was on every lip. Massacre. It was an ugly word. Frightening. She sat beneath her wagon with a blanket pulled tight around her shoulders. The chill she felt had nothing to do with the morning air, which in any event was not particularly cold.

"Victor."

"Yes, ma'am?"

"Are you sure . . . ?"

"It's what everyone is saying, ma'am. Another massacre. Someplace way far ahead. Ma'am?"

"Yes, Vic?"

"Somebody said it was Mr. Gilchrist's survey crew that was . . . you know. I . . . thought you oughta know, ma'am. Knowin' you and him was friends, like."

Megan went cold. It was odd. And very, very wrong. But when she learned that her husband Keith Gallagher had been killed, she was able to accept that news almost as a matter of course. It had hurt. Really it had. But she hadn't felt then the same wrenching, draining, stomach-twisting sense of loss that this news about Glenn Gilchrist brought.

"Are you sure . . . ?"

"Ma'am, I ain't sure of nothing. It's just what I heard."

"Yes, of course. Thank you, Vic."

36

With a sigh Megan pushed the blanket off her shoulders and crawled out from under the big, heavily laden wagon. She had chosen to sleep the night there partially to guard against pilferage, and, quite as much a reason, because she had no better prospect for a bed. The small Sibley tent that was as close to a home as she possessed these days was loaded atop the wagon along with the big tent that was her saloon. In order to find proper shelter and a bed last night, she would have had to pay an outrageous price to someone. Better, she had decided, to spread a scrap of tarp on the ground and hope for decent weather.

Well, the weather had held. That was something.

She climbed to her feet, conscious of the aches and pains brought on by a night on hard, cold ground, and began gathering up her bedding.

Glenn. Dead. She could scarcely believe it. She had seen him . . . what? . . . two weeks ago? Something like that. He had been so vital then. So handsome. Not thrilling in the same way Joshua Hood was thrilling but decent and dear and always, ever, a gentleman. Glenn Gilchrist was a man who epitomized what a gentleman, a good and gentle man, should be.

And now he was dead.

Megan fought against the tears, then realized there was no avoiding them. She gave in to her grief and began to sob.

"Ma'am? Is there anything . . . what c'n I do, ma'am?"

"Nothing, Vic."

"But, ma'am . . ."

"Go away, Vic. Please. Just . . . go away."

"Yes, ma'am." He turned and went quietly off, leaving Megan to feel even worse for having been sharp with the poor, dull boy. She continued mechanically to tuck and tie and tidy until every flap, every cord, every possible loose bit on the wagon was secure and there was nothing more she could do to prepare for the journey ahead.

As soon as Vic came back, they could harness the horses and pull out.

But oh, dear. Glenn. So handsome and fine he'd been. So staunch and true. It was hard to believe he was dead now, his life snuffed out by some savage blow.

She hoped he hadn't suffered. Awful things were said about the Indians, about the things they sometimes did to their victims. Megan hoped Glenn hadn't had to suffer. She couldn't bear it if she knew he had had to suffer.

"Morning, Miss O'Connell." Teddy Bruce, one of Joshua Hood's scouts and a particular friend of Megan's wounded brother, Liam, stopped beside her and touched the brim of his slouch hat.

"Good morning, Teddy."

"Are you all right, ma'am?"

"Yes, certainly."

"You kinda look . . ."

"Yes?"

"Never mind." He ducked his eyes and looked away from the tears that left their telltale trails across her cheeks. "I heard you was pulling out this morning, and I, uh, I was thinking maybe I'd find Liam here."

"Liam won't be riding with me this trip, Teddy. His wound hasn't healed well enough to stand the jostling. He'll stay here with Dr. Wiseman until I'm settled in the new place and come along by rail when he's up to being moved. If you want to see him, though, you can come along with me. I'll be stopping in to visit with him before I leave."

"That's real nice o' you, ma'am." Teddy grinned and touched the brim of his hat again. "I wanta make sure ol' Liam hears 'bout that scrap yesterday. He likes a fight, Liam does. Bet he'll be sorry he missed it."

"Teddy! What a perfectly awful thing for you to say."

"Ma'am?"

"All those fine young men lying dead on the prairie somewhere and you're talking about what fun it must have been?
For shame, Teddy."

"Whatever d'you mean by that, ma'am? It's a bunch o'
damn Sioux layin' dead in the grass, not white men. An' I
do say Liam woulda wanted t' be there."

"Indians, Teddy? I thought . . ."

"Ma'am, I heard twenty different stories so far, I bet, but
the last an' best word is that a bunch o' Sioux broke the
treaty an' jumped some of our boys. But Mr. Gilchrist an'
his crew was ready for 'em and wiped 'em out, ma'am.
Every last, stinkin' one of 'em."

"No."

"That's what I heard, ma'am. Cross m' heart."

"Teddy, would you do me a favor?"

"Anything, ma'am. Just you name it."

"Would you please stay here and guard my wagon please,
Teddy? Just until Victor gets back or Rachel. You know Mrs.
Foreman, don't you?"

"Yes, ma'am."

"Then wait here, please, until one of them comes. After
that you can find Liam in with Dr. Wiseman."

"You can count on me, ma'am. I won't let nothing happen
to your stuff."

"Thank you, Teddy. Ever so much." Megan lifted her
skirts and set off at a run toward the shanty where the
temporary telegraph station had been established. If there
was anyplace where she might learn the truth of yesterday's
battle that would surely be it. While she ran, she whispered
prayers under her breath, alternating the Hail Marys of old

habit with half-formed pleas that Glenn—and his crewmen too—be all right.

There was a small crowd gathered outside the telegrapher's shanty. Not so many men as she might have expected, though, and their mood seemed fairly calm. Megan began to relax a bit. Her heart left her throat for the first time since she'd heard the awful news.

Megan recognized most of the men even if she did not know their names. They obviously recognized her as well. "Ma'am." "Miz O'Connell." "Mornin', ma'am." The men touched their caps and shuffled aside to make way at her approach.

"Good morning. Can you tell me . . . that is to say, was it . . . ?"

"Nearest we can make out, ma'am, it wasn't none of our boys that got hurt," one of the men, a middle-aged fellow with yellow tobacco stains in his beard, told her. She remembered him as a sometime customer but was sure she'd never heard his name. "There was a massacre yesterday, all right, but it was a bunch o' Injuns that got killed. What we don't know is who jumped 'em. And why. They was supposed to have that peace treaty, see, that General Dodge and Mr. Hood fixed up. Now this. It's kinda confusing."

"But our people are all right?" Megan asked.

"That's what the telegraph operator at end-o'-track sent a while ago. He said an advance rider with the survey crew come in and told that much, but he didn't have details. Not yet. He said he'd send more whenever he hears."

Megan nodded and took the man's hand in both of hers. "Thank you. What is your name?"

"Kleiber, ma'am. Adolfus Kleiber."

"Well, Mr. Kleiber, the next chance you get I want you to stop by my place of business. There will be a free drink waiting for you. Along with my thanks for taking a great load off me this morning."

Kleiber blushed and grinned. "Damn it, Ad, how'd you get to be so lucky?" a voice complained from somewhere behind him. "Watch yer language, will ya?" someone else snapped. "There's a lady present."

A load off, indeed. Megan felt like a new woman, light and free and eager again.

Glenn hadn't been killed. Nor his fine young men.

The details . . . well, she would be interested in hearing the details when they became available. Of course she would. But the important news was already in. The massacre, if massacre there had been, did not involve Glenn Gilchrist's death.

That was what truly counted. All the rest seemed of scant importance at this moment.

"Don't forget, Mr. Kleiber. I'll be setting up again at end-of-track soon. Look me up whenever you wish."

"Oh, I'll not be forgetting that, Miss O'Connell. You can count on it."

Positively giddy with relief, Megan turned and retraced her steps back to the wagon, where, she saw, both Victor and Rachel were waiting for her, the horses harnessed now and standing patiently hitched in their traces.

CHAPTER

6

Joshua's rage was cold and leaden in his belly. The others in the private railcar—General Jack Casement and his brother, Dan, U.P. chief surveyor Ben Goss and half a dozen other upper-level railroad bosses—cluck-clucked and tsk-tsked with concern. But Joshua could see that none of the others understood the full and true meaning of the massacre report that Glenn Gilchrist was just now concluding.

"Did any of the Indians escape from the soldiers, Mr. Gilchrist?" General Casement asked.

"I can't be certain, sir, but I would have to assume that a few might have gotten away. Those that had been lagging behind, perhaps. They scattered in all directions. I doubt the troopers could have run them all down. I . . . I hope some got away, sir."

The bearded, pint-sized general—he stood barely over five feet in height, but his intellect was not limited by his stature—frowned and with a sad shake of his head said, "It is a terrible thing to say, Mr. Gilchrist, but in this instance it might be better for everyone—for our people and for the Sioux alike—if there were no survivors to carry the tale. If you take my meaning."

"I do, sir, but I cannot agree."

"No, of course not," Casement said mildly. "Um, sorry. Do go on with your report, Mr. Gilchrist."

"That pretty much tells it all, sir. I gathered my people up and started back before Lieutenant Wollins had his troop reassembled. Like I said, the soldiers scattered in all directions chasing the Sioux and I had no desire to linger in the area, just in case there were more bands of Indians in the vicinity. I felt the prudent thing to do was to get back here as quickly as possible, both to inform you of what happened out there and to protect my crew from any retaliation that might be mounted."

"You did the right thing, Mr. Gilchrist. No doubt about it. Mr. Hood?"

"Yes, sir?"

"What is your view of the situation?"

Joshua shook his head. "After General Dodge just got through making a peace an' those Indians coming in thinking they'd be fed an' made guests in our camp? General, I reckon it couldn't go much harder for us with the Sioux than it's gonna be once word o' this damn foolishness gets out. We're gonna have to stay armed an' ready day and night from here on out."

"You don't believe we can retrieve the situation, Mr. Hood?"

"General, let me ask you this. If it'd happened the other way 'round, sir . . . would you trust the Sioux t' be straight with you the second time?"

"I see what you mean, Mr. Hood. Once burned, twice shy. Is that about the way you see it?"

"More t' the point, sir, that's the way I expect the Sioux will see it."

"And if . . ." Whatever Casement might have asked, or said, was not to be heard by the other gentlemen in the plush railcar. There was a sharp rapping at the rear entry, and Willard Valle came inside without waiting for a response.

"Sorry to interrupt, but I thought you'd want to know. There's a detachment of soldiers coming in, and from all the brass and gilt on display the one in the middle must be General Sheridan himself."

"Excellent," General Casement said. "I'm eager to hear Phil's side of this story."

"You can be sure o' one thing," Joshua remarked.

"Oh? And what would that one thing be, Mr. Hood?"

"You can be sure the whole thing will've been the Indians' fault, General, 'cause for sure the army hasn't never made a mistake yet. And it ain't likely to start making any now neither."

Casement frowned but did not respond. By then they could hear the clatter of horses' hooves in the roadbed gravel as the small detachment of soldiers reined to a halt close by the executive railcar.

There were loud voices and a sharp-voiced peremptory command. A moment later Valle stood back and held the door so a slightly balding, middle-aged officer could stride grandly in.

The gentleman—by act of Congress if by no other measure—in question was of average size but managed to give an impression of height by way of the unusually tall heels on his knee-high riding boots and by the ostrich-plumed and gold-visored shako he wore. His uniform was bright with rows of polished brass buttons and was festooned with gilt rope and golden shoulder boards. The uniform admitted to only a passing acquaintance with standard issue and was quite obviously of custom—and baroquely gaudy—design. As for the man himself, he was lean and graying, much of his face hidden behind bushy side-whiskers and a huge sweep of mustache, as if he intended to compensate with facial hair for the impending baldness that was apparent when he removed his shako and held it stiffly under one arm.

It took the civilians in the railroad car a moment to take all of this splendor in. Then, however, there was opportunity for them to take a second look at the grandiose fellow's shoulder boards. And more than one had to turn aside to hide a choked-back snicker. General Phil Sheridan? Hardly. The rank designated on those boards was that of a mere captain. The Union Pacific's management was rife with general officers. Indeed, probably half the men assembled in the railcar at that moment had outranked this visitor when they were on active service. Starting with General Casement, who was the first to speak.

"Is there something we can do for you, Captain?"

The officer cleared his throat and gave Casement and the others a slow, critical looking over. One got the impression that he was judging them—and finding them wanting by his own high standards.

"I am Captain Medgar Taney, gentlemen, commanding officer in charge of the garrison at Fort Kearney and acting military governor of western Nebraska Territory. And may I ask who you would be . . . ?"

Jack Casement gave his own name but chose not to introduce all the others present.

"General you call yourself. May I ask if your commission is active, General?" Taney said.

"It is not, sir. I resigned my commission shortly after the recent . . . unpleasantness."

"Then you do understand that you have no authority here, do you not?" Taney persisted.

The little general smiled. "No more authority over your soldiers, Captain, than you have over my Irishmen."

Taney puffed up a bit but had no choice but to accept the former general's jab. "I see we understand each other then."

"Do we, Captain?"

"I think we do. I am in command of all military matters in

this district. It is my duty to protect your civilians from the depredations of savages. I will carry out this duty. I expect you to tell your people to obey my authority and to make my troops welcome. If you do that, I can assure you there will be no trouble between us."

"That's interesting, Captain. We were just now receiving a report about the, um, performance of some of your troops."

"Is that so?"

"Indeed. Something to do with the ambush and massacre of a band of Sioux west of here."

Taney nodded crisply. There was an expression of wolfish pleasure on his thin face. "Excellent work, that. Saved one of your work crews from annihilation, what?"

"Murdered a bunch of hungry visitors is more like it," Joshua spat, unable to hold the impulse in check.

"Ah, Mr. Hood, isn't it? Of course. We met just the other day. Nice to see you again. By the way, one of my officers was remarking at mess recently that you used to live with the savages. A squaw man or, um, something like that, I believe he said. Is that true, Hood? Do you consider yourself white again now? Or only partly so."

Joshua felt the heat rush to his cheeks. He balled his fists and took a step forward, only to be confronted by Glenn Gilchrist, who intruded himself between Joshua and the smirking army captain.

"Don't," Glenn warned. "It's what he's wanting."

"An' what he'll damn well get too."

"Not now, Joshua. Not here."

Joshua regained control of himself and spun away. He stalked away to the far end of the car and began rummaging in the cabinets there in search of a drink. He was not so far away that he couldn't hear what was going on down by the long table where all the gentlemen were gathered.

"Thin skinned, isn't he?" Taney was saying, a note of triumph in his voice.

"You were going to tell us about your, um, engagement?" Dan Casement said, returning the conversation to the original subject.

"Yes indeed," Taney agreed. "Wonderful work."

"Wonderful?" That was Glenn Gilchrist's voice. The engineer sounded quite positively dumbfounded. "Wonderful? It was murder, sir, plain and simple. Those Indians didn't have a chance."

"Really, sir, I—"

"Don't try to tell me that I don't know what I'm talking about, Captain. I was there."

"Were you now? How interesting. I've only received a field report, you understand. Haven't had a chance yet to talk with young Wollins in person. Tell me about it."

Gilchrist did. In some detail. At this second telling too Joshua could feel his stomach knot and churn. He glanced down the narrow car, toward Taney. The army captain was taking it all in with apparent pleasure, his eyes alight and his expression encouraging all the detail he could get.

"Yes? Yes? Wonderful. Oh, my. That Wollins is more clever than I thought. Goodness gracious, I shall have to cite the entire unit."

"Cite them? I should hope so. Put the whole damn lot of them under arrest. Why, those Sioux were coming in as our guests. They'd been told they would be welcome. Told they could expect food and friendship at our work camps. But your man Wollins used their belief in the sanctity of our promises to lure them under the muzzles of the troopers' guns. Murder, I said. And murder it was. Indeed you must cite those men. They belong in the guardhouse every one. I've told Wollins that, and I say it to you too."

Taney laughed. "Obviously you misunderstand me, Mr. . . . Gilchrist, was it? In any event, sir, you misunderstand me. I do intend to cite those men but for valor under arms, sir, not as a form of opprobrium. There will be no arrests for heroism like those lads displayed. More of the same, that's what is needed. More of the same."

"I cannot believe any human being could countenance . . ."

"Come now, Mr. Gilchrist. Surely you realize those savages weren't to be trusted. Had you let them come into your camp unmolested, they would have taken your food, true. They also would have turned on you the moment your backs were turned. And then it would have been you and your people who were left lying dead on the plains out there, sir. And that is the truth, whether you acknowledge it or not."

"I was there, Captain. You were not. I saw those Indians. I saw the way they approached us. Their bows weren't even strung. We were in no danger from the Sioux. Now the treaty has been broken before we ever got a chance to put it into effect. Now our people will have to fight their way through every inch of Sioux territory we have yet to cross."

Taney smiled. "Which is precisely why I've come here today, gentlemen. To coordinate your railroad construction efforts with the protection of my troops. So may I suggest we get down to business?"

Without waiting for an invitation, Captain Taney helped himself to a seat at the narrow conference table where the gentlemen of the Union Pacific were gathered.

It was too much for Joshua. He let himself quietly out the forward, service end of the railcar.

The air outside, he found, had a considerably fresher and cleaner flavor than that which he'd been breathing inside the railroad car.

CHAPTER

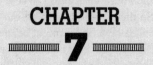

7

"We still don't know all the details," Megan told the others who were gathered around her wagon. "All I can do is relate what was told to me. And that is that there was some kind of fight, which apparently our boys won. Mr. Gilchrist and his crew all seem to have survived, at least that is what the telegrapher is reporting now." She nodded in the direction of Teddy Bruce, who was still hanging about the wagon, along with Victor Boyette and Rachel. "Just as Teddy said earlier."

The young man positively beamed, accepting Megan's simple comment as high praise.

"Naturally," Megan went on, "if either of you wants to stay here or to go back to Omaha, I won't try to discourage you. None of us knows what lies ahead, especially in light of this news."

"I don't understand, Miss Megan. Mr. Gilchrist an' them won. The Injuns is dead. Why wouldn't we wanta go on to the end-o'-track now," the hired man asked.

"Because, Vic, that fight didn't kill *all* the Sioux. Heaven forbid. It only killed some of them. And what it means . . . Well, we aren't in any position to know that, not without more details than we have here. One thing we can be sure of, though. The mere fact that there was a battle means the truce General Dodge and Mr. Hood won lasted barely long enough for the good news to spread. The fact that there was a fight means the Indian troubles aren't over yet, Vic. Not over by a long shot. So there could be danger out there along the tracks. I have no idea how bad it might be, perhaps very bad indeed or maybe it will prove to be nothing but a big scare. I only know I couldn't possibly ask you or Rachel either one to come west with me under false pretenses. I won't allow either one of you to think the treaty with the Sioux is still in force and that we will all be safe. That simply isn't so."

"Yes'm. Uh, Miss Megan, ma'am."

"Yes, Victor?"

"You're still goin', ain't you?"

"Yes, Victor, I certainly am."

"An' you still want me t' work for you? Drive the wagon an' all?"

"If you are willing, Vic, I certainly would like for you to continue helping me."

"Then I expect I'll be going wherever you say, ma'am."

"Rachel? There is no need for you to come along if you would rather stay here with Liam, you know. It might be safer later on. You could wait and bring Liam with you then."

Rachel Foreman, who had faced her share of dangers already in the great movement westward, tilted her head to one side and planted her hands on her hips. "Megan O'Connell, you'd lose half your trade if you didn't have me there for the boyos to stare at."

"I'm sure you are right about that, Rachel, but that isn't the question. Your safety is."

"Huh! No woman is safe in this country. Not with so many bachelors let loose when they all should be in cages." She laughed and gave Teddy a playful poke in the ribs. The

young man blushed mightily, and Megan suspected that poor
Teddy must have been caught making calf's eyes at Rachel
while Megan was away. Well, that wasn't so remarkable.
Rachel was certainly pretty enough, a petite blonde with
huge blue eyes, a smattering of freckles and a proud, buxom
figure that it would have been impossible for a man not
to notice. Between Rachel's blond prettiness and Megan's
own flaming red-haired Irish beauty, the two of them were
enough of an attraction to draw lonely men in off the prairie
for miles around, just to sit and look at them. And while
the lads were looking, they were also drinking. Megan's tent
saloon benefited greatly from that simple fact.

"You are welcome to come, Rachel," Megan said now,
"but we both know the sensible thing would be for you to
stay here until we have a better idea of what to expect from
all this."

"Megan, dear, you've never known me to do the sensible
thing yet, have you?"

Megan smiled. "All right then. I'm going to take a few
minutes to say good-bye to my brother. Then we'll leave.
Teddy, I believe you wanted to follow me over there?"

"Yes, ma'am."

"Rachel?"

"Me and Liam already said our good-byes, Megan. Any
more and I'm afraid I'd cry. If you don't mind, I'll stay here
and help Victor finish getting the horses ready to travel."

"Very well. Vic, have the team ready to pull out in fifteen
minutes, please."

"Yes'm."

"This way, Teddy."

The railroad doctor's office consisted of a boxcar that had
been removed from its rail truck and set down beside the
roadbed, freeing the truck to serve as a flatbed supply car

while the boxcar structure rendered separate service.

This morning, possibly as a result of the electrifying news from the west, there was no long line of workmen waiting for Dr. Thaddeus Wiseman's service. Most mornings brought a long turnout of men with real injuries and imagined illnesses, but not today. Today there was only one patient in evidence, a burly young man who was nursing a hand that was so badly swollen the skin was split over the knuckles. Megan winced just from seeing it. The poor fellow's hand looked like someone had been pounding it with rocks.

Thaddeus Wiseman finished washing the deep abrasions and began bandaging the raw but clean result. "What I'm going to do, Sam, is give you a bag of salts. For the next five days, morning and night, you're to take a palmful of the salts and dissolve them in a basin of water. Remove the bandages and soak your hand for half an hour each time. Morning and night alike, mind. Half an hour or more each soaking. Then when you're done dry off and put the wrapping back on. If the wounds go to turning green or start to stink, though, Sam, you hustle yourself back here to me and I'll try to straighten things out again without having to take the hand off."

The man called Sam blanched when Wiseman mentioned the possibility of amputation. "You don't think . . ."

"What I think, Sam, is that you'll be just fine if you soak that hand twice each day like I've told you. But if you let it go, well, that's up to you."

"I'll soak it, Doc. I promise."

"As you prefer, Sam. As you prefer." The doctor gave Thomas a pouch containing what looked to be several pounds of medicinal salts, and Sam stood. "One more thing, lad."

"Yes, Doc?"

"Try not to get into any more fights with potbellies. You hear?"

Sam went shamefacedly away, and when he was out of hearing, Megan asked the inevitable question. Thaddeus Wiseman laughed and helped himself to a seat on the stool his patient just vacated. "Sam was in his cups when he went to sleep last night, it seems, Megan dear. Not to bed, mind, but to sleep. He couldn't manage to locate his bed, but he did find the floor. Which is where he, um, chose to sleep. Some while afterward he awoke to a call of nature. The surroundings were unfamiliar. And there was this brawny figure towering over top of him. Threatening him, he swears it was. Startling. So he lashed out at it." Wiseman chuckled and reached for a pipe, which he began loading. "Punched the bejabbers out of a perfectly harmless cast-iron stove, he did. You see the result."

"All of that from one punch?"

"Oh my no. Sam and the stove had quite the scrap, I'm told. And the stove very nearly won."

Megan and Teddy both broke into laughter.

"Of course the result could be quite serious," Wiseman went on, tilting his head to one side so as to focus the rays of a burning glass and light his pipe. "Not funny at all if he should lose that hand."

"Surely you weren't serious about that, Doctor. I mean, I certainly assumed you were only trying to frighten him into using the salts when you told him that. Weren't you?"

"Not at all, my dear. This environment seems healthy enough, but a wound can fester and become gangrenous practically overnight. If that happens . . ." The doctor shuddered and looked away. When he spoke again, his voice, and his thoughts, seemed very far away. "Dear Megan, you wouldn't have believed the number of amputations we had to perform during the war. That awful war. Cartloads of arms. Wagonloads of legs. Some of my colleagues didn't even wait for sepsis to show itself. Some preferred to amputate as a preventative measure. No anesthesia, not even whiskey. Just strap the poor devils down and take up the saw." He spread his hands wide and stared down at them for a long moment as if he found them offensive. "Did you know, my dear, that I can remove a man's leg at the knee in less than a minute? It's a talent I've demonstrated many times. But not one to brag about, of course. Many of my esteemed colleagues were quicker, you see."

There was a sadness in Thaddeus Wiseman's voice now. A deeply rooted melancholy that Megan could comprehend only in the most vague of terms. But then she had never been subjected to the horrors of war the way this doctor—so odd in so very many ways—obviously had.

Since Liam had been wounded and come under Wiseman's care, Megan had come to know the railroad physician fairly well, and the more she knew him, the better she liked him.

He was not at all what she would have expected of a doctor, though.

Doctors, she had always thought, should be studious, serious men, usually mature and experienced and wise. They should be bespectacled and stoop-shouldered. Their appearance should be distinguished, even severe.

Thaddeus Wiseman was none of those things.

Thaddeus was, she thought, the physical ideal she had always expected a dashing army officer to be.

Which, now that she thought about it, was especially amusing in that the one general officer of the army with whom she was personally acquainted, Jack Casement, was so short and stocky and gremlinlike, while the one doctor she was coming to know was everything General Casement was not.

Thaddeus's hair was as red as Megan's own, and his beard and mustache flowed fierce and grand. He stood six foot five or a bit more and had shoulders as wide as an ax handle and legs as stout as young oak trees.

Whenever she saw Thaddeus, Megan thought he should be leading warriors, magnificent Gaels perhaps or Norse berserkers, to glory. A claymore would have seemed appropriate in his hands.

And yet his hands were gentle. Strong but truly gentle. She had seen the way he comforted and bandaged Sam just now. Much more to the point, she had seen the tender, gentle care he had given to her brother when Liam was first wounded and in terrible pain. Thaddeus Wiseman tried not merely to heal his patients but to comfort them as well. And Megan greatly appreciated the help Thaddeus had given to her only brother.

Thaddeus was, she thought, aged thirty or so. From the things she'd heard him say these past few weeks, she knew he was within a year or two of that. Yet there were streaks of gray showing at his temples, and salt specks of it were scattered through his beard.

It was pain that had put the gray there, she was sure. The physical pain of others, which Thaddeus insisted upon shouldering as his own burden whenever he could not take it away.

Thaddeus Wiseman, Megan thought, was a good man as well as a good doctor.

He stared down at his hands for a moment and then with a shrug seemed to resolve himself to return to the here and now. He looked up at her and smiled. Without raising his voice, he said, "As for the amputations, my dear, it is true. I would perform one on your brother's wound if only I could decide on a place to start my cutting."

Megan felt a moment of shock. And then she began to laugh.

Liam's injury had come in the form of a bullet taken in the backside. It was indelicate for her to think of it in so many words, perhaps, but the simple truth was that her brother had been shot in the butt. And where indeed would the good doctor choose to amputate if such became desirable.

"You damn quack," Liam shouted from the makeshift ward at the back of the boxcar. "Gi' me a saw t' defend myself with and I'd know where t' start the cutting. You c'n believe that, Thaddeus Quackman. Everything from the ears down, that's what I'd amputate o' yours."

Wiseman drew deeply on his pipe, wreathing his head in aromatic smoke. He grinned. "The patient, you may already have perceived, is feeling somewhat full of himself today."

Megan laughed again. "Can we go in and see him?"

"Please do. Anything to settle him down, my dear."

Megan and Teddy Bruce passed through the small, cluttered treatment room and on back to the tiny ward where Liam reclined on the only one of five cots that was occupied at the moment.

CHAPTER
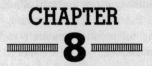
8

Joshua sat hunched over a cup of steaming coffee, morose and very deliberately alone in a shadowed corner of the mess car. During mealtimes the mess cars were as packed with swarming humanity as crickets in a bait can, but at this mid-morning hour the car was deserted save for a few swampers who were mopping down the floor, the bolted-in-place tables and the walls, all receiving the same lye soap washdown that was given—and thoroughly needed—at the end of each frenetic meal.

Just as he had taken refuge in a mess tent for the high-muck-a-mucks when he wanted to avoid his own scouts the evening before, now he had chosen to find coffee and solitude in the workingmen's mess car. There was no one connected with that meeting in the executive car that he wanted to talk to right now. Medgar Taney, captain, U.S. Army, included. No, not just included. Taney absolutely led the list of people Joshua Hood did not want to be bothered by just now.

It was still early, but the hell with it, he thought. He pulled a slim pewter flask out, unscrewed the lid and tipped a dollop of whiskey into the coffee. That should smooth it out a mite, he thought, returning the flask to his pocket.

"Before you put that away, if you wouldn't mind . . ."

Joshua blinked, surprised, and looked up to see Glenn Gilchrist standing beside him. Gilchrist had a cup in his hand and was holding it out toward Joshua.

"What?"

"I was hoping for a little something to keep my coffee warm. But never mind."

"No, I . . . I wasn't expecting you, that's all. I don't mind." Joshua once again unscrewed the lid of his flask and poured a measure of the fiery liquor.

"Thanks." Gilchrist took a seat beside Joshua.

"I didn't think you college boys ever drank before the sun was over the yardarm."

"There's lots of things college boys do that they shouldn't," Gilchrist responded. He raised his cup in a mocking salute and drank from it. "Cheers."

"Maybe you can think of something to cheer about. I can't." Reluctantly, as if drinking with the man might be construed as a truce of sorts, Joshua took a swallow from his own cup. The whiskied coffee spread its heat through his belly. "Tell me something, college boy."

"What's that?"

"What the hell is a yardarm, anyhow?"

Gilchrist smiled. "Damn if I know, actually. Something to do with a ship, I think."

"You're from Boston or some such place. I figured you to know all about ships."

"I know less about them than I should, I suppose. Probably I should have paid attention to shipping instead of this railroad. There aren't any Indians in the middle of the ocean."

"Plenty of them around here though," Joshua agreed. "Mad too." He shook his head. "That damned fool Taney. Him and his insistence that his troops fight with whatever Indians they come across. You know what I think?"

Gilchrist shook his head.

"I been thinking a lot about this, understand. Ever since I heard what happened out there. And mind, I'd already been to the fort. Maybe I should have guessed what that idiot was fixing to do, but I didn't. Anyway, I been doing some serious thinking about this. And you know how it is with the army right now, with all these officers, don't you?"

"No, I can't say that I know all that much about the military out here."

"Not just out here. Everyplace," Joshua said. "There's just too damn many officers."

"I beg your pardon?" Gilchrist swallowed away the rest of his coffee. He motioned, and one of the swampers brought a steel pitcher of hot coffee and a sack of brown, lumpy sugar to set handy on the table before the two men. Joshua grunted and brought his flask out again, this time leaving it on the table where both could reach it.

"Too many officers, I was saying," Joshua went on as if there had been no interruption. "How big was the army before the war? I dunno, likely you don't neither. Point is, it was mighty small. Then during the war it got big. I mean *real* big. There prob'ly was more officers during the war than there'd been soldiers before it. And these officers, they liked what they found in the army. A lot of 'em did, anyway. The pay wasn't so bad, and most of all they liked being saluted and made a fuss of and set up to be better than most everybody around them. So when the war ended, they didn't want to have to get out and go look for ordinary jobs again. Especially with jobs so scarce. I mean, hell, we got guys swinging hammers on the line and drawing three dollars a day, guys that used to command whole infantry companies. I have a scout that used to be a first lieutenant. And whether you know it or not, there's a stickman on one of your survey crews that used t' be a captain in the Corps of Engineers. Did you know that?"

Gilchrist shook his head. "No, I didn't."

"Well, it's true, I promise you."

"I don't doubt it."

"Yeah, well anyway, when the war ended a whole lot o' these officers stayed in the army so they wouldn't have to give up all that good fun. Which means that there's two, three times as many officers in uniform right now as is really needed." Joshua finished his drink and fixed himself another.

"What that means is that promotions . . . Well, there just aren't hardly any possible. Won't be for years an' years to come. And that Taney, you saw how old a man he is. He should've been a lieutenant colonel by now. Or higher. But all he is is a measly captain. And that's for a regular army man who was a captain before the war ever started."

"How would you know a thing like that?" Gilchrist demanded.

"I ain't making it up. I asked the man's orderly, a corporal name of Mulaney. I made like I was impressed by the idiot, Taney I mean, and was admiring him. The corporal like to wet himself he was in such a hurry to praise his captain. O' course that was the only way he *could* act about it, no matter what he really might think. Anything ever get back to Taney about one of his headquarters staff being disloyal, and the poor sap would be bucked and gagged for sure. I'm thinking Taney is that kind. Anyway, point is, I asked this Corporal Mulaney and he told me. Taney's date o' rank—that's supposed t' be important in the army, though I don't know why—is some time in '57. Hell, with that rank going into the war, you'd think he should've come out a general."

"It does make a fellow think," Gilchrist agreed.

"Sure does. But anyway, what I was saying . . . damn."

"What's the matter?"

"This flask. Damn thing's empty."

"Really?" Gilchrist turned and motioned for the swamper to come over. He had a brief conversation with the man and handed him a coin, then turned back to Joshua. "Sorry. Go on, please."

"What was I saying? Oh, right. About the army and this damn fool Taney. What I think is that he knows he's about used up in the army. Overage in grade. I think that's what they call it. Something like that, anyway. Whatever it was he did to mess up and not get promoted during the war, now he's about run out of chances to show a reason why he oughta get made a major. And whether they make him a major or not, pretty soon the army is gonna want to give his captain's spot to somebody else. They'll make room to be able to do that either by moving Taney up to be a major or by withdrawing his commission."

"They'd kick him out? Really?"

"They're starting t' have to do that sort o' thing already. They got just too many officers in uniform. Ask General Dodge. That's where I heard this part of it. Him and General Casement were talking over brandy the evening before we headed out to have our peace talk with the Sioux. I was there, Gilchrist, just kinda setting quiet and listening while them two talked, you know, about the army and fellas they'd both known and battles and such."

"About Captain Taney?"

"Naw," Joshua said with a snort. "Not him. I doubt either o' them ever heard of Medgar Taney at that point. I know I never had. They was talking about the army in general. And about getting rid of the unproductive officers, like that. It's later that I got to thinking about Taney and kinda put two an' two together. You see what I mean?"

"I think so. You think Taney wants to do something spec-
tacular, even if it means starting a totally unnecessary war
with the Sioux, if that's what it takes to get him promoted
so he can keep up the soft life in the army."

Joshua grinned. "See, college boy? You ain't as dumb as
you look. You did follow what I was gettin' at."

"I can't believe anyone would be that cold and callous,
Joshua. To take human lives . . ."

"Indian lives, remember that. Not human."

"But . . ."

"Look, you get no argument from me. I've lived with the
Arapaho. I still got friends, good an' true friends, that just
happen t' be Indian. But it ain't what I think that we're
talking about here. Nor what you think. Nor even what's
simple right an' wrong. We're talking about Medgar Taney
an' what *he* thinks. And his own boss, don't forget, is the
fella that's been quoted in all the eastern newspapers saying
the only good Indian is a dead Indian."

"But nobody . . ."

"Nobody would ever take a silly statement like that serious? Is that what you're fixing t' tell me, college boy? Don't
you never think that. There's some will take it serious. An'
I'm here t' tell you that— Say, where'd this bottle come
from? Thanks, don't mind if I do. I'm here t' tell you
that Captain Medgar Taney an' a whole lot more just like
him *will* take it serious. And there's a whole lot o' Indians,
Sioux and Cheyenne and Comanche, maybe my friends the
Arapaho, God only knows what other tribes too, there's a
whole lot o' good an' decent human bein's that just happens
t' be Indians that are likely t' be shot down dead before folks
wake up an' figure out what's wrong with thinking like that,
college boy. A whole lot."

Gilchrist fingered his chin for a moment, then reached for the pint bottle the swamper had brought and mixed the liquor with sugar and a splash of now cold coffee. "Something has to be done about this, Joshua. We can't sit back and let a man like that popinjay ruin everything you and General Dodge created."

"Too late t' change anything now, college boy. You was there. You seen what happened. There won't be an Indian this side o' the Californias that'd trust our word now. Right now, if a Union Pacific man says its daylight, the Sioux are gonna believe it's dark. Even if the words is spoke at high noon."

"There has to be—" Gilchrist slammed his cup down on the table with a bang, startling Joshua. "I have it."

"You got what?"

"An idea. *The* idea." Gilchrist grinned. "Joshua, old chap, you and I are going to take a ride."

"We are?"

"Indeed. You and I, Joshua, are going to ride out and find the Sioux encampment. We are going to explain things. Everything. And we are going to repair the cracks Medgar Taney put in our treaty with the Sioux."

"College boy, there ain't but one good thing 'bout that plan o' yours."

"What's that, Joshua?"

"The fact that you'll see it clearer when you get sober." Joshua pushed himself up from the table, amazed at how difficult that proved to be. He swayed from side to side and had to grab at the table edge to maintain his balance. Lordy, he hadn't thought he'd had that much. And in coffee too. Amazing.

"Where are you going, Joshua? We have to talk about this. We have to plan—"

"What we got t' plan, college boy, is a place where we can lay down an' not be bothered for a couple hours. Take a little siesta, like. You know what that is? No? Well I ain't feeling up t' explaining it to you, college boy. Not right now. Later maybe."

"But . . . my plan."

"Later, college boy. We'll both of us feel better later." Joshua lurched away from the table and down the folding steps to ground level. He was rather proud of himself. He wobbled a little and stumbled now and then, but he didn't fall down. Under the circumstances that seemed something of a victory.

CHAPTER
9

"There was some black man here lookin' for you, Miss Megan."

"Looking for me? A black man? You mean like . . . a Negro?"

"Yes'm," Victor told her. He was sitting on the ground, leaning against a wagon wheel, his right shoulder pressed tight against the greasy hub nut. The position looked uncomfortable to Megan, to say nothing of the filth involved, but Victor didn't seem to mind. "He said to tell you you wasn't t' go no further west, ma'am."

Megan stared incredulously down at her slow-witted hired man. Surely there couldn't . . . but then Victor would have no reason to make up a story so preposterous. And that was ignoring the question of whether he would have intelligence enough to do so. In the past she had always found Victor to be completely honest in even the slightest matters. She suspected this was mainly because he wasn't bright enough to think up lies. Whatever the reason, though, honesty was not a trait to be complained about. This news, though . . .

"Tell me again please, Vic?"

He turned his head back toward her. After he'd delivered the information, his eyes had lost their focus and he had been peering dully off toward the southern horizon. "Ma'am?"

"I want you to think back, Victor. I want you to remember, now."

"Yes, ma'am. Remember what?"

"This Negro, this black man. You say he came here to see me?"

"Yes'm."

"And he left a warning that I wasn't to go any further west?"

"Yes'm, he did."

"Did he say why?"

Victor shrugged and looked off past the rails once more.

"Vic, please pay attention to what I'm asking you."

"Yes, ma'am," he said contritely.

"Tell me again what this black man said."

"He said you wasn't t' go west no more."

"But he didn't say why?"

"No, ma'am."

"Did he make any threats, Victor?"

"What d'you mean, ma'am?"

"Did he say anything about what might happen if we do go west from here? Did he say anything about guns or . . . or fires or bombs or anything?"

Victor frowned in deep concentration for a moment, then shook his head. "No, ma'am, I don't believe he said none o' those things. Just that you wasn't t' go west. Then he left."

Megan frowned also, but her expression was due to confusion, not contemplation. A black man. A Negro. With a message for her. It seemed . . . well, it seemed incredible, that was all. Megan didn't know any Negroes. She doubted she had ever actually spoken to a black person in her entire life. Oh, she had seen Negroes before. Of course, she had. Dozens of them. On the streets here and there.

Two or three times back east. Somewhat more frequently in Omaha. And right here along the railroad there were even a few.

But she hadn't ever had reason to *speak* to a Negro. Not that she wouldn't. Why, she had nothing at all against them. And all the frightening things that were said about them, well, she doubted those things were true. Most of them. Look at all the ugly things that were said about the Irish, and she *knew* those rumors weren't so.

But still . . . a Negro. An actual Negro. With a message for her.

"Did he sound . . . mean, Vic? Or angry?"

"No, ma'am. He just kinda sounded like he was in a hurry."

"Was he armed?"

"Not that I seen, ma'am. But then he was wearing a coat. He could've been carrying a gun under that. If he was, he never said nothing about it."

The only thing Megan could think of to explain such a warning was Ike Norman trying to scare her away from end-o'-track. Ike Norman and Belle King hated her and wanted to keep her from competing with their dishonest businesses. It would be much easier for the two of them to bilk the railroad workers out of their hard-won wages if Megan were no longer in competition with them.

Megan shuddered as a cold chill ran through her body. Ike had hired a bullyboy once before and given the man instructions that he was to ruin Megan. Ike could well have done much the same thing a second time. This Negro . . .

"Rachel?"

"Yes, Megan?" Rachel was just returning from the row of privies, one of which had been reluctantly set aside for use by women.

"Victor says he had a visitor while I was gone, Rachel. A Negro with a message for me. Do you know anything about this?"

"It must have been while I was away. I'm sorry."

"Do you know of any black men in the camp, Rachel?"

"The same as you do, I suppose. None of them ever comes into the saloon to drink with the other men. But I've seen a few Negro men around. And there's that Negro woman who takes in laundry. You know, the young woman with the little girls?"

Megan shook her head. "I don't know them."

"You haven't seen those children? They're adorable. And so nice mannered. You really—"

"Rachel!"

"Yes?"

"This is serious, Rachel. Victor says this Negro man was making threats against us. You don't know of any Negroes hanging around Ike Norman's tent, do you?"

Rachel's hand flew to her throat in alarm. "No. Honestly, Megan, I don't. But I saw Ike and Belle pull out early this morning. Belle shouted . . . Well, you don't want to know what she said. It doesn't bear repeating. The important thing to know, I suppose, is that they've been on the road for hours already. I'm sure of that."

Megan frowned. "That could be deliberate, you know. Ike might have wanted to give himself a good alibi. You know. Make a scene while they were driving away to make sure everyone would know they weren't anywhere around while this henchman of theirs delivered their threats."

"What are you going to do about it?"

"Why, we're going to end-o'-track, of course. What would you think? Victor, get up now and make sure the horses are ready. We have a long way to go, and who knows what might lie between us and the next encampment. Storms, Indians . . . crazy Negroes with guns . . . anything."

Victor climbed slowly to his feet, stretched and then ambled toward the front of the hitch, where the aging draft horses stood, patient and stolid in their harness. He unclipped the iron hitching weights from the bit rings and carried them back to toss onto the floor of the driving box, then checked to make sure the reins ran loose and free through the line guides. "Reckon we're ready, Miss Megan. Ready as we're gonna be."

Megan took a last look around the wagon and underneath it to make sure they weren't leaving anything behind by accident. Then she and Rachel climbed onto the box.

"You want me t' drive, ma'am?"

"Later, Victor. You can spell me later on."

The boy grinned and happily muttered something to himself while he trotted back to crawl atop the tarp that covered the load on the cartlike trailer. Driving the wagon was something Victor truly enjoyed, and Megan knew there was little he could do that could get them into trouble. The team of elderly horses she had inherited from sweet old Walt Guthrie were so slow and steady that it practically would take an act of deliberate will to have an accident with them. As soon as they were well clear of the old encampment here, she decided, she would turn the reins over to Vic and let him enjoy himself. After all, it wasn't like he could get lost. All they had to do from here on was follow along beside the railroad tracks. Straight on until they found the new tent city at the new end-o'-track.

"Are you ready, Rachel?"

"Goodness gracious, yes. The quicker we get there the better, I say."

"It isn't too late to change your mind, you know."

"Megan!" Rachel said sharply. "Are you going to start this wagon or must I?"

Megan glanced behind her to make sure Victor was in his spot perched atop the trailer. Then she plucked the whip from its socket and snapped it noisily a good four feet over the back of her nigh leader. Moving as if they were a single creature, the team of big horses snorted and tossed their heads, then leaned into their collars. The wagon, along with everything Megan O'Connell owned in this world, began to roll slowly westward.

CHAPTER

10

Glenn Gilchrist woke to a painfully dry, rancid-cotton mouth and a throbbing headache. The fur on his tongue tasted of stale vomit, and he was so thirsty he was sure he could drain a keg at a single draft. He sat upright, an activity that caused the pounding in his head to intensify both in force and volume, and observed that he was on a cot. Inside a tent. Whose cot and whose tent he had no idea. Nothing around him looked familiar. A late afternoon—or early morning—sun beat a yellow-orange glow on one canvas wall. Late afternoon, Glenn determined after some thought. His shirt was sweat-soaked and prickly against his skin, implying that he'd slept through the afternoon heat inside this airless cocoon. There-fore the low sun announced the approach of evening and not a new day. Under the circumstances he took some small degree of pride in his ability to complete that equation of deductive reasoning. Professor Demetrios's courses in applied logic did indeed have application in the real world, Glenn decided. So there—ow! He winced as a lance of sharp pain shot from one temple all the way through to the other.

Slowly and carefully Glenn ran his hands over his scalp and down the nape of his neck, then all around his head. There seemed to be no open wounds. His hands came away free of blood. All the damage seemed to be internal. That revelation brought mixed feelings with it. It almost would have been preferable to find himself the victim of some unremembered assault. After all, a man cannot be blamed for what others may do to him, but shame on anyone fool enough to do this to himself.

With gritted teeth and grim determination, Glenn forced himself upright, swayed momentarily and then tottered unsteadily out past the door flaps.

Mm, yes. Late afternoon indeed. Over there to the south lay the roadbed with its gravel ballast and ladder-track line of fresh ties waiting for rails to be laid and spiked in place. Over there the swarming masses of laborers gathering for their evening meal. Yonder the pale, billowing smoke from a wood-fired steam engine. The sights, the sounds were all familiar. Glenn still had no idea whose guest he had been through the afternoon, but now that he was upright and moving, he was beginning to feel better. Even the pounding in his head was muted, as by a sheet of wool laid atop the drum snares. He took a look around, spied an oversized tent that he suspected was the mess tent for upper-level personnel and started toward it. Lordy but he was thirsty.

"Good evening, Mr. Gilchrist sir."

Glenn had to concentrate on focusing his eyes and consciously remembering before he could recall the name. And of his own crewman, at that. "Good evening, Laddy. Doing all right now, are you?" Laddy Sullivan, Glenn remembered now, had been badly shaken by the ugliness of the massacre.

"Yes, sir, thank you." The youngster smiled and would have gone on about his business, but Glenn stopped him with a question. "You're a friend of Liam O'Connell, aren't you, Laddy?" Glenn asked.

"I wouldna be so bold as t' say just that, Mr. Gilchrist, but I'd be knowin' Liam, I would."

"Do you know his sister then?"

"Miss Megan? Aye, sir." The boy grinned. "Name me one man in this camp that hasn't remarked on Miss Megan's appearance, an' I say you'll be naming one fey chappie."

"Have you seen her here then, Laddy?"

"Miss Megan here? No, sir, I'm sure she isn't."

"Thank you, Laddy."

"Is that all, sir?"

"Yes, thanks."

"If you don't mind me sayin' so, Mr. Gilchrist sir, you look like you could use a hand. Or somethin'."

"I'm fine now, Laddy, thank you."

"Yes sir, whatever you say, sir." The boy smiled and went on in the direction of the chow line.

Glenn stood where he was for a moment, blinking and thinking. He was disappointed to hear that Megan and her saloon were not here at the new end-o'-track. Disappointed, yes, but pleased too. They had said this morning that this spot not far from Fort Kearney would be designated the new end-of-track for administrative purposes, for stockpiling supplies and so on. That meant the hangers-on, the saloons and cafes and bawdy houses, would all gather here until it was time to move along again. And that implied that here Glenn would once again have the pleasure of seeing Megan O'Connell.

But at the same time he was afraid for her. Thanks to that damn fool Medgar Taney the treaty with the Sioux had been broken and every white man—or woman—on the Nebraska plains was at risk.

That would include Megan were she to come forward again. Thank God she'd been sensible enough to stay back this time. With luck she might have withdrawn all the way back to Omaha, where her sister operated some sort of business. Much as he would miss her, Glenn knew it was definitely for the best if Megan and her tent saloon stay far away from this spot. At least until the problems with the Sioux could be resolved.

Glenn's expression hardened at that thought. Those problems *would* be resolved, he swore. By himself if no other way. Because while he might have been in his cups earlier, he had been fully aware. He remembered full well the idea that had come to him this morning. Someone had to ride out to meet with the Sioux. To explain to them what had happened. And what had not.

Their treaty was with the Union Pacific Railroad. And the pledges of good faith that had existed between the Sioux nation and General Grenville Dodge existed still. Those pledges were unabated. Nothing Captain Medgar Taney and Lieutenant Edward Wollins—and for that matter all the rest of the United States Army too—could do would ever change that.

Someone must explain this to the Sioux.

Surely they were reasonable people. They were savages, true, but they were human beings too. They must certainly value peace or they never would have agreed to the treaty to begin with.

Well, now there had been this one small setback.

But he could explain it to the Sioux. How the army hadn't known about the peace. How peace still could be maintained if only the Sioux gave the railroad time to spread the good news.

Glenn knew good and well General Dodge could secure firm instruction from Taney's superiors if only the Sioux could be convinced that it was in their best interests to accept the pain of their losses and adhere to the original treaty.

That addendum to his idea sprang full-blown into Glenn's thoughts while he walked slowly on toward the mess tent.

Of course. He would send word east. General Dodge could handle things at that end. After all, Dodge was a brother-at-arms with Generals Sheridan and Sherman. He could speak to them. And with direct orders from that exalted level, there was nothing Medgar Taney could do to thwart the peace.

And while General Dodge was busy lobbying the military command in Omaha and St. Louis or wherever, Glenn Gilchrist would be attending to the simple task of explaining all of this to the Sioux chiefs in . . . well, wherever the Sioux chiefs were. He would have to ask Joshua Hood about that.

Glenn grunted softly to himself. He quite clearly remembered Joshua saying earlier that he would think better of his plan once he awakened.

Well, he did think better of it. He did indeed. The more he thought about it now the better and better it did sound to him.

He thought so highly of it, in fact, that he was able to muster a smile as he pushed through the door flaps to enter the mess tent.

A wall of scent greeted him inside the canvas. Smells of frying meats and rich gravies and . . . oh, Lordy.

The heavy, mingled odors struck with a force like that of a physical blow. Glenn's stomach rebelled at the thought of such greasy fare being introduced into it, and he felt a wave of acid bile rise into the back of his throat.

Clamping a hand over his mouth, Glenn turned and bolted back outside into the clearer, fresher air beyond the confines of the executive mess tent.

Perhaps, just perhaps, he wasn't feeling quite so thoroughly recovered as he'd imagined.

CHAPTER

11

"We should stop over there, I think, in that gully."

"You know what they say about staying out of low places that can flood if there's a storm, don't you?" Rachel asked.

"Take a look at the sky, dear, and tell me if you think there's more danger from rain tonight or from Ike Norman," Megan responded. "Personally I think we'll be better off if we drive in behind that brush so we can't be seen from the road. In case . . . well, never mind in case what. I just think we should drive off the road and out of sight, that's all."

Rachel nodded and sent a nervous look around the empty horizon. There was little enough to see: the railroad tracks with the road's accompanying line of telegraph poles, a few folds and wrinkles on the surface of the prairie . . . and grass. Mile after mile after endless mile of grass below and blue sky above. At this hour the blue had already turned dark to the east and a deepening purple overhead, but the cloudless effect was unchanged from what it had been ever since they began driving.

They hadn't seen another living soul since an engine and string of flatcars rolled westward late in the afternoon. The late start they'd gotten this morning had put them behind all the other end-of-track entrepreneurs who were moving west to the new assembly and supply point.

Normally Megan would have welcomed this near solitude, this rare opportunity to spend a few hours apart from the crush of noisy, unwashed men who were her friends and her customers but who placed so many demands upon her. Normally. But this evening . . . She was nervous. That was the simple truth of the matter. Not easily frightened and certainly not one to jump at shadows, she was nonetheless distressed by the thought that Ike Norman might have hired a Negro assassin to finish the job the late Lew Scudder had been unable to accomplish.

And whether her fears were well founded or not, there was no point in trying to deny the existence of her concern.

"Over there please, Victor," she said. "Pull in behind that brush, and we'll make camp for the night."

"Yes'm," Vic Boyette called back from the driving box where he had spent most of the day in a state of obvious contentment, handling the team of big, docile workhorses.

A moment later there was a change in the rhythm of the jangling trace chains, and the wagon swerved and bumped off the well-traveled ruts and onto virgin prairie.

"We have about an hour until dark," Megan said, mostly to herself. "You can help Vic with the team, Rachel, while I get supper going. We'll plan on an early start tomorrow and, who knows, perhaps we'll reach the new end-of-track by tomorrow night."

"Well, I must say, college boy, you look somewhat the better now than the last time I seen you."

Glenn gritted his teeth—figuratively anyway; he wouldn't have wanted to give Hood the satisfaction of seeing him literally do so—and slapped his plate onto the table with a deliberately loud clatter. His hope was that Joshua Hood's head was as hollow as Glenn's own, and if so, the noise would be echoing between the man's ears loud enough to make him want to yell. Not that he really expected to know if he achieved that purpose. He was sure Joshua would hide any such pain if it killed him, just as Glenn damned well was hiding his own discomforts from Hood.

"Me, leatherstocking? Is it my health you're asking after? How nice of you. But I must tell you that I'm feeling fine now. Just fine. How about yourself?" Glenn noticed that Hood's plate was laden with food no greasier than Glenn had chosen, so it was safe to assume that Hood's stomach was in no better condition now. Both men had taken mostly rice and vegetables from the serving line, opting to leave the fried meats and gravies untouched.

"What was that you called me, college boy?"

"Leatherstocking." Glenn gave the cheeky rustic a tight smile. "It's a compliment, I assure you."

"Yeah, I'm sure it is."

"But of course." Glenn eyed his rice with suspicion. The quality of the Union Pacific's supply contractors being what it was, it was not totally unknown for grains of rice or small beans to get up and walk off a man's plate. This lot, however, seemed to consist of the purported article. Or anyway had been cooked until it was dead. Glenn scooped some onto his fork and tried a mouthful, managing to do so without gagging if only because he did not want Joshua Hood to witness any such weakness. "Mm, good," he said. "Excellent. I say, leatherstocking, aren't you eating?"

Hood frowned and began attacking his own plate.

"Coffee, gennelmuns? Tea? Something a mite stronger?"

"Coffee, Henry. With a little something stronger in it," Hood said quickly. "How 'bout for you, college boy? A little hair o' the dog? Or haven't you the stomach for a taste of what brung you here."

"Fine. Make that two, please."

The colored man turned away, but Joshua called him back.

"Yes, suh?"

"I'm surprised to see you here, Henry. When did you all get in?"

"This aft'noon, suh. Came up on a work train, we did. Just had time t' set de place up an' start cookin'. Tha's why we got the servin' line over theah 'stead o' a proper selection. I hope you don' mind."

"Not at all, but did you have time this morning to do what I asked you to?"

"T' deliver yo' message t' Miss O'Connell, Mist' Hood? Oh yes, suh. I went just like you ast me to. Told 'em theah just what you said. She wasn't t' come west no mo'. She t' go back t' that Omaha instead."

"Thank you, Henry. Thank you very much."

"If you excuse me now, please, I go get them coffees with the bit o' extra warm-up in them."

"That will be fine, Henry, thanks."

"What was that all about?" Glenn asked when the waiter was gone. Normally he wouldn't have been so openly curious, but Megan's name having been raised by the man was enough to command his attention.

"If you must know, I had to leave in a hurry last night, and I was afraid Megan might be thinking about moving along with the rails again. In light of this renewed trouble with the Sioux, I figured it'd be safer for her to go back and stay with her sister until we know what's gonna happen. Since I couldn't talk to her myself, I asked Henry to carry a warning to her. You heard what he said."

"As I recall, though, all he said was that he delivered the message. He didn't say what her response was."

"Come on, college boy. Give Megan some credit. She's stubborn, sure. Independent as a hog on ice. But she's not stupid. She wouldn't come west with Indian trouble brewing. She'll see the sense in going back to stay with that sister of hers . . ."

"Aileen," Glenn prompted.

"Yeah, right. Aileen. Hell, she'll go back an' visit with Aileen an' those kids. Be a nice break for her. Then when it's safe, I'll go back an' personally escort her out to where she can set up her saloon again."

Glenn scowled. You'll go back and provide her with an escort like hell, he thought in glowering silence. Only if you can get there before me.

"The important thing," Glenn said aloud, "is that Megan is safe now. At least we can agree on that."

"Ayuh. That much you an' me can agree on, college boy."

Henry came back with a pair of exceptionally aromatic cups. The smell of the liquor wasn't as repulsive as Glenn had expected. In fact, this particular hair of the dog smelled rather good.

"Before you go and get yourself drunk again," Glenn said as he reached for the cup nearer to him, "I think we better discuss my plan."

"What plan was that, college boy?"

"You are going to take me out and introduce me to that Sioux chief, remember? What was his name again? Standing Bull?"

"Spotted."

"Come again?"

"Spotted Bull. Or Speckled Bull if you'd rather. It don't much matter which way you wanta say it in English. Spotted Bull is how it mostly comes out. But that ain't really the point here. The thing is, college boy, nobody yet has given me any kind o' good reason for you and me going out there t' get ourselves scalped an' killed."

"Scalped and killed?"

"That's right. In that order. Scalped first, then kilt later. Mad as the Sioux are bound t' be right now, I figure that's the order they'd do it in if any white man was damn fool enough t' let hisself get caught. Which I personally ain't gonna do no matter how bad you want it t' happen."

"I resent the implication, Hood. Whatever differences there may be between us, I—"

"Aw, don't get your back up s' high. That ain't what I meant. Exactly. But don't be getting no more stupid ideas about making yourself the hero by talking t' the Sioux. Captain Taney an' his pet lapdog lieutenant already made sure we won't none of us be powwowing with the Sioux no more. So just get that outa your mind, college boy. An' keep it out."

"But I know if only I had a chance—"

"Well, you ain't gonna get no such chance. Guarantee. An' don't ask me t' help you neither. Not that I'd take it so damn hard if your hair was to get lifted, mind. It's just that I wouldn't want mine taken along with yourn. So let that idea go, college boy, an' don't bring it up t' me again. It just don't wash."

Glenn frowned but said nothing. It seemed Hood's mind was made up on the subject. And Joshua, damn it, was the only guide he knew of who would be competent to take him to the Sioux encampments. If only . . . Well, no point in thinking about that, was there. He took a swallow of the whiskey-laced coffee. The beverage spread a deep warmth through his belly and quickened his appetite. You know, he thought, one of those pork chops might not be so bad

after all. And maybe a ladle of gravy to pour over the rice.
Yessir, maybe that wouldn't be so bad after all. He had
another swallow of the coffee and realized he was feeling
pretty good again.

As for Joshua Hood's stubborn refusal to guide him to
see this Speckled Bull person . . . they would just have to
see about that, wouldn't they? "Another cup of, uh, coffee
there, Hood?"

"Yeah, I reckon I'm game if you are, college boy."

Megan sighed with contentment. Their camp was a snug
and comfortable one, guarded on the east and west sides by
the sharply sloping walls of the gully and screened north and
south by dense thickets of chokecherry and wild plum and
some other low, scruffy growth that Megan did not recognize. In truth she wasn't entirely sure about the chokecherry
and wild plum bushes either. But she thought that was what
the thick brush was. She yawned and, stretching, reached
for the coffeepot that sat on a flat rock at the edge of
the coals.

"That was good, Megan," Rachel said.

"There's some bacon left in the pan. Why don't you finish it?"

"Not me." Rachel grinned boldly and said, "I don't want
to lose my girlish figure, now do I?"

"Aye, and who would it be you're keeping it for, eh?"

Rachel blushed. Both women knew it was Megan's baby
brother, Liam, whose attentions Rachel Foreman wanted
to keep.

"Never mind," Megan said. "Maybe Victor will want it."

Victor had taken a scrap of wastepaper and wandered
away into the privacy of the brush a few minutes earlier.

"That's one thing, Megan. We never have to worry what

to do with our leftovers. Not as long as we have Vic with us." She laughed softly, then tilted her head. "I think you can go ahead and take that bacon up if you want. I can hear Victor coming back."

"Really? How odd." One of Victor's many firmly established habits was that of taking a long, long time when he went off to the privy—or whatever substitute was available—each evening. Megan wouldn't have expected him back for a good twenty minutes anyway. Yet she too listened closely and could hear the approach of footsteps crackling and crunching through the underbrush, quite loudly now as they came near.

Megan set her coffee cup down on the hard clay soil and stood, bending to pick up the heavy iron skillet that contained the strips of leftover bacon and a pint or more of hot grease.

"Here, Victor, won't you take this before it— Oh, my God!"

The man who stepped out of the undergrowth and stopped, apparently as stunned by the encounter as she, was not her hired man Victor Boyette.

This man was nearly naked. And the bronze hues of his hairless chest came not from sunburn but from his own natural copper coloration. His hair hung in long braids, and his only garments were a leather breechclout, low-cut moccasins and a breastplate made of brightly colored porcupine quills. A clump of ragged feathers that had probably come from the tail of a bluejay was woven into one oiled braid, and a small leather pouch suspended from a thong around his neck. He carried no rifle or bow, but a butcher knife just like the ones in Megan's own kitchen boxes was tucked into the braided sinew cord that supported his breechclout.

The warrior—for surely that was what he was—gaped at

Megan while she stood before him as fear-frozen as any timid doe startled by a hunter.

Megan was the first to recover from the shock of discovery.

With a yelp of sheer terror she threw the skillet, hot grease and all, into the Indian's face, then turned and bolted blindly away.

Something clutched at her ankles, and she toppled forward onto the hard earth.

She felt a stunning blow at her temple.

And then felt no more, as a black and empty unconsciousness descended upon her.

CHAPTER

12

Glenn walked alone through the night. His tent had been set up by one of the camp tenders and the general location described to him, but he was not entirely sure of where he was supposed to go. Nowhere near the tent where he'd slept the afternoon away, he was sure of that. Of course he still had no idea whose guest he had been for that period. It was a fact that was somewhat embarrassing and that he did not now want to bring up, although he supposed eventually he would have to so that he could properly thank his unknown host.

He made his way through the maze of canvas and pegged-down guy lines, careful not to trip and take a nasty tumble in the dark.

End-of-track was acrawl with men living in all manner of conditions, most of them crude and some quite barbaric. The railroad provided some living accommodation in the form of massive railcars that had tiers of bunk beds built ceiling-high on each long wall, with a narrow aisle down the middle. Each car could sleep more than a hundred men. Even so, it was impossible to provide living quarters—such as those were—for all the hundreds, even thousands, of men who were engaged in the task of laying the rails west. Surveyors, road graders, muleskinners, harnessmakers, blacksmiths, tool cutters, draymen, gandy dancers, foremen, crew leaders, straw bosses, cooks and meat hunters . . . and just plain sweat-drenched laborers. All had to be provided for, fed and sheltered. And that was just the actual railroad personnel. In addition to the people who had to be there to accomplish the job of construction, there were dozens, scores, perhaps hundreds, more who chose to be there in the hope of making a profit from the men, and the payroll, of the railroad. It was a wide, wild scene and one Glenn sometimes appreciated, sometimes did not. Tonight he could have done with less wide and certainly with less wild as here a man cussed and shouted, there a pair bit and brawled. What Glenn Gilchrist wanted right here and right now was his own snug tent, his own soft blanket, his own narrow cot.

And a few hours to sleep before the dawn.

All of that was waiting for him, he knew. If only he could *find* it.

"You there."

"Yeah?"

"Is this the survey camp?"

"Hell no, bub, this's McCroy's string."

"Fishplaters," another voice came at him out of the darkness.

"Do you know where the surveyors are?"

"Try over that way." He couldn't see in which direction the respondent was pointing. If any. The man sounded too drunk to be relied on anyway.

"Thanks."

"Yeah, sure."

Glenn made his way through that clutch of tents and on to another.

"I'm looking for the surveyors."

"Try over there."

"Thank you." He went in the direction indicated, but when he reached the camp fire that was visible in that direction, he found a small group of men who'd made their beds on the prairie grass without benefit of tents for shelter. In the dim light of the dying fire, Glenn saw that he'd stumbled across Joshua Hood's scouts. Not that there was any sign of Hood himself. Which was just as well. Hood hadn't been feeling any too well the last Glenn saw him.

The scouts all seemed sound asleep, but when Glenn recognized them and would have tiptoed silently away, he found himself peering into the muzzles of at least three revolvers and into even more wide open eyes. Every man of them was alert.

"Sorry, Mr. Gilchrist," one of the scouts said with a shrug and a grin. "We thought you was Silas when you come in. You walk a lot like him. Did you know that?"

"Uh, no. I can't say that I did know it."

" 'Struth. But you stayed quiet. That's what woke us up. Silas woulda stomped around and cussed and spit a lot."

"And you would have slept through that, I suppose?"

The young scout grinned at him. "Sure. More or less."

"Now that you know who I am, though, don't you think you could put the gun away, son?"

"Oh." The grin flashed once more. "Reckon I forgot. Sorry." All the other guns and most of the other eyes had already disappeared back underneath their blankets by now, Glenn saw.

"What the hell's goin' on here?" a new voice came from the darkness.

"That you, Silas?"

"Who the hell else would it be this time o' night?"

"Whyn't all you bastards shut up an' go to sleep?" a muffled voice complained.

A man Glenn hadn't seen before stepped into the cone of weak firelight, grumbling and scratching and spitting into the coals. He was a big fellow, half a head taller than Glenn and at least fifty, sixty pounds heavier. He had a wild and shaggy mane of black hair and a huge beard to match it. He wore a flannel shirt that likely hadn't seen washing since it left the haberdasher's shelf and a pair of ragged buckskin trousers with fringes down both legs. Instead of the usual revolver, this man carried a brace of capfire horse pistols in his belt and a knife big enough to fell trees.

"Do any good, Silas?" the young scout asked.

"I come back, didn't I?"

Glenn took that to mean Silas had accomplished his purpose. Whatever it may have been. Meat hunting, probably. Much of the work assigned to Hood's scouts was the acquisition of enough meat to help feed all the many men who were employed in the construction of the iron road.

"See any Injuns?" one of the "sleeping" men asked.

"Seen some," Silas said. "They never seen me, though."

"Heard about the trouble, did you?"

"Trouble? What trouble?"

"Ask Mr. Gilchrist here. He can tell you. He was there."

"He was where?"

"Was you, Mr. Gilchrist? Is that true? You seen the massacre?"

"*What* massacre, damn it?" Silas growled.

"You really was there?"

"I was there," Glenn admitted. "I seen . . . I mean to say, I saw it happen."

"Will one o' you mouth-runnin' bastards slow down an' tell me just what the hell you're all talkin' about?" the man called Silas complained.

"There was a massacre. Mr. Gilchrist here seen it."

"Who was it got rubbed out, damn it? Us or them?"

"Mr. Gilchrist?"

Glenn introduced himself to Silas and briefly explained what had happened.

Silas growled and muttered a string of well-chosen epithets powerful enough to set his beard afire if he hadn't had a mouthful of tobacco juice to wet it down with.

"Silas has got family in the Sioux camp," one of the scouts explained to Glenn.

"Really?"

"Yeah. Couple kids," Silas admitted gruffly. "Pawnee killed their ma five, maybe six winters back." He shook his head. "Nobody never thought there'd've been Pawnee that far up the Platte that time o' year. I left the little buggers with her people. Damn shame."

Glenn wasn't sure whether Silas was saying it was a shame his Sioux wife had been killed, that the children had been left with the Sioux afterward . . . or that the short-lived treaty had been broken. Possibly the "damn shame" comment applied to all of those.

"You lived with the Sioux, you say?"

"Nope. I never said no such. She lived with me. Out near Bridger's Fort for a spell, then later on up along the Marias River. Hauled some trade goods up there an' did some swapping with what was left o' the Blackfoot. Come back south that winter t' visit with her folks, like, but I wouldn't claim I lived with 'em exactly."

"But you do have relatives there? I mean, they would know you, remember you, maybe even take you in?"

"Might. Either that or lift my hair, dependin' on what kinda mood they was in at the moment."

"You, um, don't suppose you'd want to visit your children again, do you?"

"What the hell are you drivin' at, mister?"

"Just this. I want to talk to Spotted Bull. And you might be just the man to take me to him."

"I dunno 'bout that, mister," Silas said, scratching first his crotch and then the thick mat of whiskers under his chin. He dug around in there with thumb and forefinger for a moment, then brought out something too small for Glenn to see. Silas inspected the thing with a snort of apparent satisfaction before chucking it onto the coals, where it briefly flamed and then was gone.

"I'd be willing to pay you," Glenn suggested.

"A man's hair comes dear," Silas said.

"If you aren't good enough to get us in alive and back out again, then I won't have to pay you anything," Glenn said.

Silas tipped his head back and roared with laughter. "You got you a point there, little fella."

"One conversation with Spotted Bull. That's all I want."

"You say you'd pay?"

"Twenty dollars."

"Fifty," Silas countered.

"Twenty-five."

"Forty."

"Thirty."

Silas frowned. Then nodded. "Thirty," he agreed.

Glenn grinned.

"You got a horse?"

"I have a horse."

"Then, mister, you be on 'im come daybreak. But you pay the thirty dollars up front. In case them Injuns are only takin' in kinfolk this week. You know?"

"I'll be ready whenever you are," Glenn promised.

"You, uh, wouldn't want t' give me an advance on that thirty, would you? For one last bit o' fun. You know. Just in case."

"You can have all of it if you like."

"I like that, little fella. That you'd trust me not t' welsh on you."

"Oh, I don't imagine you'd want to do that, Silas, else I'd have to give you a thrashing." Glenn smiled when he said it.

Silas drew back for a moment. Then laughed. "Yeah, I do like that. You're a real kidder, ain't you?"

"Sometimes, Silas, sometimes."

Silas blinked. Then he grinned again and shrugged. He accepted Glenn's money, all thirty dollars, and shoved it into the belt pouch he wore in lieu of pockets in his buckskin trousers. "Daybreak," he said.

"I won't be late," Glenn said and resumed his search for the surveyors' camp.

CHAPTER

13

Megan groaned and rolled onto her back. Her head hurt and her mouth was full of dry, gritty sand. When she fell, she— Her eyes flew open in alarm as she remembered those last moments. The fright. The Indian. She . . .

She sat bolt upright, twisting as if to avoid a blow and crying out.

The Indian was there, dressed just as she remembered him.

And he had the butcher knife in his hand.

But he wasn't attacking her with it, he was . . . Megan blinked and gaped, trying to take it all in, trying to comprehend.

The Indian had his knife in his hand indeed, but what he was doing with it was using the back of the blade to scrape dirt off the pieces of bacon that had been in the skillet Megan threw at him. He was scraping dirt off the bacon and slicing the overcooked meat into small portions that he handed out to more Indians who were standing now at the edge of the firelight.

There were, Megan saw, two young women and several— three, she thought—small children.

While Megan watched, the man handed the last bit of bacon to one of the children, then bent and retrieved the skillet from the ground. Smiling and bobbing his head in

Megan's direction as if in thanks—in thanks? after she'd
tried to brain him with it?—he began using the ball of his
thumb to scour bacon grease out of the pan, then licked it
off and scrubbed at the inside of the skillet once more.

One of the children, a little girl who stood barely taller
than the man's knee, toddled over to him and tugged famili-
arly at his breechclout. Indulgently the Indian scooped some
of the bacon grease onto a fingertip and held it down for the
child to suck.

The sight fairly turned Megan's stomach. Human beings
reduced to licking up scorched grease from a pan. Imagine.

With a groan—she ached from the fall, and her head was
pounding quite abominably from the blow she'd taken—she
climbed shakily to her feet. She looked around. There was
no sign of Rachel or of Vic Boyette. Rachel, bright girl, had
escaped when she could. And of course Victor had been gone
to begin with.

"Do you speak English?" she asked.

The Indians, man, women and children alike, stopped
what little they were doing to stare at her. None of them,
however, spoke in response.

"Doesn't any of you speak English?"

The man said something to the women, the nearer of
whom shook her head and said something in return. The
man looked at Megan and once again spoke. The words
might as well have been the soughing of the wind for all
the sense Megan could make of them. When she thought
about it, though, she realized that that was only reasonable,
for no doubt the English she used when she tried to speak
to them held as little meaning for these . . . whatever they
were. Sioux, she presumed. They . . .

For the second time in as many minutes Megan went cold
with fear.

Sioux. Surely these Indians were Sioux. After all, that was the sort of Indians who lived around here, weren't they?

And it was the Sioux who had been involved in General Dodge's treaty.. And in the recent collapse of that same treaty. Dear Lord, it was a party of Sioux that had been massacred just those few days ago and . . .

These particular Indians, Sioux or not, must not have heard about that incident, Megan realized. Yet.

It was her great good fortune. If true.

Still trembling but much emboldened by the idea that these people must surely believe that the treaty prevailed, Megan managed a weak smile.

"Food," she said. "Hungry?" She patted her belly and mimed the act of eating, raising her eyebrows to indicate that she was asking a question.

The Indians grinned broadly and began to chatter, all three of the adults speaking at once and the eldest of the children adding a pence worth as well.

"Wo-haw," the Indian man repeated over and over, rubbing his stomach and grinning and bobbing his head.

Wo-haw, Megan dimly remembered, was a pidgin term for beef or, by extension she presumed, for food in general. It was supposed to have something to do with Indians hearing ox drivers command their teams—gee, haw, whoa—until wo-haw became a new word and entered both languages. At least that was what Joshua Hood told her once.

Joshua, she thought. Dear Lord, what she wouldn't give to have Joshua amble in and squat by her fire right now.

Joshua would know how to speak to these people. And what to say to them.

But Joshua wasn't here right now and neither was Glenn Gilchrist. Right here and right now Megan was alone, and she alone would simply have to cope.

"Wo-haw," she repeated, nodding and trying on another smile. "Let me find you some wo-haw."

"Wo-haw," the man said again, grinning hugely now.

"Rachel," Megan said over her shoulder, "I think they aren't going to kill us after all, so it's safe for you to come in now. Bring some wood with you, please. We need to build up this fire again so we can cook a bunch of wo-haw."

"What?" Rachel's voice came from surprisingly near.

"Meat," Victor said from not much farther away.

As far as Megan knew, Victor did not own a gun or any other sort of weapon, but when he stepped into the ring of light, he was carrying a chunk of deadwood that was stout enough to have served as a club had that become necessary. Victor nodded solemnly to the Indian family—if that was what they were—and laid his club over the coals, the dry wood quickly taking fire and sending bright tongues of flame high in the air.

Megan and Rachel—Rachel had her apron pockets filled with stones, Megan saw—rummaged through the supply box on the back of the trailer for more bacon—wo-haw to some—and some hunks of stale yet edible bread.

While Rachel started slicing the meat and bread, Megan mustered her courage and marched over to stand in front of the Indians. Up close they were less frightening than they'd seemed from afar—they were much shorter and more slightly built than she'd realized, for one thing—but less attractive as well. Their body odor was foul, strong and rancid like old grease. Megan steeled herself and pointed at the skillet, then held her hand out. "I must have that if we're to cook your wo-haw," she explained. Not that the words would be understood, but she was hoping the tone of voice would help.

The Indian man looked down, hesitated for only a moment and held the skillet out for Megan to take.

She nodded her thanks and started to turn away, then paused and reached down to the little girl who was still standing beside the man—her father? probably—drawn slightly back now so she was partially hidden from the pale, flaming-haired alien creature so completely unlike her own people. But so terribly, terribly rich in comparison to them.

Megan squatted so that her eyes were on a level with the child's. "Don't worry, dear," she said softly, reaching out to gently touch the little girl's cheek. "You won't go hungry tonight."

The child smiled and then, her nerve failing, gave out a tiny cry as she spun away and fled behind the leather skirts of the women for protection.

Megan chuckled and carried her skillet to the fire, which Victor had by now revived. Rachel had the bacon sliced ready to cook.

Within minutes, or what seemed no more than minutes, Megan's entire supply of bacon was gone, consumed before it had time to cool, and the bread too, great chunks of it used to sop up grease hot from the same skillet.

Man, women and children alike gorged themselves on Megan's limited supplies, then belched loudly in obvious contentment.

Megan begrudged none of what the hungry visitors ate. It would have been unconscionable for her to turn anyone away hungry when she had food to share.

And on a more practical level, the better fed and more content these Indians were, the less apt they were to investigate the contents of the wagon and trailer for themselves.

It would be tragic, Megan was sure, if the Indians discovered that this small, virtually unguarded party of whites was transporting an entire saloon, liquor included.

Better to freely give all the wo-haw that was desired than risk the loss of her whiskeys and beer.

"More wo-haw, dear? Rachel, do we have anything else that would be quick to cook?"

"Not really, Megan, but . . . don't worry. I'll find something."

"Victor?"

"Yes'm, I know. More wood for the fire."

Megan smiled at the Indians until her jaw ached from it, and Rachel and Victor went about their unexpected chores.

"Wo-haw," the Indian man said happily, rubbing his belly and pointing to the roundly stuffed stomachs of the children. "Wo-haw."

"Right," Megan said. "Plenty damn wo-haw, you bet." She was careful not to look at the big wagon not ten paces distant, where case upon case upon keg of liquor lay hidden beneath the canvas covering.

CHAPTER

14

"Uh, g'mornin', boss." The young scout dropped his eyes, unable to meet Joshua's gaze.

"Damn it, Kenny, you know you should've been five miles gone from here by now." The sun was already close to breaking the horizon, and Kenny was supposed to be meat hunting today. "So tell me, Kenny. Why shouldn't I kick your butt from one end of this camp to the other? Why didn't you leave when you were supposed to?"

Kenny shrugged, his attention still somewhere in the vicinity of his boot toes. "D'you want the truth, Joshua, or a real good lie?"

"You can't lie anywhere near good enough to suit me, Kenny, and we both know it. Reckon you'd best try the truth. Then we'll see do I have t' fire you or not."

"Aw, Joshua, you wouldn't do that." He gulped. "Would you?"

"We'll see. First I wanta hear what you have t' say for yourself."

"Well, you see . . ." Joshua could see, all right. He could see that Kenny was fixing to make something up, that's what he could see.

"The truth, Kenny, or I'll kick your butt first an' then fire you afterward."

Kenny looked at him. Briefly. Then back down at the ground. After a moment the young scout sighed. "It's that damn Silas's fault, Joshua. We was in bed last night, all of us, an' he come in from his hunt kinda late. And that fancy surveyor fella was there and give Silas some money for a job an' so then Silas had all this money an' you know he had to go and buy a drink with it except with Silas if you got that much money in your pocket you don't buy no bottle you buy a keg and, hell, Joshua, he couldn't have a keg in camp without passing it around." Kenny sighed again. "Next thing you know it was coming first light and I was just kinda waking up. Now here I am. Figured I'd best get me a bite to eat, to settle my stomach, like. But I'll be riding outa here in fifteen minutes, Joshua. Twenty, tops. And that's a promise. I'll get my work done. You know me. You know if I say something, then it's gospel. Twenty minutes, Joshua. Half hour at the very outside. Time enough to eat an' saddle, that's all I ask."

Kenny's wheedling was of little interest to Joshua at the moment. The other things he'd had to say were much more intriguing.

"Whoa, Kenny. Back up there a mite. You said there was some surveyor fella in our camp?"

"That's right. That . . . well, I guess he ain't really a friend of yours, but you know 'im. Mr. Gilchrist. The guy that's sparking Liam's sister, Megan."

"Like hell he's sparking Megan O'Connell," Joshua snapped.

"Yessir. Anyway, he's the one I meant."

"What in tarnation was he doing in our camp?"

"Lost is what he was doing there, close as I could tell. He was asking where the surveyors was s'posed to be. He'd had a couple drinks, I think. Not that he was drunk. He wasn't.

But he wasn't cold sober neither. Somewheres in between."

"And he was in our camp?"

"That's right. Wandered in looking for his own bunch. That's about the time when Silas come in an' them two got to talking."

"And you say Gilchrist hired Silas to do something for him?"

"Yessir."

"Do you know what it was?"

"O' course. A guy couldn't forget a crazy damn thing like that."

"Like what, Kenny?"

"Like finding Spotted Bull an' introducing the two of them. Spotted Bull and your friend Mr. Gilchrist, that is. That's what he hired Silas on t' do. T' take Mr. Gilchrist out and find Spotted Bull and introduce them for some kinda peace palaver. Leastways that's what Mr. Gilchrist said last night. And like I already told you, he wasn't drunk when he said it. I believe he meant it."

"And Silas?"

Kenny shrugged. "Silas was gone when I woke up this mornin'. Him an' his horse too."

"Jesus," Joshua blurted.

"Oh, I don't know what become o' Him this mornin'," Kenny said without thinking.

It wasn't a good idea, as he quickly saw from Joshua's glare.

"Uh, if you'll excuse me, Boss, I ain't as hungry as I thought I was. Reckon I'll go get my horse now an' ride outa here, see if I can find us some nice fresh buf'lo hump for supper." Kenny didn't wait for an answer. He abandoned his place in the chow line and hurried off in the direction of the scouts' camp on the double-quick.

"No!" Quite involuntarily Megan O'Connell shouted the instruction and ran to the back of her wagon, where an Indian—it occurred to her somewhat belatedly that this was not one of the Indians she had fed the night before—was trying to unfasten the tarpaulin.

The Indian, startled, jumped back and ducked as if from a blow.

Megan came up short and settled for motioning the man away from the wagon.

The Indian said something in his own language. There was a hint of ugly menace in his voice. But then, she thought, that might only have been her own imagination supplying emphasis where none belonged. After all, the words were guttural and harsh to her ear. The implied threat might not actually exist. Certainly there had been no hostility displayed by the people they fed last night. There was no reason for this man now to—

The Indian said something in a tone of voice that was unmistakably sharp. He straightened to his full height and stuck out his chest; then, strutting, he made as if to approach the wagon once more.

"No," Megan repeated. "I don't mind feeding hungry people, but I won't stand for being bullied like this." She stepped forward. When the Indian reached for the rope holding the tarp in place, she slapped his hand away.

The Indian scowled and snatched at the haft of a butcher knife suspended at his waist.

Megan took a step backward and bent to grab up a fist-sized stone.

Before either could strike, there was a blur of motion and the young man whose family had eaten all the wo-haw the evening before jumped in between them. The friendly Indian—thank God, Megan whispered—spat a rapid torrent of the foreign tongue. The newcomer scowled again but released his grip on the knife. The two exchanged words, some of them sounding quite heated, and then the newcomer gave Megan a glowering look but turned and marched stiffly to the camp fire. There he squatted and pretended to ignore his surroundings.

Megan took a deep breath, mostly out of relief, and gave her friend from the night before a look of gratitude. He in turn motioned toward the other male Indian and said, "Wo-haw." He nodded and made some motions with his hands. The sign language Joshua had told her about, Megan presumed. It was the one common language of all the Plains tribes, he'd said. Megan wished she could read it too, or understand at least a few words of this particular Indian tongue. "Wo-haw," the warrior repeated, pointing toward the fire, where now there was not only the one newcomer Megan had already seen but four—no, five—and more coming out of the brush now—eight or maybe ten additional Indians. And this bunch, she quickly noted, was all male. This was no traveling family group but a hunting party—or worse, although none of them was painted. Indians always painted themselves if they were going to war. Didn't they? Megan was, well, almost positive that someone told her that once.

"Wo-haw," her late guest but now benefactor said.

"Yes," she agreed. "Plenty wo-haw."

"Megan?" Rachel sounded quite uneasy.

"I see them, dear, but it is all going to be perfectly fine. This, um, gentleman will see to it."

"I'm scared, Megan."

"Later, Rachel. We don't have time to be scared just now, dear. Where's Victor?"

"The last I saw him he was taking two of the little girls to look for dried grass and some other stuff. He said he was going to make dolls for them to play with."

"I think we could use him here now."

"I don't know, I—"

"Wo-haw," the friendly Indian interrupted.

"Yes, of course. Wo-haw for our, um, guests. By all means wo-haw. Rachel, you'd better bring in some wood. I'll see what foods I can find."

"I just remembered, Megan. That crate under the wagon seat?"

"Yes, what about it?"

"That's where I packed the jars of pickled eggs and that open jar of hot pickled sausages. I thought they wouldn't be so likely to get broken there."

"Perfect. Those will get them started. We have to fill them up, Rachel." Megan was already climbing onto the tall driving box and fumbling under the seat for the crate Rachel had spoken of. "If they ever find out what's in this wagon . . . so many of them . . . there won't be anything we can do to stop them."

The thought of a dozen or more armed drunks of any nationality was bad enough. And a band of drunken savage warriors? The thought lent speed to Megan's efforts.

"Go on, dear," she urged. "Build the fire up while I pass these around and see what we have left to cook for them."

When Rachel headed into the brush in search of wood, Megan noticed a pair of the newly arrived warriors rising and starting out as if to follow her. But the two Indian women who had been there the night before moved to speak to the men and turn them back to the fire. It took some persuading and a bit of shoving too, but the women prevailed after a brief argument.

Thank goodness, Megan thought.

She climbed back down to the ground, burdened by a pair of two-gallon jars, and began distributing the pickled hard-boiled eggs and the spicy little sausages, both items that tended to increase a man's thirst while taking the edge off his appetite for solid food, both items staples in the saloon trade.

Anything, she thought, anything at all. Just so this band of Sioux warriors—who also, mercifully, seemed to be ignorant of the massacre that had taken place so recently—did not discover the cargo of whiskey and beer and raw alcohol that was contained on the big wagon.

The best they could hope for was to keep the slim measure of good will they'd generated the night before when they fed that first small family band. And with their help, the danger might pass.

Megan watched the last of the sausages disappear and then, with smiles and nods and an outward cheerfulness she did not begin to feel, went back to the wagon to see what else she could find that might help pacify the Indians.

"Over there," the scout said, pointing.

"The Sioux camp?"

"Hell no, mister. We're two, three days from where I figger to find Spotted Bull. Over there's where we'll stop for lunch."

Glenn nodded his acceptance of Silas's judgment and reined his mount in the direction indicated. The horse tossed its head nervously and high-stepped along, its ears working one way and then the other. A butterfly lifted into the air on a flutter of soft wings, and the horse tried to bolt. After half a day, though, Glenn knew to ride this one with a short rein and quickly yanked its nose back in the direction he wanted. Once again, though, Glenn regretted having had to leave his own fine gelding behind.

His own horse, however, had a slight stone bruise on its off fore frog and had developed a limp. It needed several days of rest to keep what was now an annoyance from becoming an injury, so Glenn had reluctantly borrowed his friend Howard Teale's brown. Now he was wishing that his own animal had been healthy, or at least that he had borrowed some horse other than the brown. Howard's mount was large and handsomely built, but it was a spooky so-and-so, finding ghosties and goblins under the random leaf and boogering in a panic without warning. The need to pay constant attention to the brown instead of to his surroundings was taxing Glenn's good humor and his stamina too. The horse was just plain tiring to ride.

"Slow 'er down a mite, mister. We'll kinda ease along here till we see it's clear down below. Wouldn't do t' go skylinin' ourselfs till we see it's clear."

Glenn held back and watched as Silas slowed his horse to a snail's pace and moved cautiously forward, exposing as little of himself as possible as he neared the precipitous slope into a brush-choked coulee.

After several minutes Silas stopped and rose up in his stirrups, his head tilted back and his nostrils flaring. Glenn could have sworn the man was examining the air for scent in the same manner a hound or a wolf might. Except humans didn't do such things. Or did they? Whatever, Silas stayed that way for several long moments and then with a grunt of apparent satisfaction resumed his seat. He turned and motioned for Glenn to follow. "It's all right, mister. Ain't been any fire hereabouts in a long time." With that, Silas put his horse over the edge.

Glenn's stomach drew into a tight knot as he saw where the brown was expected to follow. The sides of the coulee were almost sheer, but Silas was descending as casually as if he were on a boulevard. The man's black-and-white spotted pony was sliding on its rump, its forelegs stiff and splayed wide apart, but if Silas had any concern about the route, he failed to display it. Instead his attention was on the thicket below.

Glenn bumped the brown horse with his heels and willed himself to put his trust in the creature. He too looked about while the horse reached the drop-off and pitched over it. Glenn leaned back until his cantle dug hard into his kidneys. He would have gone all the way back until he was lying on the horse's rump except for the hard ridge of the cantle preventing it. As it was, he was not quite able to remain perpendicular to the earth. He gritted his teeth and jammed his feet hard into his stirrups in an attempt to keep himself from pitching forward.

Off to the south, toward the distant mouth of the coulee, there was a crash and clatter of breaking twigs and crunching leaves, and Glenn got a brief glimpse of pale brown hide and flashing white tail as a deer was frightened off its midday bed.

"Pity we ain't wantin' t' call attention to ourselfs," Silas said. "Deer liver 'ud go good for supper."

Glenn said nothing but in truth was just as pleased that silence was in order. A nicely roasted haunch of venison was pleasing enough, or bite-sized nuggets of venison floured and fried, but the only liver he could abide was pâté and that only if caviar or salmon spread was not available.

The brown horse reached the floor of the coulee without resorting to somersaults along the way, and Glenn gratefully dismounted.

"You can go ahead an' loose your cinches, mister."

"Will we be that long with our lunch?"

"Mister, if it was just a matter o' our comfort, we'd still be ridin'. But it never pays t' let a horse tire. Not in this here country it don't. A body never knows when he's gonna have t' race some other S.O.B. with one of 'em's scalp for the winner's prize. So what we're doin' here is lettin' these here horses blow. An' they c'n breathe easier if they ain't bound up in the middle with cinches. Course, mister, that's just the way I see it. You're free t' do whatever you want."

Glenn quickly hung his near stirrup on the saddle horn and slipped the latigo on his cinches. "Should I take the saddle all the way off?"

"Me, I'd leave it in place," Silas said. "You 'member I

told you a fella never knows when he's gotta move along quick-like? Well, it's sure easier t' pull a cinch tight than it is t' saddle a horse, 'specially one that's bein' shot at."

Glenn looked around.

"No, mister, there ain't nobody close by t' go an' shoot at us. I c'n promise you that. But it's a pretty good idear t' make a habit o' doin' the right thing. You know?"

Glenn smiled. "That sounds like good advice."

"Ayuh. So it do." The big, shaggy scout rummaged through his saddlebags and brought out a hunk of . . . something . . . wrapped in a square of brown oiled paper. When he unwrapped it, Glenn thought it was pressed tobacco. The shape was not right for processed tobacco, but the color and texture seemed to be.

"What's that, Silas?"

"Lunch." Silas pulled out his knife and sliced a piece off for himself. He stuffed that into his jaw and sliced another chunk off for Glenn. "Pemmican," he said around his mouthful of the stuff.

Glenn smiled. Ever since he'd come west, he'd heard about pemmican, a winter staple of the northern plains. He'd even inquired about it once. Pemmican was said to be a mixture of dried meat and dried berries, both pounded into a coarse powder that was mixed with melted fat and placed into molds to cool. They said pemmican could be stored for several years if necessary without spoilage and that it was marvelously nutritious.

Eagerly Glenn took his first bite of the native wonder product pemmican.

And fought back an urge to gag.

"Two things you can say 'bout pemmican," Silas said dryly. "It don't rot an' it'll keep yer strength up. Everything else a body could think to say 'bout it is all bad. The taste ain't quite up t' that of pig shit, an' on a cold day it'll bust whatever teeth you got left in yer mouth. It stinks 'bout as bad as it tastes, an' if you go an' buy it from some Injun you don't know, there's no tellin' what all she coulda put in there with the edible stuff, just as a joke on the white man like, an' no way you'd ever know if she done somethin' like that 'cause good pemmican tastes s' bad anyhow." Silas chuckled and carved another slice of pemmican off the block of it he was holding. He peered closely at it and shrugged. "Beetles, worms, mayhap a bit o' dog turd . . . no way t' tell if'n somebody played a joke here, is there?"

Glenn felt his stomach lurch and roll.

Silas popped the bite of pemmican into his mouth and grinned.

"All right, damn it," Glenn said. "Give me another piece, will you?"

Silas obliged, then said, "Y' know, mister, fer a city fella you ain't all bad."

Glenn decided to take that at face value and not examine the subtleties that could be inferred.

"Two or three days to Spotted Bull's camp, you said?" he asked.

"If they're where I expect. Won't know till we get there. Now, if you don't mind, mister, I'm gonna stretch out in that grass over there an' take me a nap whilst them horses rest up. Wake me if you see any Sioux tryin' t' sneak up on us."

"I'll be sure and do that, Silas. I surely will." Glenn too looked for a spot on the ground that might prove to be soft and comfortable.

Soft was unobtainable but, he was pleased to discover, comfortable was not. It was actually quite pleasant lying there in the shade with the delicate scent of grass sweet in his nostrils and a touch of breeze to cool his brow. He closed his eyes and before he knew it floated gently into a refreshing sleep.

CHAPTER
17

"Settle down now, boys, and mind your manners. We'll be open as quick as we're ready and not a minute sooner." It was pleasing—and mildly exasperating too—to see how eagerly the men awaited the reopening of Megan's tent saloon. Word had spread in advance of the wagon's arrival, and by the time Megan, Rachel and Victor reached the patch of bare, beaten earth that was designated as the new town site, a crowd had already gathered, ready to buy those first refreshing rounds. That part of it was all pleasure. The exasperation came from the way the crowd, good-natured though it was, got underfoot and in the way. The process of setting up the mobile saloon really would have been much easier without so many thirsty men milling about at arm's length.

"Miss Megan?"

"Yes, Victor?"

"Would you mind, ma'am, if I was to say something?"

"Of course not, Victor."

The youngster looked around and licked his lips nervously, then leaned close so he could whisper in Megan's ear without being overheard by the men nearby.

"Why, Victor. What an excellent idea. Thank you."

He beamed with pleasure from the compliment.

With a quick hand up from Victor, Megan mounted the tailgate of the trailer. There was ample room inside the trailer

110

for her to stand, due to the amount of supplies that had been taken from it to feed that first small group of Sioux and the much larger hunting party that came afterward. All that was two days past, however, and no longer seemed important.

"Listen to me. Hush a minute, will you?"

The buzz of excited conversation continued. After a moment Rachel winked at Megan and then stuffed the tips of two fingers into her mouth. She whistled, the sound as piercing, and very nearly as loud, as an end-of-shift screech from one of the steam whistles.

"Yes'm?"

"That's better. My friend Victor had a suggestion that some of you boys may want to adopt. If some of you want to pitch in and help us unload and set up—I'm sure you all know how to handle a field tent and carry some boxes inside—everyone who helps will go to the head of the line when it comes to—" She was not able to finish the sentence. Before another word could issue from Megan's mouth there was a great cry, and half a hundred grizzled workmen descended upon the wagon like a swarm of locusts denuding a clover patch.

"Oh, dear," Megan said. "I hadn't thought . . ." She grinned and shook her head as she jumped down to the relative safety of ground level and gripped Rachel's hand.

"I just hope they don't steal us blind," Rachel said.

Megan gave her a startled look.

"You didn't think about that?"

Megan shook her head.

As it happened, however, if anyone snitched a single drink, Megan was unaware of the loss.

The heavy tent canvas was laid out in no time and as quickly rose high into the air as scores of hands grabbed poles, pegs and guy ropes alike. Men who couldn't find mauls used rocks or whatever else they could find to drive the tent pegs into the hard Nebraska earth. Others began hauling the many crates and boxes inside almost before the tent was sufficiently raised to create head room for them.

Within moments Megan was surrounded by calls of "Where's this go, ma'am?" and "What d'you want me t' do with this here box, Miss O'Connell?"

"I'll direct traffic, Rachel," Megan said. "You can start unloading. Don't try to be neat about it. Just get everything out where we can see it. We'll sort things out and put it all in order later on."

Rachel nodded and picked up her skirts. Megan headed the other way. Between their efforts, and Victor's, wagon and trailer were swiftly stripped of their contents and everything was transferred inside the newly erected tent.

Planks and barrels became a bar. Tables were knocked together and chairs and stools distributed. Kegs, mugs and tankards were stacked in untidy piles behind the bar. Lamps were hung, their mantles bare of the globes and glass chimneys that were still packed away in sawdust somewhere.

Not everything was done exactly as Megan might have wished. She saw a one-armed youth with a wispy blond beard gnaw at his cheek in intense concentration as he tried not to spill the fluid he was pouring into a lamp. Megan recognized him as a former regimental drummer who'd lost his limb to cannon fire, and more recently a water boy serving the needs of the track layers. Unfortunately the liquid he was so studiously introducing into her lamp was a rather expensive aged brandy. The brandy, she subsequently learned, burned quite nicely. But oil—coal or whale, either one—gave off the better light.

Someone else stepped on a small box that had fallen out of an incoming armload. The misstep turned fifty fine cheroots into an unappetizing melange of tobacco dust and wood splinters.

A crate of tin mugs survived an uproariously loud crash, but Megan's favorite snack platter did not.

Not that she needed a snack platter. Not for the time being. Thanks to the voracious appetites of the Sioux visitors, there was no free lunch to put out, nor would there be until Megan could resupply.

Still, things got done. And quickly.

Within ten minutes of Victor's suggestion, the tent had been erected, everything had been brought inside and enough containers had been breached that Rachel and Megan could begin serving customers.

"All right, boys. Is everyone inside? Everyone who helped this afternoon? Are you all inside now? Yes? All right then." She smiled and added, "The first drink is free to each one of you, and thank you for helping out."

She was positive her last few words were heard by no one, because before she could utter them, all other sound was drowned out by a roar of approval from the workingmen who had been so generous with their efforts.

Megan gave Rachel a grin and a nod. "Welcome to . . . wherever this place is. I think we're in business again."

Rachel, though, was not listening. She was already drawing foamy mugs of beer and splashing generous tots of whiskey and water into tin cups—and handing them out just as quickly as she could get them filled.

Business, Megan saw, was booming. At least until they started collecting money for their wares.

CHAPTER

18

"It's gonna be dark soon. Reckon we'd best think about holin' up." Silas brought his horse to a halt and stood in his stirrups to better survey the possibilities. "There. Toward the head o' that draw. If'n I remember right, there's a seep o' fresh water there."

It amazed Glenn how Silas and the other scouts could recognize and remember so much of the uncharted country they covered in the course of their travels. Yet rarely did one of them prove wrong about what to expect of an area, even if they had not seen it in years.

Without waiting for Glenn to comment, Silas resumed his seat and heeled his horse forward. Glenn obediently jogged along behind, his concentration focused on the clumsy, hardheaded brown horse he was riding.

Silas was frowning as they neared the edge of the slope leading down into this latest wrinkle cut into the face of the earth. The scout tipped his head back, and Glenn could almost have sworn Silas was smelling the air. Almost. No human would bother trying to smell out an enemy, though. Would he?

Instead of pausing to make his usual slow survey before proceeding, Silas made straight for the edge and over it.

Glenn followed close behind, pleased to find that for once the descent was relatively shallow and easy to negotiate.

The floor of the coulee was thick with brush, alder and chokecherry in the bottom and on the fringes dense tangles of scrub oak and shrubs that Glenn did not recognize.

Off to the north, to their right, Glenn could see a glint of shimmering reflection off water just as Silas had predicted. But instead of turning their thirsty horses in that direction, the scout plunged straight on into a thicket.

Once more Glenn followed, but he couldn't help being curious.

"Why aren't we . . . ?"

"Shut up!" Silas snapped, his voice low and threatening.

Glenn recoiled, his feelings hurt. He and Silas had not become bosom friends during the past few days, but the big scout had not acted so unpleasant before now.

"Really now, can't you at least—"

"I tol' you to shut your yap, damn you," Silas said without looking around.

"But—"

"Shit!"

"I say now, there's no need for that sort of language. If you want to discuss—"

Silas yanked his horse's head around with a cruel snatch of rein. The animal reacted to its pain by wheeling and plunging in protest.

"Here now—" Glenn started.

He was interrupted by a low-pitched thrumming sound that started somewhere in front of him and whisked rapidly past just to his left, immediately disappearing somewhere behind.

"What was that?"

A matter of paces ahead Silas was grimly fighting with his rearing horse, clinging to the animal with his legs and wildly thrashing it left and right with hard, cutting slashes of his rein ends.

Glenn backed the brown out of the way, making room for Silas and his horse.

With a strangled cry that sounded like . . . fear? Glenn was not sure . . . Silas brought his mount under some small measure of control and immediately booted it into motion, back the way they'd just come.

"Silas," Glenn said with no small amount of exasperation. "Whatever do you think you are doing?"

His answer came not from the scout but from the far rim of the coulee, where a sharp, ululating yell cut through the cool evening air.

It was a sound Glenn had never in his life heard before that moment. And one he knew he would never forget.

It was, it had to be, the war cry of a savage Indian.

Glenn looked up in time to see an arrow zoom past him a foot or less to the right of his head. The sound was the same faint sibilance he'd already heard moments earlier without realizing what it was.

Outlined stark and bold against the fading daylight he could see mounted men, mounted warriors. Four, five, perhaps as many as a dozen of them.

They were armed with bows, not rifles, thank goodness.

The bows seemed quite bad enough.

One of the Sioux jerked his pony to a halt. The warrior's cry of challenge and defiance came loud across the coulee, and he did something with his hands and arms Glenn could barely see.

Glenn recoiled and, much too late, ducked as another arrow hissed past too close for comfort.

"Silas. Talk to them, Silas. Damn it, man, talk to them."

But Silas was no longer in a position to talk. Not to the Indians and not to Glenn.

In fact, Glenn was not entirely sure just where Silas had got to. Somewhere down the coulee and out of sight. Glenn could hear a loud crackling of brush in the direction where he'd last seen Silas.

"Damn it, Silas," Glenn shouted. "This is what we came here for. You can't go running off now."

The only response he got was more crashing and thrashing in the brush toward the mouth of the coulee.

Glenn felt something brush across the back of his hand, and when he looked down, there was a line of bright blood welling to the surface of a shallow cut.

The brown horse grunted and stumbled. The feathered shaft of an arrow protruded from the fatty ridge of flesh at the base of its tangled mane. It was only luck that had kept the tip of the arrow from finding the animal's spinal cord and dropping it out from under Glenn.

"Jesus!" Glenn blurted. "Jesus, Mary and Joseph."

These Indians were *shooting* at him, for God's sake. And they *meant* it too.

For an ugly instant Glenn imagined himself back on the field where those Sioux warriors had been massacred. For that moment he once again could see the surprise and fear in the eyes of that Indian boy who'd been shot in the face and coldly murdered. Except this time, in Glenn's imagination, it was he who stood before the muzzle of that soldier's weapon, he who took the force of the gunfire full on, he who fell, he whose substance was snuffed out as swiftly and as thoroughly as a candle's flame in a whirlwind.

Dear Lord, Glenn wildly thought.

And as wildly he sawed at the reins of the brown.

Silas, damn him, had reacted at the first hint of danger, racing to save himself without a word of warning to Glenn.

Still and all at this moment Silas's actions were to be

emulated, not dissected. There would be time enough for recriminations later.

If Glenn lived that long.

He yanked the panicking brown about and spurred the animal hard in Silas's wake.

The horse burst into a choppy run that carried Glenn out of the thicket into the open.

Arrows hissed by to spend themselves clattering on the pebbled soil.

The brown stumbled and lurched, nearly throwing Glenn. He lost a stirrup and wound up clinging frantically to saddle horn and mane with both hands.

More arrows whizzed by, and Glenn felt someone punch him high in the back. Coup, he thought. One of the Indians had gotten close enough to rap him with a coup stick. What had he been told about that? Something about it being even more of an honor for an Indian to count coup on a live enemy than to take the life of one. Ha! Let them count coup all they damn well wanted, then. Better to be battered with sticks than shot.

Funny, he thought. The motion of the horse wasn't bothering him anymore.

In fact, now that he gave the matter some attention, the brown was really quite steady.

Everything felt steady, at any rate.

He . . .

He blinked. He was not on the brown any longer. He frowned, concentrated. He must have fallen off. Damned odd, that. He'd fallen off the horse and hadn't even noticed it at the time. My, wasn't that something to tell about. Why, he would have to tell . . .

Glenn felt a sense of emptiness wash through him.

He was alone here except for enemies who would kill him.

There was no one to tell.

Not Megan O'Connell. Not the scout Silas. Not . . . anyone.

Dear Lord, indeed.

He was . . . He had to work on it. He was lying in a nest of sorts made of ancient, dried-out leaves and moist gravel and gray, gnarled twigs. He seemed to be lying mostly underneath the overhanging spread of a clump of scrub oak.

Somewhere close by he could hear the churn of horses' hooves and the excited babble of some Indians. The Indians seemed to be looking for something. It took Glenn a few moments to appreciate that the Indians were looking for him.

He had fallen off the horse, and in the poor light at the bottom of the coulee they must not have seen the place where he fell. Or perhaps they were not even sure that he had fallen, for the brown must have raced on without him.

Jesus!

Glenn lay still, his stomach a ball of ice and his bowels watery with terror, while the feet of the Indian ponies crashed through the brush all around.

He had his revolver, he supposed. At least he hoped he did. Unless it had been dislodged from its holster when he struck the ground, he did. If the Indians found him . . .
He would have felt at least a little better if he could have checked to see that he still had the gun, but he did not want to move and risk making noise that would draw attention. But if they found him . . .

He had come here hoping to talk, to make peace. Yet now he had gone to ground like a harried fox, and if one of those Sioux warriors discovered him, well, Glenn intended to do his level best to kill that warrior before the Indian could kill him. That was probably a very uncivilized attitude, he acknowledged, but it was the attitude he held right now. If he survived this experience, he could moralize about the situation then. Right now the only thing that mattered to him was sheer, simple survival. That and nothing else.

A horse walked by close enough that Glenn could have reached out and grabbed the animal's hock. He cringed, willing himself small and invisible. Cold, greasy sweat beaded his forehead, and his stomach churned and gurgled so that he was afraid the sound of it would give him away. The horse moved on, the Indian riding it calling out a question to someone else.

Glenn lay still, scarcely breathing.

The Indians rode around and through the area where Glenn lay hiding for what seemed an interminable amount of time, although he judged that it was likely no longer than two or three minutes in truth.

Then, with a renewal of the shrill war cries that were even more chilling from this close up, they rode off down the coulee in the direction Silas had taken.

Glenn lay quiet a good five minutes lest they return, then slowly and with great care to make little noise, he tried to sit upright inside his clump of scrub oak.

He got halfway up, then gave out a startled yip as a jolt of pain lanced through him.

The upper left quarter of his back felt as if it were being seared with a white-hot brand.

He remembered feeling something there before and deciding he'd been struck by a coup stick. Yet no tap from a stick, or even a war club he would have thought, would leave this kind of pain behind.

Lying down again, he reached back in an attempt to explore the area.

His searching fingers encountered wood. Slim, cylindrical,

jagged. The broken shaft of an arrow.

Lord God Almighty, he'd been shot. By a Sioux arrow. And the arrow tip was still lodged somewhere inside his flesh.

The rest of the shaft must have been broken off when he fell from the horse, but the cutting point was still inside him.

Did the Sioux poison the tips of their arrows? Glenn was sure he'd been told that some tribes poisoned their arrows. But he couldn't recall now if the Sioux did or not.

For that matter, one Indian tribe was the same as another as far as he could tell. He was only assuming that it was a Sioux arrow that had shot him. Sioux, Cheyenne, Otoe, Pawnee . . . he would not know, and at this point did not care to, one from another.

The point was that he'd been abandoned by Silas, wounded and left afoot two-and-a-half-days' ride from the rail end.

A less stubborn man would have concluded that Joshua Hood's advice had been good and that perhaps he should not have embarked on this one-man peace mission to speak with Spotted Bull.

Glenn grinned ruefully into the gathering night. It was probably a damn good thing, then, that he could be as stubborn as the next fellow. And as determined.

Having gotten himself into this fix, he thought, he was just going to have to get himself out of it.

As for how to best go about that . . . He coughed, the shuddering movement of it causing another spear point of pain to shoot through him . . . Well, as for that, he hadn't a clue.

It was something he would have to give some thought to, though. Just as soon as he felt up to the task.

For the moment what he wanted, what he needed, was some rest.

He put his head down on his sweaty, grime-covered forearm. And passed out cold.

Every muscle hurt, and every joint was filled with aches and small, shooting pains, yet exhaustion acted as anesthesia to numb the worst of it. Exhaustion numbed Megan's brain too, making her thought processes slow and unreliable. Even her balance was off, and she stumbled more than once as she made one last round through the empty tent, extinguishing lamps as she went.

She had no idea what the hour was. Something close to the dawning, she suspected. She—Rachel and Victor too, of course—had been on the go nearly twenty-four hours, driving, then setting up, and finally that frenetic night of dispensing drinks and trying to oversee the gaming.

Megan had already sent Rachel and Victor off. She herself did not intend to be far behind them in seeking out the comforts of her bed.

Tired as she was, though, and as pleased as she should have been after such a successful start in business at this new location, she could not help feeling a twinge of disappointment.

She had hoped—no, she told herself, be honest; she had fully expected—that Glenn Gilchrist would stop by to see her safely settled in the new place. And Joshua Hood too.

Yet neither man had bothered to so much as drop by and say hello.

Megan found herself mildly irked by their disregard. Both of them too. Humph!

Well, that was just fine by her. She didn't need their help and she didn't need them. Not either one of them, she didn't.

She lifted the globe of a lamp and blew, the puff of breath bringing darkness to that corner of the big tent, then tripped and almost fell as she turned to go toward the last remaining lamp.

A hand, firm and supportive, grasped her elbow and kept her from falling.

Megan cried out, startled. Then her eyes widened and her heart began to race with a surge of quick fear.

"Ike, I mean . . . Mr. Norman. I didn't see you come in."

Ike Norman was no benefactor. Far from it, in fact. If there were anyone, anywhere who could be said to wish her ill, she suspected it would have to be Ike.

A big man, Ike must once have been a handsome, perhaps even a distinguished-looking man. Now, although still only in his thirties, Norman had put on far too much weight and was becoming somewhat seedy under a brash and fancy veneer of frock coat, brocade vest and diamond stickpin.

"No one else saw me come in either," Ike said.

The implications that could be taken from that message chilled Megan and brought her fully awake and alert. Ike had tried to ruin her business before. And there had been the threats made by that unknown Negro back at the old camp. Surely Ike Norman had been behind that . . . whatever it was. Not that anything had materialized on the road, but that could have been because Megan and her wagon were surrounded by Indians so much of the time. Of course, she thought. That had to be the reason Ike's hired assassin hadn't put in an appearance before. And now here was Ike himself, sneaking in in the middle of the night.

Megan cleared her throat and, thinking rapidly, slid gracefully away from Ike's supporting hand beneath her elbow. "Can I offer you a drink, Mr. Norman?"

"Mister, is it, Miss O'Connell? If we must be so formal, then would you prefer Mrs. Gallagher?"

"It's Miss O'Connell if you please," Megan said, inwardly wincing at the reminder of her dead husband, Keith. Keith had been a charming Irish boy, gay and laughing. But utterly unreliable, a poor excuse of a man and an even poorer husband. It was God's blessing that there had been no children born of the marriage. As it was, Megan still felt guilty that she hadn't been able to truly grieve after Keith's death. The marriage had been a failure long before that, and she accepted the belief that the failure must surely have been hers. If she had been a better wife to him, he would not have remained so wild, he would not have strayed the way he did.

After Keith died, Megan had resumed her maiden name of O'Connell in an effort to distance herself from the failed vows. But in her heart that was not enough to assuage the guilts that weighed on her. That was not, and nothing else ever would be either. Guilt was something she was going to have to live with for the rest of her life.

But that, darn it, was for her to know. Not Ike Norman.

Megan steeled herself and held her chin high. She gave Norman a level gaze and said, "You haven't answered my question, Mr. Norman."

"Haven't I?" He smiled. "Forgive me, Miss O'Connell. Yes, I would like a drink, thank you."

Megan pointed to a chair. "Whiskey?"

"Brandy, I think. I'm told you have a nice Portuguese brandy."

Megan sniffed. "If you are trying to show off about your spies, Mr. Norman, you shall have to think of something better than that. Anyone who comes in with a dime in his pocket can learn all he wants about my brandies and my cordials."

"I'm not trying to show off, Miss O'Connell. Just asking for something that sounds pleasant."

"If you aren't here to show off, Mr. Norman, what is it that brings you around after hours?" She hoped she did not already know the answer to that. When she bent to fetch the brandy bottle out of the box where she kept her better spirits, she surreptitiously picked up a bung starter too, hiding the hardwood mallet in a fold of her skirts while she carried the brandy to Norman and took a seat opposite him. If it came to that, she would reach over and brain him with the bung starter.

Ike took his time about savoring the brandy, smelling it first, then taking a tiny sip that he swished around in his mouth before swallowing. "Mm, yes. Just as I was told. Very nice. D'you have much on hand?"

"Not terribly, but I can get more. Why?"

"A question of inventory, of course." He smiled again, then leaned back and pulled a pale, expensive-looking cigar from inside his coat. When he reached for it, Megan at first thought he intended to pull a gun and very nearly bashed him with her bung starter.

"Are you all right, Miss O'Connell?"

"Yes. Why do you ask?"

"You look worried about something. Jumpy."

"Not at all, Mr. Norman. I certainly wouldn't worry about the likes of you. Not even after you sent that blackamoor after me."

"I beg your pardon?"

"You know perfectly good and well what I mean, Mr. Norman."

"As a matter of fact, dear lady, I do not."

"Are you trying to tell me you didn't hire a Negro to . . . you know."

"I have no idea what you are talking about, Miss O'Connell."

"So you say," she sniffed.

"That's right. So I do say." If he was lying, he was doing a remarkable job of it, Megan conceded. Norman did not act the least bit guilty when she brought up the matter of the Negro assassin.

"What I came here for tonight," Ike went on, "is to make you a business offer."

"Oh?"

"That's right. I was doing just fine here until you showed up, Miss O'Connell. Doing the best trade that I can remember in a very long time. Then you roll in and start giving drinks away. That was very bad for my business, Miss O'Connell. I probably shouldn't admit that, but it's true. You took a good many of my customers away, you and Mrs. Foreman with your, ahem, large bosoms and who knows what else."

"Mr. Norman, I will not sit here and listen to—"

"No, I didn't come here tonight to start anything with you. I'm sorry." Ike held his hands up as if in surrender. "Really."

"And so you should be, sir."

"I apologize, Miss O'Connell. I came here tonight hoping to end the, um, disagreements that have been between us."

"If you mean that, Mr. Norman, I can assure you I would be willing to let bygones be bygones. I'll make a fresh start if you will."

"Yes, well, um, let's consider how best we can go about that, Miss O'Connell."

"It seems simple enough to me, Mr. Norman. We each go about our own business without animosity toward the other. What else could be required beyond that?"

"Well, you see," Ike cleared his throat and shot his cuffs and stared off in the direction of the canvas roof, "what I was thinking was that, um, you might consider selling your, um, interest in the business."

"You were thinking I should sell, were you now?"

"As a matter of fact, um, yes. I was."

"Cash on the barrelhead?"

"Cash, yes indeed."

"And what offer is it you're making to me, Mr. Norman, this cash on the barrelhead offer of yours?"

"Well, um, what I had in mind is four thousand—"

"*Mister* Norman," she began. The thing was, her saloon was worth at least twenty thousand for the goodwill alone. She'd worked hard to build a reputation for honesty with her customers, and Ike Norman knew that quite as well as Megan did herself.

"No, now, I'm not done, Miss O'Connell. Hear me out. Please."

Megan was still frowning, but she did settle down to the extent of allowing him to speak again.

"Four thousand cash plus a twenty percent holding in this saloon *and* my place. Plus a salary for you and Mrs. Foreman to stay on and operate this business." Norman's smile returned, wider than ever. "No one would need to know about our, um, arrangement, Miss O'Connell. In fact, we could pretend to be rivals still. Make a fuss every once in a while. Pretend to fight. You know. I'm sure you understand what I'm talking about here. And, hey, I won't even mind if you want to keep on selling liquor that hasn't been diluted very much. That's okay. In fact I kind of like the idea. It'd keep the suckers thinking they're being taken care of."

"But of course they won't be." Megan smiled too, hers artificially sweet. "Will they, Mr. Norman?"

"Everything will be on the up-and-up, Miss O'Connell. You'll see. Why, I'll leave the liquor entirely up to you. I won't put in so much as a gill from the Platte. How does that sound? I won't water a single keg, not one."

"If you would be leaving the liquor to me, Mr. Norman, what is it you would want to control for yourself?"

"I thought perhaps—and mind, I know how much difficulty you've had in this area in the past, trying to get someone knowledgeable to operate things for you—but I was thinking perhaps I would take charge of the gaming. Not openly, you understand, but I would, um, suggest who you should hire. That's all. You would still be in full charge of everything else. And you would have a twenty percent stake in the profits from both saloons. Believe me, Miss O'Connell, your income would be considerable. With the two of us working together . . ."

Angry now, Megan stood. "Good night, Mr. Norman."

"Won't you at least consider my offer?"

"Good night, sir."

"We could negotiate the details. I could go as high as eight thousand cash and a twenty-five percent share in the businesses, Miss O'Connell."

"I asked you to leave, Mr. Norman. Would you prefer that I scream?" She gave him a cold look. "Just think what those men out there would do to anyone who laid an unwelcome hand on me or Rachel Foreman. Think about that, Mr. Norman. Then decide if you will leave as I asked. Or stand there while I scream."

Norman shot to his feet. "I've tried to be reasonable about this. I've tried to be nice to you. Whatever else may happen, woman, is on your head alone. Remember that." He spun on his heels and stalked outside. Through the tent flap as Ike Norman pushed his way out, Megan could see a hint of crimson dawn.

She was tired. Lord, but she was tired. The weariness swept over her once more and this time a measure of despair with it. She felt so alone here. So vulnerable. And now she did not even have the support of Glenn Gilchrist or of Joshua Hood to buttress her resolve.

What she needed, she thought, was sleep.

About a week of it for starters. Then perhaps a good breakfast and go back to bed for another few days.

She sighed.

And went to blow out the last lamp so she could stumble off and find her cot for a few hours of rest. Then she would have to get up and face a new day.

Damn you, Keith Gallagher, she thought as consciousness faded away.

CHAPTER

20

Ah, God, the pain. Glenn bit down hard on a piece of broken oak limb and tried to keep himself from crying. He'd never known pain like this. Never known it was possible for anything to hurt so much.

But it did, and it would continue to hurt no matter what he did, so he might just as well go ahead and do what had to be done.

For the moment the thing he had to do was get up to the head of this damned coulee and find the seep that bastard Silas had told him about.

Silas, Glenn thought darkly. That son of a bitch. But thinking about Silas now would accomplish nothing. Better to wait and savor his notions about Silas another time. Right now there were more pressing considerations.

A man can go a long time without food. Glenn knew that. Between the accounts reported by wagon-train émigrés over the past dozen years and the more recent stories of prisoner deprivation to come out of the war, it was no secret at all that food was of little immediate importance to someone in Glenn's distressed condition.

But water, that was another matter entirely. A man needs water often, although not necessarily in great quantity, if he is to survive. That too Glenn knew from the accounts of travelers and other unfortunates.

Lying half on his side and using his legs to drive himself forward, he scooted another foot or foot-and-a-half closer to his objective, then stopped to catch his breath and rest.

He could not be certain, but he suspected that the arrow that had entered his back had damaged his lung, because he was finding it remarkably difficult to breathe now and he had precious little strength.

If there was other damage, he could not tell. But then the whole of his upper back was one vast sea of pain, so much so that it was hard to distinguish one hurt from another.

What Glenn knew for sure was that he was in dire straits and would soon have died if he had continued to lie within the patch of oak scrub that had hidden him from the Sioux.

Of course he would die immediately if the Sioux party returned and discovered him away from the protective cover of that scrub oak.

On the whole, he had determined, he would rather die quickly than linger to suffer a slow and pain-filled end. Hence his current efforts to reach the water that lay so impossibly far away.

And if the Sioux returned, well, he would do what he could. He still had his Colt's Patent revolver. He'd determined that soon after regaining consciousness this morning. He still had that and his pouch of paper-wrapped cartridges and most of a tin of percussion caps. Call it—he hadn't counted—call it thirty or so rounds of ammunition including the five already loaded in the cylinder. Not that he would expect to have time to reload if the Sioux returned. They would be too quick for that, he suspected, they and their evil arrows. Five shots in the revolver, he reminded himself once again. Four to fire at the murderous savages and one final ball for himself.

Funny, Glenn thought without mirth. He'd come on a mission of peace. And the Sioux had tried their very best to kill him. May very well have accomplished that end, in fact. So now here he was, thinking of Spotted Bull's people as murderous savages when yesterday at this time he'd persisted in thinking of them as the innocent victims of Captain Medgar Taney's treachery.

Funny, sure. It was all a matter of whose ox was being gored. That was a truth Glenn had never particularly appreciated until now.

But truth it most certainly was.

And, Lord, it most certainly did feel to him at this moment as if an ox had indeed gored him. High on the left side of his back.

The arrow wound throbbed with every rush of heart-pumped blood, and sometimes sharp jolts of pain like ragged, jagged bolts of lightning would shoot through his body—for no reason at all, even when he held himself completely still in an effort to avoid the bitterness of pain.

Yet another jab of fire sliced through his flesh, and he bit down hard on the spit-slickened piece of wood that he clenched tight between his teeth.

Despite his resolve, a groan of agony escaped him, and he felt shame to compound the pain of his wound.

A man should be able to bear his burdens, damn it. A man should—"Ahhhh!" He rocked facedown into the dirt, then back onto his side again. But there was no way to escape the cutting, tearing pain. There was no place to hide, no way to run. From the Sioux perhaps but not from this.

Glenn shuddered and reached up to wipe the sweat out of his eyes, then with a conscious effort of will forced himself forward another foot and then again. Moving like some gigantic inchworm toppled over onto its side, he pushed and kicked and shoved himself across the gravel-pocked soil inch by painful inch.

The water he so sorely needed remained an impossible distance away.

But each time he moved, damn it, that impossible distance was shortened by six inches, eight, sometimes by as much as a foot.

Glenn had no idea what he would do if he ever did succeed in reaching the water. Drink, he supposed. And sleep. After that, well, after that he would just have to see.

For the moment all that was important was to reach the water.

That seemed quite enough of a goal for the time being.

He gathered himself, steeled his nerves and once more used waning leg strength to push himself a few inches onward.

Ten more shoves, he decided. Then he would rest. Ten more. He bit down hard on the bit of wood wedged in his jaw and pushed again. Nine more. Just nine more. He closed his eyes against the salt sting of the sweat that was coursing off his flesh and, once again, pushed. Eight more, he thought. Just eight times more.

He cut short a cry but could not keep himself from whimpering aloud in the lonely emptiness of the coulee bottom.

Seven pushes more, damn it. Seven more. Then he could rest.

21

With so many men employed in the construction of the railroad—Megan did not know what the number would be, but she was sure it was in the thousands by now—some were sure to be free at any given hour of the day or night. Whether because they had a day off, were recovering from an injury and could not work, or were simply malingering, there were always customers available to the businessmen and women who followed end-of-track, day and night, and these were men who drew their wages, good wages, in hard cash. Business at the Union Pacific end-of-track was in a state of perpetual boom.

So why, Megan wondered, was her saloon empty of customers now?

It was a little past noon, and in anticipation of the normal noontime trade, she had opened her doors—figuratively speaking, that is; what she had in fact done was to tie open her tent flaps—an hour ago.

So far she had served one beer. And that was to Jimmy Horlick, the telegrapher who was going to transmit her food order back to Aileen in Omaha. They needed to replace the free lunch items that had been eaten by the Sioux, and Megan was counting on her sister to handle that small chore for her.

Apart from Jimmy, though, the only people she'd seen so far were Rachel and Victor. And they were as puzzled as she. All three of them sat now at one of the tables where customers—when they had customers, that is—were allowed to play whatever games they wished. Megan supplied the men with cards and asked them to return a rake-off from each pot. It would have been easy for the men to cheat the house, she knew, but few of her customers took advantage of her. On the rare occasion when someone spent an evening in play and did not pony up a house share, she simply made a mental note of who it was and refused him cards the next time he asked. The system was not an especially profitable one for Megan, but at least it enabled the men to play and enjoy themselves. And remain on hand to buy more beer or spirits as the evenings progressed.

And this system was infinitely preferable to the one she'd had when her gaming manager Lew Scudder had proved to be working for Ike Norman. That had been an unmitigated disaster, and Megan would much rather earn little than earn much and be robbed of it, which had been the case under Scudder's management.

Besides, this way the games were as honest as the players chose to make them. And no fault or blame could blemish Megan's reputation for honesty in her business dealings. Here the house was impartial and completely uninvolved in the gambling.

But in order to make any profit at all, whether from gaming or from liquid refreshments, there first had to be customers.

And today those seemed to be in remarkably short supply.

A shadow momentarily darkened the entrance, and Megan looked up to see a short, very handsomely dressed gentleman come in. Her worried frown immediately spread into a smiling welcome.

"Dan. It's so nice to see you. I was afraid all my friends had forgotten me."

Megan motioned for Rachel to fetch the U.P. boss a drink and pushed out a chair so Dan could join her.

The Casement brothers, Jack and Dan, had been awarded a contract by the Union Pacific to hire the workmen and perform the actual labor of laying track while the Union Pacific, under the overall direction of Thomas Durant and General Grenville Dodge, attended to the logistical and political ends of the enormous project.

Like Dodge, Jack Casement had been a general in the Grand Army of the Republic during the recent war. Megan knew the brothers, both of whom were short and stocky, with closely trimmed spade beards and measures of confidence that belied their diminutive physical stature. Megan knew both but was particularly fond of Dan. After all, it had been Dan Casement who suggested she convert her workingman's restaurant into this much more lucrative saloon and who had quietly helped her make the transition.

"I can't tell you how pleased I am to see you today, Dan."

"What was that you were saying about old friends deserting you, Megan?" He took the seat Megan indicated and accepted a cup of coffee from Rachel with a smile and a nod of thanks.

"Oh, I didn't mean anything by it, really. I guess I'm feeling a little low today, that's all. I mean, there isn't any reason why Glenn and Joshua have to visit just because we've set up in a new place. But I'd hoped . . . well, you know."

Casement smiled and patted her wrist. "Whichever one of those young men you choose, Megan, will be most fortunate indeed. Why, if I weren't married . . ." He laughed.

Megan squeezed his hand. "Thanks, Dan. I was needing a compliment today. And if you weren't married, I would certainly welcome you as a suitor too." Her words were lightly spoken but carried a full measure of truth within them. Megan might be a head taller than Dan Casement, but she doubted she had ever known a man who was more decent or thoughtful. And had he been single, she would indeed have considered him a most attractive gentleman.

"You make me blush, my dear. So much so that I'm almost loath to tell you why your gentleman friends haven't paid you the attention you so richly deserve."

"Oh? You mean they have a reason?"

"I should say so. Several nights ago your friend Gilchrist embarked on a most ill-advised if deucedly brave venture. He hired one of Joshua Hood's scouts and rode off to the west. Claimed he intended to find Spotted Bull and see if he couldn't restore the truce between the Sioux and the Union Pacific. Of course after what the army did . . ." Casement shrugged. "Like I said, the young man was as brave as he was foolish about this. He hasn't a hope of pulling it off. The only question is whether he can be found and called back before anything . . . untoward, shall we say . . . happens to him."

Megan's hands flew to her mouth to cover an exclamation of alarm.

"Please," Casement said. "You shouldn't be upset. This scout he went out with is known to be more bluster and braggadocio than substance. I suspect he'll merely run Gilchrist about for a few days and then claim he can't locate Spotted Bull. You know. Raise enough smoke and dust to justify his pay but not risk his neck while he's doing it."

"I certainly hope that's what they do," Megan said.

"Yes, well, we hold your young Mr. Gilchrist in rather high regard too, you know. So the chief surveyor and I asked Mr. Hood to toddle along after them and fetch them back before there is trouble."

"Thank goodness."

"Mmm, as you say." Casement smiled and patted Megan's wrist again. "In any event, that is why neither of them has come to call. I suspect they will both be back in, oh, another day or two."

"I hope so. Safely back."

"Indeed, dear lady, that is what we all hope. And in the meantime, perhaps we can think of some way to get you out of your predicament."

Megan raised her eyebrows.

"Do you mean . . . you don't even know?"

"Know what, Dan?"

"The whiskey price war that's started."

"Dan, honestly, I have no earthly idea what you are talking about."

"Surely you've noticed that your place is empty."

Megan rolled her eyes. "Oh, I've noticed that, all right. But I've been assuming, sort of, that the railroad is doing something special today to keep everyone busy."

"I wish that were so, Megan, but the truth is that one of your competitors has been sending boys all through the camp announcing a price reduction at his saloon. Three-cent drinks or two for a nickel."

Megan felt an emptiness in her belly. Two-and-a-half cents a drink.

"Ike Norman," she blurted.

"That's right, it is Norman. He's posting signs, calling men in with a barker. He's being quite aggressive about the whole thing."

"He's trying to ruin me, Dan, that's what he's really doing. He wants to undercut the prices and force me to follow at a loss until I can't stay in business any longer. Then he can buy me out or simply take over whatever property I have to abandon, and he will be able to charge anything he likes."

"Can he do it, Megan? Force you out of business, I mean?"

"There is a strong chance that he can, Dan. That's the awful truth of it. You see, I won't water my drinks the way he does. I insist on giving my customers full measure. Ike Norman serves whiskey so weak I'm surprised the minnows don't survive in it when he pours the Platte in. And that is the problem, of course. Two-and-a-half cents is pretty much cost for me. Ike can sell at that price and make at least a penny a drink. Maybe more depending on how deep he cuts his measure."

"The answer seems simple enough to me then, Megan."

"It does?"

"Certainly. You know you have to meet his price or he will take all the trade away from you. So do it. Cut your prices and cut your liquor." Casement smiled. "Just remember to strain all the minnows out before you introduce the water. It would be rather awkward to find the tiny corpses floating, wouldn't it?"

"Dan, I'm trying to be serious here."

"So am I, Megan. So am I."

"But . . ."

"But nothing, Megan. I don't see that you have much choice in the matter. It's a question of survival, and you shall have to do whatever it takes."

Megan set her jaw and shook her head. "No. I won't do that, Dan. I won't cheat my customers just for the sake of profit."

"Profit, Megan? Or survival?"

"Profit, of course. I won't try to rationalize it as anything else. If my business fails, Dan, the sun will still rise tomorrow morning. I'll still be alive. I won't be defeated. I just simply won't be. If I can't make a go with this, then I'll do something else. I'll do whatever I have to, Dan, but I'll do it on my terms, not Ike Norman's. And I'll do it with my chin high and able to look anyone, man or woman, straight in the eye and never have to flinch. I'll do that, Dan. I promise you that I will."

"You know, Megan, I believe perhaps you will at that." Casement nodded and pushed away from the table, rising. "If there is anything I can do . . ."

"Thank you, Dan. You've already done more than you know."

The construction boss over the entire Union Pacific railroad effort reached deep into his pockets . . . and came up empty. "Megan, I can't believe I've come away this morning with not a cent to my name."

She laughed. "The coffee is on the house, Dan. Surely you know that."

"No indeed. I insist. That is, I would insist. If I had anything to pay you."

"Forget it, Dan. I don't think the price of a cup of coffee is going to break me." Her smile faded. "The price of a drink, now, that could be another thing entirely."

"We'll think of something, Megan."

"If you do, Dan, please tell me what it is, because right at this minute I don't have an idea in my head about how to stop Ike Norman from ruining me."

"You aren't a quitter. That's the most important thing. And if I do think of anything I can suggest or better yet anything I can do, well, you will be the first to know."

"Thanks, Dan. Thank you ever so much."

Casement turned and walked out into the midday sunshine while Megan, aghast now that the impact of the news had had time to hit home, slumped wearily back onto her chair.

CHAPTER

22

Joshua reined his horse to a stop and froze at the warning signal from Dave Pettis on the point. The three men riding behind Joshua halted as well.

Dave remained still for a moment, listening, then turned in his saddle and quickly sketched a series of designs in the air with rapid hand movements, the universal sign language of the plains.

Rider coming. Two, maybe three. Not far. Quiet. Pettis's hands flew.

Two, maybe three, Joshua thought. No wonder they were moving quiet. It wasn't any war party. Unlike white men, Indians generally rode as a group when they traveled. A large party of whites would put out vedettes in advance of the line of march. Indians rarely bothered with such precaution. So whoever was approaching was no war party. But they still could be trouble. It would only take one wanderer to spot them and ride to warn other Sioux that there was a party of whites intruding onto the Sioux lands.

And after what those fools Taney and Wollins did in their ambush, no white man was likely to be welcomed into a Sioux camp or onto Sioux lands again for a very long time to come.

Two, maybe three.

Joshua had four men with him. Four rifles should easily take care of two or three Sioux.

That would be rather rough on the unsuspecting Sioux, who might well be innocent travelers out in search of bullberries or just going to the next village south for a visit with the kinfolk.

Rough on the Sioux, perhaps, but better rough on these few than to allow some larger band of Sioux to slaughter Joshua and his scouts.

It had come to that, damn it. Thanks to Medgar Taney and his popinjay lieutenant Wollins.

Joshua gave the order, still using the silent sign language.

Dave nudged his horse into a sidepass, man and mount alike disappearing into the sun-dappled foliage beside this trail along the Platte River.

Behind Joshua the other scouts too disappeared from sight as completely as so many puffs of smoke drifting away on a summer's breeze.

Joshua waited a moment to make sure everyone was well hidden, then he too guided his horse quietly into the brush.

He stopped at the edge of a clump of screening willow, the sunshine hard and hot on his left shoulder. A bright-winged deerfly flittered around the ears of his horse, and Joshua slapped it away lest its bite cause the horse to stamp or whinny. The approaching riders were close enough now that Joshua could hear their passage through the grass.

Slowly and careful to make no noise he pulled his slim but deceptively heavy Winchester rifle from its scabbard. All of his scouts were armed now with the new Winchesters, courtesy of General Dodge's appeal to the factory back east. The new Winchesters were a marked improvement over the old Henry pattern. Both used the squat and highly effective,

if short-ranged, .44 rimfire self-contained cartridge, but the
new rifle did away with the fragile tube feed mechanism of
the Henry in favor of a much more reliable breech feed. Not
only was the new model stronger, it could be reloaded in the
midst of action with no more effort than the twist of a wrist
or the stab of a finger. Joshua doubted any Sioux had yet
faced this newest offering from the Winchester factory.

Not that two or three riders would put the Winchesters to a test. Still, it was comforting to know that his
scouts were as well prepared for a fight as he could make
them.

Now all they needed to do was wait for the oncoming
riders to reach a point midway along the line of ambushing
scouts. Joshua would open the scrap by firing the first shot.
He doubted any Sioux would survive the first volley even
if there proved to be four of them. Not that there would
be so many. If Dave said there were two or three, then
there probably were only two and certainly no more than
three.

Joshua felt a constriction deep in his throat and fought
back an urge to cough. He settled for swallowing hard several times in succession. When that failed to bring comfort,
he simply accepted the annoyance as a nearly welcome
distraction from the tension of waiting to gun down an
unsuspecting human.

The footsteps were very close now.

Joshua held the Winchester near his belly so as to muffle
the sound of its action and carefully earred the thick hammer
back to full cock. He did not have to look to make sure there
was a live cartridge in the chamber. He made it a point
always to carry one there. Although wouldn't it be a kick
in the teeth if this one time he'd forgotten to chamber a
cartridge? The night before, when he last cleaned the rifle?

He'd remembered to seat a fresh round then, hadn't he?

He stifled an impulse, a wildly strong impulse, to crank the lever and make sure a cartridge was chambered.

Nerves, he acknowledged. Nothing that couldn't be overcome.

The sound of the riders was close now.

Two horses. He was sure there were no more than two. This was almost too easy. He would much rather . . . Damn it, it didn't matter what he wanted. What mattered was that he keep his men alive and safe. That was what was at stake here. Never mind fairness. Nor even right and wrong. What mattered was that these scouts ride safely back to end-of-track once they found that imbecile Gilchrist and that equally mush-brained Silas Short.

Joshua cocked his rifle and lifted himself in his stirrups. Saddle leather creaked softly but not so loud it would be heard from more than a few feet away.

Ready. Ready.

"Aw, shit!"

The voice was Dave Pettis's, from off toward Joshua's left. The unexpected break in the silence was darn near enough to make Joshua jump and blow off a round by accident.

Joshua was not the only one who was startled by Dave's exclamation.

Out ahead and to the left there was a gasp and immediately afterward a pounding of hooves as two horses jumped into a run.

"Damn you, Silas," Dave called out, "it's us."

By then the horses had bolted into view and Joshua understood. The riders they'd been laying their ambush for weren't a pair of Sioux warriors, they were Silas Short and . . . and nobody, that's who else.

Silas came tearing down the trail astride his spotted pony, and alongside him on a lead rope he was dragging a stout brown. But the saddle on the brown was empty. Joshua would have sworn the saddle that brown was wearing was Glenn Gilchrist's. Would almost have sworn it anyway.

"Silas," he called, stepping his own mount out of the willows. "Whoa up there, Silas."

The rest of the scouts moved into the open also as Silas and his horses charged past.

"Damn you, Short, you come back here right now."

"Hell's bells, Joshua, I'm a-tryin'."

Man and mounts disappeared around a bend, Silas leaning back in his seat and sawing hard with his reins. A minute or two later they returned, this time at a much slower pace.

"We like to shot your head off, Silas. What're you doin' out here by yourself? Come t' that, where's the college boy you come out with? What's happened to Gilchrist?"

The big scout came to a halt close to Joshua's right stirrup and dropped his gaze sheepishly toward the dirt.

"That Mr. Gilchrist, Joshua, he's dead."

"What?"

"It's true. We was jumped by a bunch o' Sioux. Musta been forty, fifty of 'em. They had us surrounded, Joshua. By this spring where we was stopped fer the night. They snuck up on us an' opened fire without no warning. I tried t' fight 'em off, but they was too much for one man t' handle. I shot an' shot an' kept 'em off long enough for Mr. Gilchrist t' get the horses, but he was knocked down just as he was gettin' mounted. It was awful, Joshua. Wasn't nothin' I could do by then. The man was a regular pincushion o' arrers. Looked like a half-nekkid porkypine. So I done what I could. I went fer my own horse here an' skedaddled. Got away somehow, I'll never know how. Come the next mornin' I found this brown followin' along behind, nose t' the ground an' smellin' out my trail like a damn hound dog. You know how horses will do that sometimes. Well, he caught up with me. Lucky for me them Sioux didn't know t' follow him, for I never seen more o' them oncet I got clear o' the camp. But your friend Mr. Gilchrist, Joshua, he's cold meat just as sure as God made little apples."

"I'm sorry t' hear that, Silas."

"Well I'm sorry t' tell it to you, but I got t' tell you what I seen with my own eyes. And that there is what happened, all right. I done the best I could t' save him, Joshua, but there was just too many o' them red bastards. Wasn't nothing I could do more'n what I done. I swear t' you the truth o' that statement."

"Yeah, well, damn. I'm gonna hate to take this news back to Ben Goss."

"Can't be helped, Joshua. It's the simple truth. Can't nothin' change that."

"No, I don't suppose so." It occurred to Joshua that there was another party back there who would also have to be told.

And while in one way there was a sneaking, unwelcome bit of relief in the knowledge that Glenn Gilchrist would no longer be his rival for Megan O'Connell's affections, there was also the fact that this news would cause her pain.

If there was anything Joshua Hood did not want to do it was to bring pain into Megan O'Connell's life.

Still, like Silas said, nothing can change simple truth. And the loss of Gilchrist was something Megan would get over someday. With any kind of luck, Joshua himself would be there to help ease her through the hurt.

Joshua cleared his throat, taking considerable comfort from being able to freely cough now if he wished, and looked at his men, who were gathered around the brown horse, examining an arrow wound in its crest.

"That horse gonna be all right?" he asked.

"Silas shoulda cut this arrow out before now, but I think it'll heal okay," Wilbur Newell said. Wilbur was a good man with horses, and Joshua was willing to accept his opinion on the subject.

"You can doctor the horse when we stop for supper then, Wilbur. Right now I expect we'd best move along. We got a lotta ground t' cover, and I'd just as soon not be hangin' around where that war party can find us any longer'n we got to."

"Whatever you think, Joshua."

Joshua gave them just long enough for the horses to be watered and the men to relieve themselves. Then the little party of scouts, six men now and seven horses, resumed their trek through hostile territory.

CHAPTER

23

Megan had given Victor the rest of the day off—it didn't
seem there would be much need for him to remove empty
kegs or bring replacements out—and now she and Rachel
were having supper in the empty, cavernous saloon tent.
They were the only two in the place, and there was certainly
nothing better for them to do at the moment.

Across the table from Megan, Rachel winced.

"What's the matter, dear?"

"If I hear another chorus of 'For He's a Jolly Good
Fellow,' Megan, I think I'm going to . . . to . . . I'm going
to just scream."

The sounds of merriment filtered all too easily through the
canvas walls, the noise coming from Ike Norman's place. It
had been bad enough earlier in the afternoon, but ever since
the work day ended, it had been unbearable.

"It's a wonder they all fit inside," Megan said, a note of
bitterness creeping into her voice despite her best resolve to
pretend she was unaffected.

"As a matter of fact, ladies, they do not. They've rolled
the tent side walls up and hired extra help to manage the
overload."

Megan jumped, startled. She hadn't noticed the little man
come in.

"Sorry," he said with a disarming smile. "I didn't mean to frighten you."

"You didn't. Well, yes, I suppose you did. But . . ." Megan cleared her throat. "Can we help you?"

"I came for a whiskey, but that stew smells divine. I don't suppose you could be persuaded to serve a meal along with the drink?"

"Of course we serve meals," Rachel volunteered before Megan had time to inform the gentleman that this was a saloon and no longer a cafe. "Sit wherever you like. I won't be a moment." And she was gone, slipping quickly away before Megan might contradict the invitation.

Megan sighed. Trust Rachel to try to salvage a half-bit profit from this worst of all possible days. To the customer she shrugged and said, "You're welcome to join us if you want company, sir, or enjoy the privacy if that is what you crave." In an effort to put a twist of good humor into the situation, she added, "We have all the privacy anyone could want here, and a bargain it is by anyone's standards. Help yourself if that would be your pleasure."

"If it's all the same to you then, Miss O'Connell, I would be honored to join you."

"Help yourself, friend."

Megan received a bit of a surprise when the man moved slowly and with a quiet dignity to her table. He was short, not a whit taller than Dan Casement and perhaps not even that tall. But she'd seen that to begin with. What she hadn't noticed while he stood still was that at least part of his lack of height could be attributed to a withered right leg that, now that she paid attention, she saw was inches shorter and much slighter of structure than his left limb. Yet instead of walking with a dwarfish swing-and-hop on the abbreviated leg, he managed a slow but somehow rather stately glide across the as yet unbeaten prairie sod that served as a floor.

The gentleman—and she was certain from his demeanor and dress that this fellow was indeed a gentleman, very much the real thing—wore a handsomely cut if much used suit of charcoal-colored broadcloth, a silk vest and maroon cravat and a ruby stickpin so garishly large that it had to be a glass fake rather than the genuine article. His hat was an old-fashioned low-crowned beaver of Planter design, and he wore, incredibly, spats and kidskin gloves. A cane would not have been out of place with such a getup, but perhaps because it would have drawn attention to his infirmity, he chose not to carry one.

Apart from the twisted leg, his physique was exceptionally small and slight, and he was so emaciated, with sunken cheeks and dark hollows under his eyes, that he seemed almost skeletal. Yet he did not appear to be in poor health. If anything he exuded an air of strength and competence.

He had, Megan thought, an exceptionally strong force of character about him. She liked this little man virtually upon sight.

"I am sure we haven't met before, sir, so how is it that you know my name?"

"I took the liberty of making inquiries," he explained. "Please, though. Don't let me interrupt your supper. Do go ahead and eat."

"I'll wait for you and Rachel, thank you. I believe you were telling me about the reason for those inquiries?"

"Was I?"

"Oh, I'm sure you were about to. Please don't let me interrupt that, sir."

The fellow laughed and leaned back in his chair. He had an infectious smile when he chose to use it, the sort of smile that could warm an entire audience with its spell.

Megan wondered if perhaps he were an actor or balladeer or such. "You are direct, Miss O'Connell. And I'm told you are honest. Is that true?"

"Honest enough to remind you you can buy your whiskey for half the price at Ike Norman's. And honest enough to admit to wondering why you've come here when you obviously know that a'ready."

Rachel came back with a bowl of stew for the gentleman and a glass of whiskey to accompany it. "Coffee, sir?"

"Later will be fine. Sit down now before your meal gets cold, eh?"

Rachel joined them, and Megan prompted, "You were saying . . . ?"

"As a matter of fact, Miss O'Connell, I did stop by to take in the sights over there. Had a look at the tables Mr. Norman operates." He grinned and feigned a shiver. "Wintry, the prospects there. If you're a mark, that is. The house is what you might call exceptionally secure."

"Oh?"

"Pinpricks on the cards before they ever come out of their wrappings."

"I didn't think that was possible," Megan said.

"Ah, the naïveté of the blindly honest," the little man said with no hint of censure, or of condescension, in his voice. "Of course it is possible. A little steam, a little glue, a little time, that's all that is required. For that matter, madam, there are certain brands of cards—you'd be surprised which ones—that can be purchased new from the printer with certain smudges and omissions. If you know the code, you can read suit and number from the back as easily as from the face. Then there are the wheels. Squeeze pedals and wires on every one. Not that that's surprising. It's all too common. And the dice?" He rolled his eyes and chuckled. "Whoever loaded those did such a sloppy job of it he should be ashamed of himself. Why, where has pride in workmanship got to anymore? A mechanic of the green cloth should at least be good at what he does." He lifted his glass and took a tiny, birdlike sip from it.

"You sound like you know what you're talking about."

The little fellow remained seated but gave Megan a half bow. "If I do say so, Miss O'Connell, I know more about gambling than anyone else this side of the continent. Both the licit forms and, um, otherwise."

"You still haven't explained what brings you here, though, when you could be enjoying cheap drinks—and whatever else—in Ike Norman's place."

The little man beamed. "But of course I have, Miss O'Connell. I've come in search of honesty. And it seems my information was correct. I've found it."

"I'm not sure I know what you mean."

"This whiskey, Miss O'Connell. By the bye, did I mention to you that my palate is as keen as my gambling sense? No? My, imagine the oversight." He grinned. "Still, this whiskey proves my point. You haven't adulterated it by so much as a cupful of water. Believe me, I would know if you had. Yet even though your competitor is undercutting your prices by half, you haven't given in to temptation. You aren't cheating your customers. That is what I heard about you down the line, and that is what I now find in your establishment. Bravo for you, Miss O'Connell. Bravo for you, I say."

"Thank you, I'm sure."

"No thanks necessary. You deserve the compliment."

What an odd little man, Megan thought. But likable. She wondered if he really was as good as he claimed with cards and liquor.

"Now," he said, "shall we get to business first or strike

our deal after we eat?"

"Deal? Whatever deal are you talking about?"

The broad, happy smile returned in full, sunny force, and the little man spread his hands wide. "My dear Miss O'Connell, in gaming circles I have a certain renown. One might even say, well, fame and following. If I undertake to run your gambling tables, there are two things I can guarantee: impeccable honesty and a great deal of play."

"Come again, sir?"

"You see, if I do say so, Miss O'Connell, my reputation for honest dealing is at least as great as yours, albeit in a slightly different line of, um, work. I insist on it. I demand it. Which is why I walked out on Mr. Norman after he invited me here. He wanted to draw the clientele that I would bring along with me. And I can't blame him. Men have been known to travel from New Orleans all the way to Cincinnati to face me across a table. My presence would have lent your friend Norman the panache he himself is unable to generate. It would have been, if I do say so, a feather in his cap. But first I listened, then I looked. I did not like what I heard and liked even less what I saw. And by then I'd already heard about you. And so, *voilà,* I am here." Again he bowed from his chair.

"Fascinating," Megan admitted.

"It is done then? We are partners?"

"Partners!" Megan yelped.

"No, no, dear lady. Not in the saloon business. In that I have no interest anyway. But you will allow me to play my little games and, we shall say, supervise your tables? I would return to you fifteen percent of my profit. Mind, though. I give you no guarantees. There will be times when the cards do not come my way. There will be days when I make nothing." He tipped his head back and laughed quite happily. "There will be days when I profit in the thousands too. One never knows. That is what makes it the game and not the business, yes?"

"How do I know you are what you say you are?"

"Madam. Please. You wound me."

"It isn't like you're probably thinking, mister," Rachel put in. "The last gambling boss Miss Megan hired turned out to be a plant, a phony run in on her by Ike Norman. The guy was stealing her blind and all the while telling her he was just having bad days. You know. Because he was playing honest and there wasn't no guarantees. Kinda like another speech we just now heard. So if she ain't real quick to jump at your offer, well . . ."

"Ah, now I understand. And what can I say except that I am not of that cloth? I tell you what. We will speak no more of this tonight. We will eat. We will drink. I will pay full measure for whatever I take. Then at your leisure, dear lady, you ask about me. Ask anyone who would be familiar with the gentlemanly art of the wager. You ask anyone about Henry Harrison Armbruster. Then we will talk again later. How does that sound to you, eh?"

"Henry Harrison Armbruster, huh?"

"That's me!" the little fellow cried happily.

Megan liked him. In spite of herself, in spite of her history of bad experience, the last time she thought she'd found someone to take over her tables, darned if she didn't just plain like Henry Harrison Armbruster.

As for his offer, though . . . they would just have to wait and see.

"This stew is cold," Rachel said. "Let me bring the pot out and I'll warm everybody's bowls."

"Bring the coffee too, please, Rachel. And more whiskey for Mr. Armbruster."

"Please, Miss O'Connell. Call me Henry Harrison. Everyone does."

"Very well, Henry Harrison. Whatever you prefer."

"Should I give him the good stuff again, Megan?" Rachel asked with a wink. "Or can we switch him to the cheap stuff now?"

Henry Harrison Armbruster roared so hard he almost toppled off his chair. "Oh, ladies. I do believe I am going to like it here."

"We'll see about that, won't we? When we talk. Later."

"Later. Right." He howled with laughter again and took another tiny sip of his whiskey, then dug into his bowl of stew with a right goodwill. When it came to his appetites, it seemed that little Henry Harrison Armbruster could match any man twice his size and then some.

CHAPTER

24

Megan. Ah, Megan. So beautiful. So pure. Her skin was milky white and soft as eiderdown.

Her hair was loose and flowing. A bright, flaming red. Lightly curling. Full and free across her shoulders, its color crisp, almost startling against the white silk of the dressing gown.

She sat at a low table, a mirror in a gilt frame before her and lamps placed to either side. She was brushing her hair. One long, sensuous stroke after another.

When she lifted her arms to begin each new stroke the flimsy material of the gown pulled tight over her full bosom, the outline of each firm breast clear and lovely.

Her waist was small for so tall and buxom a woman, and her complexion was an example of the perfection that is possible but so rarely found in nature.

As she brushed her hair, the silk material of her dressing gown slid gently off her leg, the belt at her middle unable to hold the two halves together when she was seated. The falling silk revealed a shapely leg, slim and lovely and pale. Her ankle was small and her calf sleek.

She counted aloud as she brushed. Ninety-eight, ninety-nine, one hundred.

She laid the brush down and leaned forward. Picked up a glass-stoppered vial and shook it, then touched the tip of the stopper lightly to each side of her throat, behind each ear, once more to the deep valley of her decolletage. Carefully, turning her head first this way and then that, she inspected herself critically in the mirror.

Finally she rose.

Turned.

Opened her arms.

She took a step forward, the creamy perfection of her leg again showing itself through the folds of the silk gown.

She tossed her head, throwing that thick mane of flaming red hair back off her shoulders.

She held herself tall and proud.

Shrugged first one shoulder and then the next, deliberately causing the silk covering to slide first down one shoulder and then off the next until . . .

Ahh!

He parted his lips in anticipation of the embrace.

His mouth trembled and sought.

And pain from the dry, cracking corners of his own caked lips brought him out of the half-sleep reverie that had claimed and comforted him.

Glenn Gilchrist woke to pain. The pain of thirst and a parched, burning throat.

His tongue felt swollen and his lips were split and oozing blood from the dryness.

For a moment there he had thought his dream real, and for a moment more he wished he could return to it, return to the much more pleasant world of fantasy and the hell with this ugliness of reality.

Had he really been able to take Megan O'Connell into his arms, to hold her, to touch her face and stroke her hair, to feel the press of her lips against his and to taste of her sweet breath . . . had he really been able to do any of those imagined things, he would gladly have relinquished what little hold he still had on life and all that went with it.

But the choice was not his.

Megan was, thank goodness, safe in Omaha with Aileen and Aileen's children.

There was that to be grateful for. And to regret.

For, oh, the dream had been a grand one.

A mite short, of course. He would have preferred for it to run a tad longer so that he could have imagined . . . no, now that he thought about it, it was probably just as well that he'd wakened when he did. A man could abide just so much torment, and Glenn felt that he'd used up most of his own ability to endure.

It would be better, he was sure, if he could just find the water seep.

He knew it was somewhere close by. It had to be. But he'd crawled and struggled and fought his way along and hadn't ever managed to locate the life-giving water.

Life-giving, that was the thing.

The water meant life. Being unable to reach it meant . . . something else again.

If he could just see . . .

But he couldn't.

There was a haze over his vision like a layer of cheese-cloth drawn across his eyes.

That had happened . . . when? He wasn't sure. Time had gotten away from him lately.

He'd been shot . . . He had no idea how long ago that had been.

He'd been shot by an arrow. He was pretty sure that was what had happened.

Yet, funny, it wasn't the arrow that was bothering him so very much now. Rather it was the throbbing in his hand. His hand was swollen up like a rubber bladder. And it hurt. Oh, Lord, it hurt something awful.

It hurt so bad he couldn't bear for it to keep on hurting, and yet there wasn't anything he could do to make it stop either.

It hurt so bad that whenever he passed out he welcomed the loss of consciousness.

He knew that every time he passed out like that, he was kept from finding the water and therefore was that much closer to dying, but, oh Lord, it hurt so bad that he just didn't care any longer. He truly didn't. He would have given anything, including life itself, just to make the hurting stop.

But it wouldn't stop. It didn't stop. And he just had to . . . had to what? He tried to remember but could not.

Not that it mattered anyway. Not really.

Glenn closed his eyes and sighed. What he thought he would do was to lie here just a little longer. Lie here with his eyes closed and think about Megan.

If he was lucky, really and truly lucky, he would drift off again. But close enough to the surface that he could think about Megan. Think about the way she looked. The way her hair smelled. The firm and yet ineffably soft feel of her body inside the circle of his arms. Think about . . .

Oh, Jesus. Jesus and Mary and Megan and . . .

Glenn Gilchrist wept a little before once again consciousness left him and he descended slowly into a place that held no pain.

CHAPTER

25

"Hold it," Joshua hissed, motioning the men behind him to halt.

"What d'ya see, boss?" someone whispered.

"Sioux. A whole bunch of 'em. Riding up through the bottom."

Joshua and his scouts were approaching the east side of a north-south–running gully or shallow coulee north of the Platte River. It was, Silas said, the place where the Indians killed Glenn Gilchrist. Retrieving Gilchrist's body and taking it back for burial was the reason they'd backtracked Silas Short's route. That was only the right thing to do. And besides, Joshua was sure Megan O'Connell would appreciate the sentiment of it. But Joshua and his men hadn't expected to encounter another party of Sioux warriors here.

"Lemme see now," Joshua said in a low voice. "There's . . . I make them out t' be twelve . . . No, there's thirteen of 'em. Can't be the same crowd that jumped you, Silas. Not all of 'em anyway. You said that was a big party."

"That's right. Forty or more. I didn't take no time t' count, but there was at least that many."

"You know what I bet this is then," Joshua suggested. "I bet this bunch has come back t' scavenge any arrows or iron heads that're still good."

One of the few advantages the primitive bow had over a rifle or revolver was that you could reuse an arrow. Unbroken arrows could simply be picked up and shot again. And even shattered arrows retained salvageable materials. Feathers could be glued onto new shafts and arrow points made from soft, malleable sheet iron could be reshaped and sharpened over and over again. Difficult and time-consuming as it was to fashion good arrows, it was no wonder the Indian warriors made a habit of reclaiming all they could, with such spoils going to the victors in their frequent battles with other warring tribes.

"You don't think they're gonna chop Mr. Gilchrist up, do you, Joshua?" Dave Pettis asked. "I've heard Injuns do awful things t' the bodies of folks they've murdered." Joshua thought Dave sounded a mite queasy at the thought.

"Won't make no never mind if they do, Dave. Gilchrist is dead. He won't feel it, whatever they do."

"Whether he does or not, Joshua, it ain't right to let that happen. It ain't Christian."

"I know, Dave, but I'm not gonna risk our lives to stop it." Joshua fingered his chin and scratched idly at the side of his neck. "On t'other hand, boys, that bunch down there killed one o' our own. I'd kinda hate t' see them gather up their ammunition an' ride away unharmed. Seein' as how we're right here an' have them outgunned."

"Outgunned, Joshua?"

"I only see two of 'em with rifles. The rest just have bows and spears and like that."

"Bad enough at close range," Silas said. "Them sonsa-bitches shoot fast an' hard at close range. B'lieve me, I seen 'em. I know."

"They don't know we're here," Joshua went on, ignoring Silas. "One aimed volley from up above an' then a run down onto 'em, I bet we'd cut down the most of them right from the get-go. The rest'd skedaddle, an' we'd have plenty time t' grab Gilchrist's body an' get the hell out afore they could fetch the main party down onto us. If you're with me, I say we do it. What d'you think, boys?"

With the exception of Silas Short, the response was a round of grinning nods from the scouts.

"That's it then. We'll give 'em a taste o' these new Winchesters."

Joshua pulled his own carbine from its scabbard, and the rest of the men, Silas included, followed suit.

"We'll come up in a line," Joshua ordered, "an' shoot one volley, no, make it two. Fire the first one on my command, then crank an' fire a second quick as you can manage. After the second volley, we charge. All right?"

The men calmly nodded and drew their hammers back, ready to fire. There wasn't a man among them who hadn't faced hostile fire before. Nor was there any group of men he could think of who Joshua would rather be with at a moment like this. He motioned for them to bring their horses into line just below the crest above the coulee.

It took another few moments for each man to position his horse the way he wanted it, then Joshua bumped his mount onto the skyline looking down into the coulee.

The Indians below were unaware as yet. They continued to ride single file along a narrow game trail at the bottom. They were roughly abreast of the line of scouts now and no more than sixty yards downslope from them.

"Fire," Joshua said without waiting for them to be noticed by their foes.

Wreaths of white smoke and sharp lances of yellow fire spat from the six rifles on the skyline, and down below five Sioux warriors twisted in sudden pain.

The scouts' horses pranced and reared at the sudden commotion, but Joshua and his men controlled the horses with their knees, without conscious thought to what they were doing, as they swiftly yanked the levers of the Winchester rifles down and back up.

When they'd reloaded, there was another volley, this one slightly ragged, and three more Indians died before they had time to flee.

There was confusion and some amount of panic among the remaining Indians.

Horses pitched and bucked at the noise of the onslaught, and one warrior lost his seat and went flying to the ground.

"Hit 'em hard now, boys. Charge!" Joshua shouted, his own horse already three or four flying paces ahead of the rest of the scouts.

Joshua transferred the Winchester to his rein hand and drew his .44 Colt for the close-in work that was to come.

Below him the Sioux scattered, spare horses and the animals that had belonged to the newly dead impeding the progress of the warriors who were trying to flee.

Rifles and revolvers crackled and spat as the scouts charged into the confused Indians.

A warrior with half his face painted black dropped his bow and the arrow he couldn't manage to nock. The man snatched a feather-decorated war club from his waist and sent an ululating cry of defiance across the few yards that separated him from the onrushing Joshua.

Joshua admired the Indian's courage. But not so much so that he would allow the Sioux to brain him with the pointed granite head of the war club. Joshua shot the man square in the chest, thumbed back his hammer again and at a range of little more than inches shot the man a second time in the face. Then his horse carried him past the Sioux and the now harmless war club, and Joshua looked for a second threat.

The Indian who'd been thrown from his horse lay half-hidden in a clump of scrub oak. An arrow sprang into view from within the foliage, and Wilbur Newell's brother Tyrone reeled, the arrow lodged in his calf.

More gunshots sounded, but Joshua could not see what his men were firing at.

As suddenly as if they'd been made of smoke and caught on a rising wind, the few remaining Sioux were gone, the only evidence of their presence being the bodies they left behind and a pair of horses that couldn't decide which way to run to catch up with the others.

"Damn!" someone said.

"Yeah. Ain't that the natural truth." Two Left Puckett—so named because he'd worn moccasins for so many years that when he finally bought a pair of boots, he picked up two left boots and wore them, not noticing the difference, for days before someone else discovered the error—took out a plug of tobacco and used a huge Arkansas toothpick to whittle a chew from it. Then he threw his right leg over the horn of his saddle and slithered to the ground, still holding the knife in his hand.

"Got a chaw t' spare, Two?"

"Ayuh." Puckett handed the plug up to Dave Pettis and calmly went about scalping the dead Sioux. Silas Short hurried to jump down and join Two Left before all the opportunities for trophy taking were exhausted.

"How you doin'?" Wilbur Newell asked his brother.

"It kinda hurts."

Wilbur had dismounted and was standing at Tyrone's side. The feathered shaft of the Sioux arrow barely protruded from the buckskin-clad calf of Tyrone's left leg.

"It went clean through, Ty," Wilbur said.

"Didn't stick m' horse, did it?"

"No, he's all right, but I got bad news."

"What's that?"

"The point of the arrow here is stuck into your stirrup leather."

"That's bad?"

"Hell yes. Means we'll have t' dig a extra big hole t' bury you in, you bein' attached t' this saddle permanent now."

"Damn you, Wil."

"Yeah, I expect I will be, Ty." In a louder voice Wilbur called, "Two Left, when you get done operatin' on them departed heathen, whyn't you fetch that knife over here an' chop Tyrone free of his saddle, will you?"

"Sure, Wilbur. I won't be a minute more." Two Left leaned down, sliced and tugged. With a grunt he came upright again, a hank of black, greasy hair in one hand and his big knife in the other. "What'd you say needs cuttin'?"

"Tyrone's leg."

"Damn you, Wilbur, Two Left—"

"Aw, he ain't gonna cut you, Ty." Wilbur spat. " 'Less he has to."

"It ain't funny, damn it."

Two Left glanced at Tyrone's problem and, almost casually, ran the blade of his knife between Tyrone's slowly bleeding leg and the stirrup leather. The sharp Arkansas blade made quick work of the arrow shaft, and Tyrone was free.

"Tyrone. Quick. Look up there!"

"Where? Ow!"

Too late, Tyrone jerked his leg away. But by then Wilbur had yanked the headless arrow shaft back out of Tyrone's calf. Blood began to flow freely once the arrow was removed.

"Anybody got any whiskey to pour in this hole?" Wilbur asked.

No one confessed to having any—which Joshua thought was improbable, except that they'd been away from camp a number of days, so perhaps everyone was dry after all—and after a moment Wilbur said, "Reckon we'll have to make do with water. Sorry, Ty."

"There's a seep up there," Silas said, hooking a thumb toward the head of the coulee. Silas was busy investigating the contents of the dead warriors' medicine pouches, every now and then finding something that he wanted to keep and tossing the rest aside.

Wilbur legged it off in the direction Silas indicated. Joshua stepped down and rummaged through his saddlebags for the box of cartridges he carried there. His Winchester took the same .44 rimfire round that the older Henrys had used, and lately he'd had his .44 Army cap-and-ball revolver converted to use the same self-contained brass cartridge. All that was necessary to accomplish that was the services of a good gunsmith who could bore the cylinder chambers out and add a loading gate and hammer extension to the Colt. Except for a few pipsqueak and mostly useless little Smith and Wesson revolvers, Joshua's was about the only cartridge-firing revolver west of Connecticut. At least it was as far as Joshua knew. The cartridge conversion was such a good idea, though, that he was sure everyone would be doing it soon.

He found the pasteboard box of cartridges and was busy reloading his rifle and revolver when Wilbur shouted from up toward the water hole.

"Hey, Joshua, come quick."

"What is it, Wilbur? Can't you see I'm busy here."

"You ain't too busy for this, Joshua. I done found Mr. Gilchrist. An' he's alive. Just barely, by gar, but he's alive."

Joshua slammed the Winchester back into its scabbard and set out at a run toward Wilbur.

Megan poured generous tots from her best bottle of rye whiskey and set the glasses onto a tray for Rachel to carry to the big table where half a dozen exceptionally well-dressed gentlemen were engaged in combat over a deck of cards.

Two drinks this time. That made a total of eight whiskeys and two dozen or fewer beers she'd sold today. If Henry Harrison Armbruster didn't deliver a profit today—No, there was no point in thinking about it. Either he would or he wouldn't. There was nothing she could do to alter things either way.

At least Henry Harrison had been right. His presence did bring in some serious gamblers eager to play against him.

Thank goodness, too. If it weren't for that, she would have no business at all. That damned Ike Norman had dropped his prices even further. Whiskey—more water and tobacco juice than liquor, but the customers either didn't know or didn't care—two for a nickel still, and now he was advertising beer at two cents a mug.

Victor claimed Ike put wax in the bottom of his mugs to shorten the measure and that the beer was watered in the keg, but again the customers seemed to be deluded into thinking they were getting bargains at Ike Norman's rock-bottom prices.

Megan would have put her nose in the air and said the men were getting what they paid for, except that she herself was getting nothing at all at this point. Her saloon's earnings had virtually disappeared, and she could not even afford to put out a free lunch.

The sensible thing for her to do now would be to let Victor go. She didn't have work enough now to justify paying him a wage. But he didn't ask for much. And wherever would he go, whatever would become of him if she shoved him aside?

She sighed. No one ever promised her that times would be easy.

And a damn good thing no one had, or she very likely would've looked them up and . . . kicked them right in the shins, that's what she would've done.

Having decided upon that as a vent for her tightly pent anger, she felt a little bit better. Not much, but any improvement was welcome.

"Do you want me to fix you some lunch, Megan?"

"What? I was, uh, woolgathering, I'm afraid."

"I asked d'you want some lunch yet."

"Oh. No. Thank you." Megan managed a smile. "If you keep on feeding me whenever I look down at the mouth, Rachel, you're going to have me fat as an old cow before this month is out."

"Well, I know something that will make you feel lots better," Rachel said.

"And what would that something be, I ask you?"

"Take a look to the doorway there and tell me what you see," Rachel said.

Megan looked outside. And immediately smiled. "Joshua!" Still smiling, she hurried to greet him.

To her surprise, though, Joshua did not try to sweep her into his arms. Nor did he so much as mention the near-empty condition of the saloon. Instead he yanked his hat off and stood before her holding the hat in both hands and twisting its brim as if he expected to throttle it. Except he appeared far more distracted than angry, she thought.

"Joshua? What is it, Joshua? Is something wrong?"

"I just . . . I just come from Doc Wiseman's place," Joshua said haltingly.

"Liam!" It was her first thought and quickly out of her mouth. But even as she said it, she knew that wasn't likely. Dr. Wiseman had kept Liam back at the old town site, abandoned by the railroad but already becoming occupied by farmers eager for the cheap lands the railroad was selling.

"No, Megan, it isn't Liam. It's the college boy. I mean, it's Gilchrist."

"Glenn? But I don't . . . the Indians. That's it, isn't it? He went out with that crazy idea of talking to Spotted Bull. Did they . . . Have they . . . ?"

"He wants to see you, Megan. Doc Wiseman said I oughta come get you."

"Go on, Megan. I'll watch out for things here," Rachel quickly offered.

Megan barely heard. She gathered up her skirts and hurried outside, Joshua Hood's long legs hard-pressed to catch her.

For a moment Megan could not remember where Dr. Wiseman had established his surgery. She felt an instant of panic as she stood gaping helplessly first one way and then another until Joshua took her gently by the elbow and said, "This way, Megan. I'll help you."

Gratefully she accepted his lead and trotted meekly beside him as Joshua guided her through the busy, sprawling camp that had sprung up on this previously barren stretch of prairie.

As before, the emergency surgery was situated in a railroad boxcar, the same modified and fully equipped one she'd seen before, set off its truck carriage so that it did not have to be shunted around on the rails to make way for other cars. The next time end-of-track moved, so would Thaddeus Wiseman's surgery.

Even if she hadn't known which car was the doctor's, though, Megan would have been able to locate it now by the small group of Joshua's scouts who were gathered outside it, their horses dust-covered and weary. In the middle of them was one horse with a travois drag rigged behind it. Megan assumed that was the way they'd brought Glenn in from . . . from wherever he'd been.

She hurried into the surgery and had to pause for a moment inside the door so her eyes could adjust after the bright glare.

"Thaddeus? Is that . . . ?"

"It's all right, Megan. You can come closer. In fact, I hope you will. Mr. Gilchrist has been asking for you, and frankly, dear, I've been hoping you will help me talk some sense into him."

Megan moved closer. Glenn—he was so pale and emaciated, with the beginnings of a beard and with sunken, bloodshot eyes, that she scarcely recognized him—was lying on the sheet-covered collapsible table that Wiseman used as his operating theater.

Glenn's shirt had been removed, and there was a huge swath of white bandage affixed around his left shoulder. His right hand was secured to the side of the table by stout leather straps, though, and it was there that Dr. Wiseman seemed to be concentrating his attentions.

"What . . . is it, Thaddeus?"

"Apart from suffering from dehydration and exposure, the patient has an arrow wound in the left shoulder. I've

successfully removed the arrow and probed for the projec-
tile head, which was lodged against his scapula . . . That's
the shoulder blade to you, dear. That wound seems clean
enough, and I would expect it to heal without complication.
By far the more serious injury is this small scratch the patient
received across the back of his right hand. If you care to
look, although I don't advise it, you will see that it has
begun to fester and suppurate. The recommended procedure
is clear-cut and entirely effective. It—"

"Megan. Is that you, Megan?"

Glenn's voice was almost as shocking as his appearance. It
was little better than a controlled croak, rasping in his throat
and rattling about in there on its way out.

"Yes, Glenn, I'm here." She moved around to his left side
and grasped that hand between both of hers, lifting it to her
lips and lightly brushing his knuckles with a kiss intended
to convey comfort. "I'm here for you, Glenn."

"Tell them, Megan. Tell them for me. Please."

"Tell them what, Glenn?"

"Tell them. Mustn't . . . mustn't cut. Won't lose . . . damn
it, won't lose it. Not after so much. Been through too much
already. Won't lose it now. Tell them, Megan. Help me.
Please help me."

"I'll help you, Glenn. I promise I will."

"Thank you. Thank you." As if suddenly relieved of a
great burden, Glenn Gilchrist closed his eyes and lapsed into
unconsciousness.

"Glenn? Glenn?"

"He can't hear you, Megan."

"You mean he's . . . ?"

"No, not that. At least not yet. But it is my considered
medical opinion, Megan, that he will indeed die if the sepsis
in that hand is not corrected immediately. It may already

have gone too far as it is. I have to act at once if there is any hope of saving him."

"Then by all means do it, Thaddeus. You have to save him."

"Good," the doctor declared. "If I have your permission, then I'm sure he will accept the loss when he wakens. That's what I was hoping for when I sent for you."

"Loss, Thaddeus? I'm not sure I know what you mean."

"Excuse me, Megan, I thought you understood. There is only one standard treatment for something like this, Megan. One sure remedy."

"Yes?"

"Why, amputation, of course."

"You mean . . ."

"He won't lose the entire arm, dear. Just the hand. You can see right here if you care to look. The infection has barely begun to spread. I can separate the hand at the wrist, and there will be no danger of the infection moving further. If I take a good fold of flesh from the palm and thumb pocket, I'm sure I can make a very durable stump. In a few months he can have a hook fitted or a pad, whichever he prefers. He'll be back on his feet in . . . Megan, are you all right, dear? You look a little pale. Do you feel woozy, dear?"

Megan did not notice Thaddeus leaving his patient and moving swiftly around to her side of the operating table, but as if by magic she felt his arm support her and guide her onto a stool nearby. "There. Better now?" There was a tin cup of water pressing against her lower lip. She didn't know where it came from, but she welcomed it. She drank, paused for a moment and drank again, more deeply this time. She felt light-headed and unsteady, and there was a mild buzzing in her ears. Her forehead was beaded with exceptionally chill perspiration, and it took a conscious effort for her to focus her eyes.

"I thought we were going to lose you for a second there," Thaddeus said.

"I'm sorry. That was awfully silly of me, wasn't it?"

"Not at all. It happens to people all the time. You were in a state of mild shock induced by the unpleasantness of what I was saying. It is I who should apologize, not you. Anyway you can leave now. In fact it will be best if you do. I'll call in my assistant, and in fifteen minutes we'll be all done and your friend Gilchrist will be well on his way to recovery."

"He is right-handed, Thaddeus."

"Yes, so I gathered. It's a pity, but what can you do? The important thing is to save his life."

"But Thaddeus . . ."

"Please, Megan. Trust me. We have to save his life. That is what is important here."

"But Thaddeus, I promised Glenn. I promised to help him. And he doesn't want you to take his hand."

"Do you want to see, Megan? I can show you the line of infection if you want. The hand has to come off. If it doesn't . . ." Wiseman spread his hands in resignation and shrugged his massive shoulders. "If it doesn't, Megan, he will almost certainly die."

"Almost, Thaddeus? A minute ago you were talking like it was certain. Now you are saying almost. For that matter I seem to remember some fellow, I forget his name, who hurt himself punching a stove. You warned him he could lose his hand, but you saved it. At least you said he could save it if he used that medicine you gave him. Why couldn't you use that medicine on Glenn now, Thaddeus? Why must you cut Glenn's hand off when you let that other fellow keep his?"

"They are entirely different circumstances, Megan. In the case of that other boy, no infection had yet commenced. I was able to prescribe salts as a preventative. In Mr. Gilchrist's case, dear, there is already clear indication that infection has set in. It would be entirely too dangerous to wait at this point."

"And the alternatives, Thaddeus? What would be the danger of trying the medication and waiting a little longer?"

"If the infection becomes gangrenous, dear, he will most surely die."

"But if you can prevent that by removing the hand, wouldn't there be time later on to still prevent it by removing the lower arm?"

"Are you suggesting that I gamble with a man's life, Megan?"

"No, Thaddeus, but I am suggesting you gamble with a part of his arm. He bets his hand against his forearm that you're a good enough doctor to save them both. That's the wager, Thaddeus. I believe it's a wager Glenn would make if he were able."

Wiseman gave Megan a level look and walked around to the far side of the table. He stood there for a time, peering down at his patient. "You ask a great deal of me, Megan."

"No, Thaddeus. I only ask you to do your best. And do you know what? I think your best will be good enough to save Glenn's hand for him. That's what I think."

Wiseman rubbed the back of his neck and stared off toward the ceiling for a moment, then back down at the unconscious Gilchrist. He walked over to the line of cabinets built onto the wall of his movable surgery and opened one. He took down first one heavy brown jar and then another. He poked and pried among the medications, mumbling to himself now and then as if thinking aloud.

"It might . . . mind now, I'm only saying might . . . but it might be possible to halt the infection with an application of these unguents and frequent salt baths. If, that is, I could somehow . . . damn it, I don't know why it mightn't work. Not that there are any guarantees. But if I were to scrape away the pus and visible suppurants . . . to clean it out, as it were, and start the healing process over again. I wouldn't want to use a cauter because that would fuse the tendons and tend to make the hand unusable, I should think. The hand is a very complicated and delicate instrument. But scraping or cutting away the . . . Megan, I'm not sure. But if you believe he is willing to take this chance, well, I will do whatever I can to save the hand. You do understand, though—"

"I do understand, Thaddeus, and so will Glenn. I'll explain it all to him. We're betting his hand and forearm against being able to keep him whole, or you could take just the hand now and be done with it."

"It will take a great deal of care afterward if I attempt this, Megan. Near constant bathing with the salts to prevent the formation of new infections. I don't know that I would be able to find the manpower—"

"I can help, Thaddeus. God knows I have nothing better to do with my time lately, not with the way business has been. I can take care of him afterward if you will just see to him now."

"This isn't an ordinary procedure, you understand. But . . . it just might work."

"Please, Thaddeus. Give him a chance. Try to save his hand."

Wiseman cleared his throat and turned his head to cough. "Yes, well, um, I think probably you should leave now, Megan. And send some of those lads in from outside, would you. The pain of cutting away that infection will be extreme.

I'll need help holding him down."

"Is there anything I can do, Thaddeus?"

"Yes." He gave her a gentle but pain-wracked smile. "Go somewhere else. I'll send for you when it's over."

"And then?"

"And then, dear, we will have to wait. It will be days before we have an inkling. A week or more before we can be sure even if we do somehow succeed."

"Thank you, Thaddeus. Thank you ever so much." Megan paused beside Wiseman to rise onto her tiptoes—she was a tall woman, but Thaddeus Wiseman was huge—and buss him briefly on the cheek. "I'll ask Joshua's men to come help you."

Thaddeus stopped her at the door.

"Yes?"

"One other thing you might do, Megan."

"Anything at all."

"Pray, Megan. Pray."

She smiled. "I already have been." And then she was gone.

CHAPTER

27

Glenn Gilchrist's eyes fluttered and came open. The first thing he saw in . . . he had no idea how long it had been . . . was Megan O'Connell's lovely face. And his first expression in ever so long was a smile.

"I've died and gone to Heaven," he ventured, "for there's an angel hovering over me."

He tried to reach out to her but winced at the sudden thrust of pain through his hand and right arm.

"Are you all right?" she said quickly, leaning forward to wipe his brow with a cool, damp cloth.

"Fine. I just . . . What's happened, Megan? Where am I and what's happened to me?"

She explained, placing the burden for failure—if failure there was to be—on herself.

"You don't, that is the doctor doesn't, know anything yet?"

Megan shook her head. "It's only been three days, Glenn. Thaddeus says it will be another week before he can be sure."

"And I've been out all that time?"

"You were in a very weak state when Joshua and his men brought you in. Thaddeus says you nearly died out there. You're very lucky to be alive now."

"Hood found me?"

Megan nodded and explained that too.

"And it was Silas who led them to me after I was wounded?"

"Sort of. He told Joshua where you were, but of course he thought you'd been killed. Really it's a marvel that you weren't with all those dozens and dozens of Indians shooting at you and only Silas to try and hold them off. He was terribly brave to keep them at bay as long as he did."

"I don't remember all that much about the fight. Would you mind telling me what you've heard about it please, Megan?"

"Of course." She complied, speaking at some length while occasionally leaning near to lave his cheeks and forehead with the wet washcloth.

"Interesting," Glenn said when she was done.

"Everyone thinks it was very brave of him," Megan added. "General Dodge commended Silas in person and ordered a bonus payment of fifty dollars to him for saving your life like he did."

"That was decent of the general."

"Mr. Goss said if General Dodge hadn't done something then, he would have rewarded Silas out of his own pocket." Megan patted Glenn's sound shoulder and told him, "You proved to be awfully popular when people thought you were dead."

"The true test of a gentleman's character, eh? Just let him die and see what everyone says at his wake."

Megan laughed. Then, more soberly, she said, "It's about time for your bath."

Glenn blushed furiously.

"No, I didn't mean *that* kind of bath, silly. I mean your *hand*."

"Well, in that case . . ."

With the dexterity of much practice, Megan took a kettle of water off the top of a small stove at the back of the recovering room and poured a small amount into an enameled basin. She measured out a portion of sandy-colored crystals from a wide-mouthed jar and stirred them into the water with a glass rod. When the crystals were completely dissolved, she soaked a square of cotton gauze in the medicine and brought both pad and basin to Glenn's bedside, settling herself onto a stool at the right side of the narrow cot.

"Is this going to hurt?" he asked.

"I have no idea, actually. You've been unconscious every time up until now. You didn't twitch or groan or anything, though."

"I'll take that as a good sign then. Does, uh, does this bathing have to be done very often?"

"Every half hour, all the way round the clock," she told him.

"But that's . . . that's awful."

"Not really. Not if it saves your hand it isn't."

"But . . . every half hour?"

"It's what Thaddeus recommended."

"You must be exhausted, Megan."

"Oh, it isn't all that bad. Thaddeus does it sometimes during the afternoons, and Rachel has been helping out some at night. So has Victor. Among us . . ." She shrugged.

"I owe you all . . . *so* much." His voice thickened with emotion, and choking, he was unable to say more.

"Nonsense," Megan said easily. "Hold your hand over the basin now. That's right, just rest your fingers over the edge here. Now hold still."

She squeezed the medicated fluid over the top of the pink, open wound that cut across the back of his hand. "Does that hurt?"

"Nope. It's a little warm."

"Too warm?"

"Not really. It surprised me a little, that's all."

"But it doesn't sting?"

He shook his head.

"I hope that's a good sign." She repeated the process, dribbling the mild antiseptic solution onto the wound, over and over again, occasionally dabbing and even scrubbing at it.

Glenn winced and tried to draw back the first time she scrubbed inside the wound with the rough gauze. "Hey, you aren't doing laundry against river rocks here, you know."

"Sorry, but this is the way Thaddeus showed me to do it. He says it might hurt a little but it's best."

Glenn clenched his jaw and kept his mouth shut the next time she rubbed the medication into his wound.

"There," she said finally. "That's enough for this time." She looked at the big clock mounted above the door. "We'll do it again in half an hour."

"Do you know what?" he asked.

She shook her head and, biting her underlip in concentration, began cleaning up and getting everything ready for the next treatment.

"I still think this must be Heaven, for there really is an angel hovering over me."

"Go on with you," she protested. But he thought she looked pleased nonetheless.

CHAPTER

28

"Yes, sir?"

"Come in. Sit there if you please." General Grenville Dodge laid his pen aside and shook himself as if trying to waken and bring his attention back from wherever his jottings had taken him. He blinked several times and pinched the bridge of his nose, then motioned in the direction of a sideboard. "Drink, Mr. Hood?"

"No, thank you, sir."

"Cigar?"

"No, sir."

"You're probably wondering why I asked you here," Dodge ventured.

"Yes, sir, that I am."

The former major general of the G.A.R. nodded and swiveled his desk chair around to face Joshua, who was sitting in one of a pair of wing-back chairs that flanked a low table with a chessboard inlaid on the surface. The general's private railcar was handsomely appointed, the walls paneled in burled walnut and the ornate moldings gilded. The sconces and gimballed lamps were made of brass so brightly polished as to look like gold, and a small chandelier with crystal teardrop highlights was suspended from the ceiling. Surely, Joshua thought, the chandelier had to be packed away when the car was in motion. He suspected it would be a mighty pretty thing, though, when all its many tiny candles were lighted.

The forward part of the general's car was given over to the parlor or sitting area where they now were. The rear part Joshua assumed to be sleeping quarters and who knew what else, kitchen and servants quarters or whatever.

"Tell me, Mr. Hood," the general said, leaning back in the oak armchair and crossing his legs, "what is your opinion about the peace mission Gilchrist and your man Short were embarked upon when they encountered their, um, difficulty?"

"Damn foolishness, sir."

"Oh? How so?"

"For reasons I know you understand, sir, Spotted Bull and the Sioux nation have good cause to feel betrayed. Their response to the sight of a white man, any white man, is only to be expected. They will attack, General. They will fight us. They've proven that. I told Gilchrist as much when he first mentioned his plan to me. I thought I'd talked him out of it then. Obviously I hadn't, but it wasn't for lack of trying. And if you're asking me now, sir, if I think maybe we . . . you, me, any of us . . . can put the peace back t'gether again, sir, well, my answer now is the same as I gave Gilchrist then. It won't work, sir. Forget it."

Dodge smiled. "I admire forthrightness in a man's responses, Mr. Hood. Thank you for your candor."

"Does that mean you aren't thinkin' about a peace mission o' your own, sir?"

"No, Mr. Hood, it does not. In fact I have been giving thought to a plan on the order of what Mr. Gilchrist was attempting."

"Don't try it, General. It'd just get somebody killed. And

I reckon I'd rather it wasn't me as winds up losing his scalp, sir."

"I understand what you are trying to tell me, Mr. Hood, but have you considered what is at stake here? We have obstacles enough in the building of this magnificent road without adding Indian depredations into the equation. The threat of attack alone, and I do mean the threat not the actuality, is enough to slow the production of our workmen. Why, even tracklaying crews are not immune from attack. And those men who have to work ahead of the main construction parties, the surveyors and road graders, the mule skinners and fresno operators, the tie men, water haulers . . . under these current conditions they all must keep one eye on their work and the other on the horizon, searching constantly for threat or encroachment. It unnerves them, Mr. Hood, and disrupts their efforts. We can't have that. Every mile of effort we lose to the Sioux is a mile of subsidy payment that we turn over to the Central Pacific. We can't afford that, Mr. Hood. The Union Pacific needs those mileage payments. We need the grant lands along the right-of-way, Mr. Hood. We cannot afford to abandon a single mile in favor of the Central Pacific, sir. We must press on with all possible speed. And warfare with the Sioux will hold us back. It must. There simply aren't enough troops in Nebraska Territory to protect the railroad and all our people."

"Then we'll just have to protect ourselves, General," Joshua said. "I don't know no other way t' do it."

Dodge looked tired, Joshua thought. Tired and troubled. "Do you know General Sherman, Hood?"

"No, sir, not really. I've seen him now an' then, but I wouldn't say that I know him."

"He's a good man, Sherman. A bulldog. Set him a task to do and he'll worry it like a dog with a bone. He'll gnaw and chew and keep right on keeping on until he's accomplished whatever it is that he's to do. That is a good thing in a commander. A very good thing. And the Union Pacific has Sherman's complete endorsement. The general has pledged to me that he will do whatever he must to maintain the security of our effort. But you know, Hood, and I know that a military presence is not enough. The army does not have half enough manpower in the entire Department of the Missouri to subdue the Sioux nation if it comes to an all-out war. Oh, we would eventually prevail, of course. The savage red man can never hope to overcome the weight of superior numbers and intellect that we possess. But, damn it all anyway, Hood, even the United States Army cannot hope to quash the Sioux nation without a struggle. And for every day of struggle, sir, the Central Pacific gains an advantage on us. We can't have that, Mr. Hood. We simply cannot."

"What is it you're tryin' to tell me, General?"

Dodge hesitated for a moment. Then he spoke. "I am telling you, Mr. Hood, that I think we must consider taking up the torch where Mr. Gilchrist and Short left off. I am telling you, sir, that we may yet find it advantageous to reopen peace talks with Spotted Bull."

"Impossible, General. I'm sorry t' tell you that, but it just ain't possible."

"Then think of a way, Mr. Hood." Dodge leaned forward in his chair and gave Joshua a long, level look. "Think it over very carefully, Mr. Hood, then come back tomorrow and tell me what you've come up with. Surely there must be *some* way we can resolve this without further bloodshed on either side. Find that way, Mr. Hood. That is what I ask of you now, sir. Find me a path to peace."

Joshua stood. "Yes, sir. I'll give it my best," he said. But in his heart of hearts he knew that what the general asked of him was not a path to peace but a path to the grave.

"That's all I ask of you, Mr. Hood."

"Yes, sir. G'day, General."

CHAPTER

29

Megan was beat. Her eyes burned with fatigue, and her head felt as if it were filled with cotton wool. Between trying to oversee the saloon—not that there was any appreciable amount of business to oversee—and tend to Glenn Gilchrist's needs, she had only a moment here, fifteen minutes there, in which to doze. Real sleep was out of the question. Not that it mattered at this point anyway. Her exhaustion had reached the stage where if she lay down and tried to go to sleep now, she only lay there, aching eyes peering into the darkness, so tired she was unable to sleep.

And on top of that, Ike Norman continued to apply pressure, taking and holding all the liquor and beer trade with his undercut prices and overwatered products. Megan was taking in practically nothing.

That wouldn't have been so bad, really. Her only regular outlay was salaries for Rachel Foreman and Victor Boyette. And she knew that if push came to shove, they both would delay receiving their pay without so much as pausing to think about it. Megan was blessed to have such wonderful people working for her—no, *with* her—and she knew it.

But unfortunately that was not the whole of her problem.

When she first arrived and set up here, she'd wired her sister, Aileen, back in Omaha to buy and ship supplies. There would be cases of pickled sausages and kegs of hard-boiled eggs packed in water glass for preservation, salt-cured hams—the salt helped induce a thirst that beer slaked rather nicely—and great tins of soda crackers. Moreover, she'd asked Aileen to find and ship two dozen sixteen-gallon pony kegs of best-quality lager beer, from one of the excellent St. Louis breweries if possible.

At the moment she had need of neither the free lunch items nor the beer. She was far from exhausting the supply of beer she'd brought here with her, thanks to Ike Norman.

The problem, though, was that when the shipment arrived, she would have to pay for it.

And she had fully expected to make that payment from income generated here.

Most of Megan's money was already tied up in equipment and inventory. She had suffered severe losses when Lew Scudder was managing her gaming tables, and much of what she'd had over and above that she had already sent back to Aileen to help her and her children.

It was not something she had ever admitted to anyone, not even to Rachel, but the simple truth was that Megan O'Connell was close to being flat broke.

That financial pressure was doing nothing to help her get some rest.

She sat now, woozy and silent in her chair, while Henry Harrison Armbruster's poker game broke up for the night. Rachel was at the doctor's, bathing Glenn Gilchrist's hand. Megan had no idea what had become of Victor this evening. That is, she dimly recalled him asking her something, and she had the impression that she'd agreed to his request, whatever it was, but she could no longer recall what that might have been. Wherever he was and whatever he was doing, he had her permission for it. She supposed that should be good for something.

She yawned and stood, weaving just a little and blinking in an effort to convince her eyes to focus, then began moving slowly about, extinguishing the lamps.

Lamps. That was another thing. She needed lamp oil, was almost out of it, and she could not remember now if she'd asked Aileen to put lamp oil on the list of purchases or not.

She noticed that the last of Henry Harrison's gentlemen was gone, and the little man was making his way across the floor to her. She stopped where she was and waited for him. "Yes?"

He smiled and shrugged. "Not so good tonight. Only twenty dollars to show for a full day's work."

"I'm sorry to hear that."

"Tomorrow will be better." The gambler meticulously counted out three dollars in small silver and handed it to Megan.

Three dollars. Two months ago that amount of change would have been an annoyance, a burden to be sneered at for its awkward bulk. Tonight—no, it was morning, wasn't it?— three dollars in change seemed a small fortune. She dropped it into her apron pocket, hoping that Henry Harrison could not tell how gratefully his contribution was received.

"Is there anything I can do to help you close, Miss O'Connell?"

"Nothing, Henry Harrison, but I thank you."

"In that case, I'll say good night."

"And good night to you."

Henry Harrison bowed with courtly ease and glided away with that slow, fluid, strange gait he had.

Megan sighed and blew out the last lamp. Her thoughts were of her bed, and the question of whether she should selfishly run to it now or—it was the right thing to do and she knew it—go instead and relieve Rachel at the infirmary.

She sighed again. Rachel would be tired too. And Glenn's care was Megan's task. She was the one who'd volunteered to undertake the constant salt baths, not Rachel. She was the one who'd convinced Thaddeus to risk Glenn's arm, indeed to risk his life if the infections sprang up and raced out of control.

Megan fetched her shawl from behind the bar and walked wearily to the closed but unsecured tent flap that served as her doorway.

She stepped out, intending to tie the flap down, and froze at a harsh, threatening hiss from the darkness.

"You ain't changed your mind?"

Megan's thoughts raced as she tried to recall what the question could possibly refer to. She could think of nothing in her recent experience that would apply.

"I presume you mean the generous offer of employment?" a second voice responded. After a few seconds Megan recognized this voice as belonging to Henry Harrison Armbruster and realized as well that the first man had not been speaking to her after all.

"That's right, crip. You're outa time. You come real polite an' tell the gentleman you'll take him up on his offer. Or you'll take yer medicine. The choice is yours, crip. What's it t' be?"

"Oh, I really do not believe I would enjoy working for Mr. Norman. I'm sure he will understand."

Megan thought Henry Harrison seemed calm enough under the circumstances. She tried to see the two men. She could tell from their voices that they were not far away, but the night was dark and the sky cloudy and overcast, making it almost impossible to see.

She saw, or sensed, movement twenty or thirty feet to her left and thought that might be Henry Harrison. She had no idea where the other man was hiding.

"You sure, crip? Lemme give you a hint, maybe convince you t' change your mind. Y'know how that one leg o' yourn is all gimpy an' twisted an' short? Ha. Sure you do. Well, lemme give you this t' chew on, crip. My orders is that if you don't do what the man wants, time I'm done with you that gimpy leg o' yourn will be your good'un. 'Cause I'll bust hell out o' the other, just as sure as nits turn inta lice."

"My," Henry Harrison said mildly. "Poetic imagery like that is wasted on an audience this small. You should be on the stage, my good man. Or a scaffold at the very least."

"You're funning me, aren't you?"

"Somewhat," Henry Harrison admitted.

"That's as may be, little feller, but you ain't gonna turn my mind from what's gotta be done. Now, you tell me. Are you gonna take the man's offer or are you gonna learn to walk all over again?"

"Oh, I suppose I shall just have to take my medicine like a good little fellow," Henry Harrison said.

A shadow detached itself from the side of Megan's own tent, and she could see a burly, towering figure advance on the tiny, crippled gambler.

With a hoarse cry of rage, and with no forethought whatsoever, Megan balled her hands into upraised fists and launched herself at the big man who'd said he would break Henry Harrison's one good leg.

CHAPTER

30

Megan flung her weight into the half-seen bully before he got within ten feet of little Henry Harrison Armbruster. Kicking and clawing, she quite literally bowled the man over, her unexpected assault toppling him sideways onto the ground.

She landed atop the sprawling man and began pummeling him just as hard and fast as she could manage, striking with both clubbed fists, with her knees, and once even with her teeth when a stray ear happened past in close enough proximity.

The man howled with pain when she bit him and squirmed madly in an effort to get away from this shrieking harpy.

He elbowed her painfully in the chest and ribs but still she battered and kicked at him for all she was worth.

"Megan. It's all right. Come away now, Megan. Back off."

She heard the words clearly enough. They didn't particularly register at first, but she heard them. Long seconds later she understood what Henry Harrison was saying.

By then Henry Harrison, or somebody, had grasped the collar of her dress and, as if taking her by the nape of the neck, lifted her away from her prey.

For a moment she thought someone else had heard the commotion and come to help, because the person who picked her up did so by main strength. And a good deal of it at that.

Still, close inspection proved that the gentleman was, in fact, little Henry Harrison.

Continuing to claw and kick so long as she was within range of the cowardly bully who would have attacked her friend in the night, Megan was dragged off the downed bone-breaker.

The man who'd been facedown on the ground now came to his knees and with a great leap went sprinting away into the dark.

Henry Harrison, Megan was distressed to discover, was laughing.

"And what is it that's so funny, I ask you?" Megan demanded.

"Funny? No, that isn't quite it. But . . . amusing, yes. And touching too. Thank you, Miss O'Connell. I truly mean that." He let go of her collar, substituting a firm hold on her elbow to make sure she did not lose her balance. Once he was sure she was upright and able to manage on her own, he released his hold on her.

Megan was puffing as hard as if she'd just come in from Omaha. By way of footrace. She sniffed loudly and patted at her hair. Her bun was in shocking disarray, with tufts and strands and strings and things popping out in all directions. "Oh, dear. I must look a perfect sight."

"Your hair," Henry Harrison said, "is nothing compared to that shirtwaist. May I suggest you, um, tuck yourself in and tidy up a bit?" As he spoke, he took her elbow once more and began gently but firmly guiding her back inside her saloon, where prying eyes could not follow.

Once they were indoors and Henry Harrison had a lamp lighted, she could see why he'd wanted her in from the

public areas. Even at night. The bodice of her shirtwaist had
come completely out of her skirt and was bunched beneath
her breasts, exposing slivers of skin and white cotton alike in
ways no gentleman save a husband should ever be permitted
to see.

Her hair was a medusa-like mess of snakes and coils, and
her skirt was soiled and rumpled and dusty.

"I look awful!" she cried.

Henry Harrison gave her an indulgent smile, then bus-
ied himself behind the bar—a place he had never ventured
before now despite his status as a quasi employee—finding
a basin, water, and cloth so Megan could clean up. He was
careful not to look her way while she pulled the rumpled
shirtwaist down where it belonged and hastily stuffed the
shirttail ends inside the waistband of her skirt. Her assault on
the man outside had been so violent and strenuous that she'd
even twisted her underthings about. Not that she intended straightening those while in the presence of a man, of
course. But she could not help but be acutely conscious of
the unusual and therefore highly uncomfortable positioning
of . . . things.

"Are you all right now?" Henry Harrison asked once she'd
had time to more or less put herself back together.

"Yes, but shouldn't I be asking you that? I was . . . I was
afraid that man really was going to . . . He really was, wasn't
he?" she asked.

"Break my other leg?" Henry Harrison smiled. "I do
believe he had that intent, yes."

"But you didn't act frightened at all," Megan said. "You
were so brave. That's why I just couldn't stand it, I think.
You couldn't run away and yet you wouldn't give in to him
either. You were so terribly brave, and I simply couldn't bear
the thought of anyone hurting you like that."

Henry Harrison's smile was gentle and, she thought, indulgent. Kindly might be a better way to put it. But indulgent fit perfectly well also.

"You are a fine, dear lady, and I thank you for coming to my aid. If, um, it were to occur again, however, it might be for the better if you stand well clear. It wouldn't do for you to be injured, now would it?"

"Nor for you, Henry Harrison."

He smiled again. "Oh, there's little enough danger of that, I think."

"But that man. He was so big. And mean. And you couldn't have run away from him."

"I wouldn't have thought of trying, my dear. But I wouldn't have considered allowing him to do me harm either."

"No? I don't understand."

"One might say that it was he that you saved this evening, Megan, not I. Had you not dissuaded him, you see, I would have shot the revolting creature."

"Really?"

"I am sure it would be considered a character flaw in polite company, but yes. I have this unfortunate and unalterable policy by which I defend myself from physical harm. I simply do not countenance pain, you see. It's been known to plunge me into all manner of difficulty from time to time, but I simply can't bring myself to allow anyone like him to get their hands on me."

"But I've never seen you with a firearm, Henry Harrison."

"Appearances, my dear, can be deceiving." Henry Harrison spread his hands wide in a gesture of innocence. Then he dropped his hands and, winking, spread them again. This time there was a palm-sized derringer in each of his impeccably manicured hands.

"How did you . . . ?"

"Rather well, I thought," he said, laughing.

"Henry Harrison! I never suspected."

"If you don't mind, Megan, I would prefer that you not mention my, um, personal defenses to anyone."

"No, of course not. But, two of them? I don't think I've ever seen anything like that before."

"I am what is known as ambidextrous," Henry Harrison said. "I have equal facility with either hand. And if I do say, I'm a rather good shot. So I was in rather less danger tonight than you believed. The other . . . shall we be generous and say gentleman? . . . was the one who had cause to fear."

"Should I apologize then?"

"Not at all, Megan. What you did was a great and generous act of truest friendship." Henry Harrison's amiable demeanor changed, and he became serious for the moment. "Believe me, dear lady, I'll not forget how you acted to save me, even at risk to yourself."

"But you said yourself you have everything under control. You weren't in any danger."

"You didn't know that, Megan. You saw me in danger, and you placed yourself at risk to save me. That means . . . you cannot know how much I appreciate what you did tonight." He turned half away from her and hesitated for a moment. "We don't know each other well, Megan. But . . . I am a man who has many acquaintances but few friends. From this night on, with your permission of course, I would like to regard you as a true friend."

"You don't need my permission for that, Henry Harrison. I would be honored if you would call me your friend."

He turned back to face her, his smile back as brilliant and sparkling as ever. "Would you do a favor for a friend then, Megan?"

"If I can, Henry Harrison."

"I'm wide awake now, my dear. Would you allow me to take over at the infirmary from Miss Rachel for what's left of the night?"

"Oh, I can manage. Really, I can."

"Of course you could, but I really am wide awake now. And if I do say so, I have rather good hands. Quite soft and delicate. I'm sure I can manage the medicine and the water baths with a little instruction."

"It isn't that, Henry Harrison. I know you could do everything that needs—"

"Fine. That settles it. You go off to your slumbers now. I shall relieve Mrs. Foreman and wake you in the morning."

"Henry Harrison! Really . . ."

But he would have none of it. He insisted on bustling her off to bed, and in the end she gave in, concluding that she either had to allow the little gambler to do this for her or hurt his feelings quite desperately. And she did not want to risk doing that.

Furthermore, Megan discovered with pleasant surprise that, tired as she was, she was no longer at that state of exhaustion that precluded sleep.

In fact, her head barely had time to burrow into the downy softness of her pillow before cleansing sleep overtook her and she sank into the best rest she'd known in days.

"Good morning, sir. D'you have a minute?"

General Dodge glanced up from the eggcup where a four-minute egg was resisting his efforts to uncap the shell. "Just a second . . . wait . . . there," he said triumphantly as a thin section of shell finally came free. "Now, Hood. Yes, by all means do come in. Breakfast?"

"No, thank you, sir."

"You'll take coffee at least, won't you?"

"That would be nice, sir, thank you."

The general motioned toward the side of the car, and a Negro steward in white jacket and dark trousers hurried to comply with the request.

Dodge pointed down at the plate and eggcup before him. "Damn things never cooperate, have you noticed? Don't know why I persist in asking the cook for them. Or could it be that that is the reason why I do, that a soft-boiled egg served in the shell remains a challenge whereas an ordinary fried egg, or a poached one that tastes virtually the same as boiled, holds no mystery for me, eh?"

"If you say so, sir." The steward brought the coffee—it tasted no better than that served in the private mess for U.P. management and for that matter seemed to Joshua identical to that slopped into tin cups and handed out to the workmen. Boiled coffee was boiled coffee no matter how fancy the cup that held it.

"I take it you've given some thought to that little problem I laid before you last night?" the general suggested.

"Yes, sir, I have. Do you want the long an' flowery way around it or should I just lay it on out?"

Dodge smiled around a spoonful of dripping egg white and pale, runny yolk. "The short version if you please, Mr. Hood."

"Yes, sir," Joshua said with a smile of his own. He hadn't expected this sensible and clear-thinking man to ask for anything else. "Getting right down to it, General, I don't really think it can be done."

"But—"

Joshua cut Dodge short with a quickly upraised hand. "Let me finish, sir, please."

"Very well," Dodge acceded, returning his gaze if not his actual attention, to the egg.

"Like I say, sir, I don't really believe it can be done. I don't think any white man, including me, could approach Spotted Bull right now without getting his hair lifted.

"If it could be done—which o' course it can't—it'd only be by a party carrying a white flag an' armed heavy enough that the Sioux would think twice about shooting."

General Dodge acted like he wanted to say something, but he held his question in check, settling instead for attacking the remainder of the boiled egg and sopping up the last gobbets of yellow yolk with a triangle of toast. The steward moved quickly in to take that place setting away and replace it with a slab of fried ham and a huge mound of fried potatoes. Boiled egg and cold toast were no inducement, but at the sight of the ham and potatoes, Joshua wondered if he'd been a mite too quick in his refusal of the general's breakfast offer.

"Go ahead, man," Dodge prompted, returning Joshua's attention to the needs of the moment.

"Yes, sir, like I was saying, there ain't really anybody gonna get close to Spotted Bull after Taney an' Wollins had their say. But if it was gonna be possible—which it ain't— it'd be by a strong party. Say, a troop o' cavalry. No more'n two troops, for sure. A bunch big enough t' be respected but not so big as t' scare the Sioux right off. An' they'd have t' march under a white flag. Spotted Bull'd hear 'bout that before the yella legs got anywhere close. He'd know what it meant. Mightn't believe it—I wouldn't if'n I was him, not after Wollins an' that ambush—but it's anyway some small kinda chance. Then go in slow an' easy without waving guns an' swords around, and if we could get inta the village at all, start passin' out presents. I mean, sir, fetch along five, six, maybe a dozen mule loads o' foofaraw. Beads, blankets, mirrors, brass kettles, Green River knives, trade rifles an' ammunition—some o' them cheap pinfire ca'tridge guns would be good, that'd impress hell outa the Sioux what with them bein' ca'tridge firing—the best o' everything, sir, an' just heaps an' heaps of it. Point is, sir, you'd have t' show the glad hand right t' begin with. Give the whole shebang away before ever the talk got started. That's t' let Spotted Bull know you haven't come t' try an' buy a new treaty but t' apologize for the problems with the old one. You see?"

Dodge nodded solemnly and seemed to be in deep concentration, his eyes unfocused and his brow furrowed. Joshua figured either the man was paying close attention or maybe he had gas. One of those.

"One last thing'd have t' be done, sir, least the way I see it."

"I asked for your opinion, Mr. Hood. Please give me the rest of it."

"Yes, sir, well, this here would be the hard part. I think, sir, that idjit Cap'n Taney would have t' go along an' apologize for there t' be any chance at all that Spotted Bull would relent."

"Taney?" Dodge asked. "Why Taney? He wasn't in the field that day, Wollins was."

"No, sir, but we wouldn't dare let Lieutenant Wollins come along on a expedition like this here."

"No? Why not?"

"General, I know a mite about these Indians. I never spent all that much time with the Sioux themselves, but I've sure lived with their neighbors, an' I know more'n just a bit about 'em."

"I know that, Hood."

"Yes, sir, an' I'm trying t' impress on you that I got a pretty good idea o' what Spotted Bull an' his council will be thinkin' an' how they'll react to things. An' to a white man the sensible an' logical thing here would be for the fella that done the stupidity to come along an' do the apologizing too."

"Exactly my point," Dodge agreed.

"Yes, sir, but that'd be the exact wrong thing t' do if anybody was able t' get inta Spotted Bull's village without shooting his way in."

"And why is that, Mr. Hood?"

"T' the Indian way o' thinkin', General, an apology is one thing, but it ain't restitution. Neither is a whole carload o' trade goods. I mean, them things are good. They'll soften things up an' set the mood. But they ain't restitution."

"What is, Mr. Hood?"

"Blood, sir. It takes blood t' be genuine restitution for blood spilled. At least t' the Indian mind as I figure it."

"We can't have that, Mr. Hood."

"No, sir, we damn sure can't. An' if Wollins was t' walk inta Spotted Bull's village, he damn sure wouldn't never be allowed t' walk out again. Not if the whole tribe had t' go down under soldier guns t' get that accomplished. Worse, if we took him in there an' didn't agree t' turn him over to the Sioux for blood punishment, Spotted Bull would figure we wasn't serious about sayin' we was sorry. He'd just think it was another pack o' white man's lies an' tell us what t' do with our words. And, um, what we could do with certain other things too, most likely. So we wouldn't dare take Wollins in. But we could take Taney an' let Spotted Bull know that he's the soldier chief that sent Wollins t' make war on the Sioux. Since Taney himself didn't spill no Sioux blood, I figure we can get away with an apology from him an' not have the Sioux hotheads demanding his scalp like they would if Wollins was there."

"Complicated, isn't it?" Dodge mused.

Joshua took a swallow of his coffee and leaned back with a shrug. "Actually, sir, it ain't really s' complicated as you might think." He smiled. "In fact, General, I don't reckon none of it will ever happen."

"Don't be so certain, Mr. Hood. If I ask General Sherman for the services of Captain Taney, I am quite sure the orders will be issued. And in the exact terms that I request. Bill Sherman and Phil Sheridan have been friends of mine for a very long time, you see."

Joshua smiled. "General, I never for one second doubted your ability t' get things done. What I mean is that I don't really reckon any of us could ever get close to Spotted Bull."

"No?"

"No, sir. What I really expect will happen isn't what I just told you, which'd be the best possible outcome. What I expect t' be the realistic outcome, sir, is one o' two things. Either we ride out with a party small enough that the Sioux feel safe in jumping us an' we all lose our hair. Or we take along a party big enough that the Sioux don't wanta tangle an' we never see their camp. They'll know we're coming long before we get there, y'know, General. And it don't take a Sioux housewife very dang long t' pack her stuff an' skedaddle."

"You suggest poor prospects, Mr. Hood."

"Yes, sir, but I've give it my best thinkin', an' this is what I come up with. Poor chance t' none at all, it's all I can see there is t' shoot for now that the army's gone an' messed things up so bad."

"I'll think it over, Hood, and let you know."

"Yes, sir."

"Thank you for getting back to me so promptly, Mr. Hood."

"Yes, sir." The general's expression, his attentions shifting far from this railcar and Joshua Hood, clearly told Joshua that the interview was ended. Quietly and without bothering the busy man again, Joshua slid out of the chair at Dodge's breakfast table and made his way out of the luxurious railroad car.

CHAPTER

32

Eight days later Megan was in the saloon trying to find things that needed doing. Henry Harrison Armbruster and the inevitable poker game were active on the far side of the room, but except for the little gambler and his few opponents and hangers-on, there was no activity in the place. Ike Norman continued to apply financial pressure against her, and Megan had not had a good day's trade since she arrived at this spot.

Moreover, she was concerned that those supplies she'd asked Aileen to send would arrive any time now. And she hadn't the money to pay for them. She doubted she had enough cash left at this point to pay the freight charges on her purchases, much less the principal amount.

In spite of her worries, though, Megan found herself trying to fight off a bout of simple boredom.

She hadn't had this little to occupy herself with since she was . . . She thought back, trying to recall just when it would have been. If ever. As a girl she'd had to help around home, taking care of Liam almost as if he were her own baby from the time she was seven or eight, doing part of the cleaning and all the family's laundry from when she was ten or thereabouts.

Once she thought about it, she realized she probably hadn't been this lazy and lackadaisical since she was . . . seven?

About that. Certainly since Liam was wee.

She smiled a little. She'd nursed baby Liam's hurts then, and she nursed Glenn Gilchrist's hurts now. It seemed she hadn't come very far in all the intervening years.

Still and all . . . She sighed and bit back a yawn, her jaw chittering . . . Still and all, things could have been worse. She supposed. She picked up a box of tin mugs that hadn't been unpacked since the recent move and began dropping them one by one into a bucket of soapy water, swishing them briefly about and then transferring them into a second bucket of clean water. Might as well clean things up while she had the chance to do so, she thought.

"Miss Megan?"

"Yes, Victor?" she asked. There was little enough for her to do these days and virtually nothing that required Victor's strength. The only tasks she set him lately were the routine ones of tending to the horses daily and helping see to Glenn Gilchrist. And half of that was make-work by now. At this point Glenn was fully capable of preparing his own salt baths and moistening his own wound. The arrow wound in his shoulder was almost fully healed, and he would have been completely mobile had Dr. Wiseman permitted it. Victor's task was not to bathe Glenn's hand but to watch over the vigorous young engineer and keep him from sneaking out and getting into something that might retard the progress of his recovery. As a consequence of this, Megan rarely knew where Victor was during the days and even less often saw him. His appearance at the saloon now was something of an event. She looked up and waited for Victor to continue.

"You're wanted over to the doctor's office, Miss Megan."

Megan felt a brief thrill of fear. "Is it . . . Did Thaddeus say what he wants me for?"

"No'm, but I seen him showing his bone saws to Mr. Gilchrist, Miss Megan."

"Oh, Lord. Did he, did they . . . ?"

"They didn't neither one of them say nothing to me, Miss Megan, 'cept that I was to bring you."

"This morning . . . did his hand look red to you, Victor? More than it did yesterday, say?"

"I didn't see it today, Miss Megan. Mr. Gilchrist, he told me he'd take care of it. But I don't know if he did or not."

Megan blanched. If Glenn had gotten lazy and skipped even a few of the desperately necessary treatments . . . Why oh why hadn't she been there herself, done the bathing herself. Why had she allowed others to take over from her? Why on earth had she trusted Glenn to take care of himself these past days?

Megan was berating herself for her laziness and general shiftlessness even while she dried her hands and removed her apron. Her hands fluttered uselessly about her face as she tried to tidy straying strands of hair. She grabbed a shawl and hurriedly flung it about her shoulders, then followed Victor outside and at a rapid pace toward the rails.

Glenn Gilchrist and Dr. Thaddeus Wiseman were in the surgery when Megan arrived. Glenn was perched atop the operating table. Well, at least he wasn't strapped onto it yet.

Both gentlemen seemed in high enough spirits. Thaddeus stood at Glenn's side, holding Glenn's injured hand and examining it closely with the aid of a looking glass.

"Come in, Megan. I thought you should have a look at this yourself."

"Is . . . Has it gone bad, doctor?"

"Bad? You mean infection? Heavens, no. That's what I want you to see," Thaddeus said happily. "The wound is pink and clean and healthy as healthy can be. And Mr. Gilchrist here can thank you and your friends for saving his hand. It's your diligence that brought this about, you know, not anything my poor profession knows how to accomplish."

"Oh, my. I thought . . . Well, you probably know what I thought. When Victor said you wanted me here . . . Say, he told me you were looking at bone saws when he left."

"Yes, certainly. Having escaped the experience, Glenn expressed curiosity about it. I was just explaining to him what would have happened if you hadn't been so insistent on saving him."

"As an exercise in theoretical science," Glenn said, "it was fascinating. But I'm just as glad to miss out on the practical applications."

"You really are all right now?" Megan asked.

"Just take a look." Glenn proudly extended his hand to her, twisting it this way and that so she could see.

The flesh was pale and wrinkled from the often repeated immersions, but it did indeed look healthy enough to Megan's untrained eye.

The wound, caused as much by the doctor's cutting and scraping as by the cut of the Sioux arrow, was beginning to heal now. The puckered edges were a light and healthy pink, as Thaddeus said, without the ugly threat of dark scarlet infection. And no red tendrils of infection radiated out into the surrounding flesh as she'd seen before Thaddeus excised the pus and other suppurants.

"It looks practically new, doesn't it?" Megan said.

"As good as," Thaddeus agreed. "I haven't wanted to speak too soon and give false hopes, but I believe at this point we can safely declare the crisis at an end. Another few days and that hand will be fully healed. I don't believe there is any danger of infection now."

This was a result Megan had fully expected. Yet she found herself with tears glimmering in her eyes at the joy of the pronouncement by Thaddeus. She grasped Glenn's good hand and squeezed it. Glenn responded by trying to hug Megan.

Slightly embarrassed because Thaddeus was in the room and several other men were looking in from the doorway, Megan resisted the embrace, moving lightly away as if she hadn't recognized what Glenn was trying to do. At least that was the appearance she hoped she gave. She did not want to offend Glenn, but she did not want him laying a public claim to her either. She was not ready for that. There was too much else on her mind right now for her to be thinking about suitors in any event.

Glenn coughed into his fist and pretended the aborted embrace hadn't happened.

"What shall we do to celebrate?" Thaddeus asked, his voice a trifle overloud. "Coffee? Brandy? What would you like, Megan?"

"Tea, I think. Would that be all right?"

"Anything you want is all right with me," the doctor said emphatically. "Victor? Are you out there? Good. Trot over to the kitchen like a good lad, would you, and bring back a kettle of tea. Some of that dark brew they make for the Irish lads, right? Milk and sugar too and any sweet tidbits they have lying about, cookies or whatever. That's the good lad, Victor, thank you."

"It sounds like a party," Glenn said.

"And so it is. Can you think of a better reason?"

Neither Megan nor Glenn admitted that they could.

Ah, it was a fine, fair day, and so it was. Laddy Sullivan tipped his head back and peered into the blue glory that was the sky, cloudless save for a few white wisps drifting lazily above.

As lazy as Laddy himself felt at this moment late in the forenoon. This was entirely too fine a day to waste it in labor. But then labor was what was required to sustain a man—or a boy soon to be a man—through days both fine and foul.

A boy, Laddy thought, who was indeed to be a man soon.

For Laddy Sullivan had fallen in love.

It had happened just six days past. Six nights, actually. He'd tagged along with the others of the survey party, and they'd all gone to that movable pub where the drinks came cheap. They'd all had their drams, Laddy included, and after a bit he'd felt the least bit woozy.

Not ill, mind. But a trifle woozy. And so as to walk off the fumes and take a snootful of atmosphere that would have more air than smoke in it, he'd stepped out behind the tent, onto the path that led both to the sinks and to the second, smaller tent, where the dark-haired lady Miss Belle King conducted her own wee enterprise.

Laddy'd been told about that business and had promised not to go there. Lads who frequented Belle King's place

came out often as not with the sort of disease no sensible
fellow wants. Others woke the following day with their
purses empty and their heads aching. Or worse. No, it was
not a fit place for man or boy, that was what Laddy'd been
told on the excellent authority of those that'd been there.

But there was nothing wrong with walking past it whilst
a fellow sought out a breath of purest air, was there? Nor
was there any harm in appreciating the scents of incense and
perfume that clung to the breeze close by.

Those smells alone were enough to excite Laddy's fervid
imagination and set his blood to racing.

He'd filled his lungs with the exciting scents, drinking
them deep into his pores and becoming intoxicated with the
headiness of anticipation.

It was then that he'd seen his ladylove.

She was a wee bit of a thing. Tiny and pale. Wrapped
tight around with a tattered kimono that was too flimsy to
fend off the chill night air, so that she held her arms close
to her meager chest and shivered.

"Are you all right?" he asked timidly.

"Aye," she said. "Havin' a taste o' the fresh air, is all."
Her brogue was music to him, her voice as lovely as her
face. And her face . . . He came near to her on the path,
and a beam of benevolent moonlight slid gracefully down
from above to illuminate her just for Laddy Sullivan's benefit.

She was thin, a wee and wasted slip of loveliness. Her
eyes were huge and moist and glimmering bright in the
moonlight. Her cheeks were hollow and her lips thin. Her
face was heart-shaped, her chin sharp and her neck too
narrow to be. Her hair was drawn hard back and coiled
into a bun at her nape. Moist bits of it escaped confinement.
Laddy thought these wee sweaty bits quite dear.

"You look . . . Forgive me if I'm forward, but you look most tired. Is there naught I can do for ye, pretty lassie?"

She held something to her lips and sucked on it, and there was a red glow competing with the moonlight to illuminate her beauty. It took Laddy a moment to realize she was smoking something. Not a cigar or a pipe but something he'd never seen, something with the shape of a cigar but smaller and wrapped in paper. She took the smoke deep, paused a moment and exhaled. Twin streams of the smoke seeped from her nostrils—he noticed then how delicate and fine and lovely her nose was—and wreathed round her head in the still night air.

"It's likin' your voice that I am, laddy," she said, and for a moment Laddy thought this elfin vision of beauty somehow already knew his name. Then he recognized the truth. He wasn't disappointed. The other would have been beyond hope anyway. "Where is it you'd be from now?"

When he told her, she gave him a wide-eyed stare. "You'd not be lyin' to me na, would ye?"

"Of course not. Whyever 'ud I do a thing like that?"

"Whyever? Why, because I myself 'ud be from Glennach Brae, laddy, not five minutes' stroll from where ye say ye're reared, that's why."

"No! D'ye know Father Eaton, then?"

"Know him? It was him as gave me my confirmation, wasn't it?" she returned.

"No."

"Aye, I swear."

They both smiled then, and the girl seemed to relax.

They talked, the words fairly flying from their mouths, and after a bit Laddy got bold enough to offer the girl his sweater for a wrap against the chill, and she was bold enough to take it, placing it about her thin shoulders and accepting the lingering warmth from his body into hers.

They'd have talked the night through, Laddy was sure, and mayhap done more than talk, except that after a while Belle King herself came out, pretty as a picture but snapping mad, to grab the lass by the arm and yank her off inside without a word to Laddy.

"What did I tell you about giving it away?" Miss King snarled. "Worse, there's half a dozen paying customers waiting in there, and here you stand doing nothing but talking, damn you. Now, get inside and get to work before I teach you a lesson you won't forget."

The girl had gone then, and Laddy still did not know her name.

But he knew he was fair in love.

And he knew he'd be seeing her again just as quick as they finished staking this next bit o' line and pulled the survey crew back to end-o'-track.

That couldn't come too soon for Laddy, no indeed.

Smiling and whistling a gay tune, he gathered up the heavy tripod and a pair of red-and-white striped sticks and began lugging them forward.

"Hey, Laddy," one of the other boys called.

"Aye?"

"Put those down, son. We're breaking for lunch now."

"Go ahead an' start. I'm this far, I'll set 'em out ready to pick up after dinner, 'eh?"

"Whatever you want to do, Laddy."

The other men in the crew were gathered close by the string of light but rugged wagons that hauled all the men and equipment. And their rations.

Laddy ordinarily could pack away as much food as any pair of his older companions, but for the past day or two— say, roughly since he'd made the acquaintance of his own true ladylove—his appetite had been off. Certainly he did not mind doing a bit extra now while the others sat and smoked their pipes and fixed dinner. Every chore completed put them that much closer to returning, that much closer to his being able to find out what the lassie's name might be.

He walked out ahead of the party, trying to guess where the party engineer, Mr. Dumbrough, would want the stakes. He dropped off the tripod first, then first one marker, followed by the other.

He glanced back at his chums, intent on the fire to boil their coffee. It would be a while before dinner was ready.

Laddy looked again to the sky. Such a grand day, clear and glorious.

He'd dropped the last stake at the edge of a narrow slough that extended like a slightly curving tongue to the north of the river. Cattails filled the moist depression. The slough was more swampy muck than pond, but out in the center there was a patch of open water. The day was warm, and Laddy found the prospect of a bath inviting. He could as good as feel the cool pleasure of it on his skin, and thinking about getting clean, he became conscious of the clammy feel of clothes that had been too long unchanged against his skin.

Another look behind convinced him. They hadn't even started to cook lunch yet. He could have a quick dip and still get back to the wagons in time for dinner.

Why not? he asked himself.

He trotted down to the edge of the slough and kicked his shoes off, then quickly stripped, tossing his clothes into a heap atop a clump of wiry grass where they wouldn't get any more filthy than they already were. Already he was regretting not having anything clean to wear when he came out of the water. But that lack was not going to keep him from enjoying his bath. Not hardly.

The thick, spongy water grasses and cattails felt odd underfoot as he picked his way out toward the bit of open water, and the air moving on bare skin felt invigorating and free but also a trifle intimidating. In his nakedness Laddy felt vulnerable and defenseless, and of course he was.

Still, it was a fine and fabulous day, and Laddy had a future to think of, and a lady fair, that was much more interesting to dwell upon than discomforts and fretfulness.

He laughed and splashed his way out into the middle of the slough, the sun unaccustomedly warm on his bare backside. A rising breeze tickled as it passed over him, and the mud he waded through was calf deep and almost cold. It occurred to him that he would be muddy when he returned to shore because there was no water except beyond this patch of mud, so he would have to wipe himself off with leaves or bunches of grass before he could put his stockings and shoes back on again.

He reached deeper water and waded in to his thighs, then finally achieved waist-high water in the middle of the slough. He sat, allowing the water to engulf him chin-high and enjoying the cool, refreshing feel of it. This was better than any bathhouse tub, never mind the chill and the lack of soap. This was clean and free and fine.

But then all of this land seemed clean and free and fine to Laddy Sullivan.

He was glad he'd taken the ship from home. He was even more glad that he'd found his way here, to this place, to this job, to that pretty lassie whose name he would soon know.

Aye, this truly was near to as grand as life could possibly offer. Work to do, food to eat . . . and a lassie to look forward to. What more could any man—or boy—ask?

Laddy whirled and sloshed and splashed for a bit. But only for a bit. A rumbling in his belly reminded him that dinner should be ready by now, and so he stood upright and began making his way back.

He waded into the shallow water until it came but knee-deep and started then into the cattails.

His thoughts were on the pretty lassie from Glennach Brae.

Something, a swish of movement where there was no wind or a hint of sound too low to register, gave him pause.

He stopped, frowning, and stared about in all directions.

It occurred to him that he was standing naked in a slough somewhere on the unmarked prairie of wild Nebraska in the American wilderness and not in safe and settled old Ireland.

There were dangers here, as he'd well seen with his own disbelieving eyes.

Dangers of many sorts. And his companions were all far distant from him at this moment.

His heart suddenly thumping in his throat, Laddy took a step forward into the thick cattails and then another.

A moment of panic clutched at his belly, and he tried to run.

The cattail roots and stringy shafts trapped his ankles, and he fell sprawling face-forward into the muck.

Frantic for no reason but frantic nonetheless, he stumbled to his knees and plunged blindly ahead.

A bird's song twittered and lilted in front of him, and for a moment the soft, mundane naturalness of it gave Laddy ease.

Then it occurred to him to wonder what manner of song-bird would hold its ground in the path of an onrushing intruder.

He stopped. Turned this way and that. His heart was racing again. Chest heaving. His bowels were watery and gurgled with fear.

He heard the rattle of cattail stalks, the plop of sucking mud and more rattling of cattails.

Laddy heard a groan and realized he had uttered the sound himself.

Jesus, he said to himself. Hail Mary, full of grace, be with me now and at the hour of my death. Hail Mary. Be with me now. Now and at the hour . . . Be with me now.

A hand materialized through the green screen of cattail rushes.

Laddy cried out.

The hand, dark and unclean with nails bitten into the quick, pulled the cattails aside.

Laddy found himself staring into a flat, dark face with obsidian eyes and an unspeakably hideous mask of streaked paint, black and vermilion and white blotches.

"No." It was a whisper. It was a prayer.

The Indian was holding something. A hatchet. An ordinary hatchet like anyone might use to split shingles, an ordinary hatchet such as the one Laddy used himself to make the marker pegs for the surveyor flags. Except this hatchet had brass tacks driven into the handle, and a bundle of blue and pale gray feathers fluttered at the end of a thong tied to the steel head of the thing.

Oh, God, Laddy thought or possibly said aloud.

He felt his bladder loosen, and his sphincter lost its ability to control his bowel.

"Please. Don't."

The painted warrior stood tall, his chest expanded and muscles bulging. The Sioux cried out something Laddy could not understand and lifted his hatchet high overhead.

Trembling, kneeling in the cold mud of the slough, Laddy closed his eyes and tried to remember how to pray.

Mercifully, all he felt was a jarring thump high on the forehead.

CHAPTER

34

Glenn formed his hand into a fist then flexed his fingers, extending them as wide as he could manage.

"Well?" Thaddeus Wiseman asked.

"Fine."

"No pain?"

"None," Glenn said. "A bit of tenderness behind the knuckles, but I wouldn't call it pain. It's more like a stiffness."

"That's because you haven't been using the hand," the doctor said. "In a few weeks, a month at the most, I would suspect you'll hardly know you were ever hurt. Is the shoulder doing as well?"

"That hasn't much bothered me right from the first except for a little soreness when I lay on it."

"Good." Wiseman chuckled. "The shoulder would have bothered you a great deal, I think, if you hadn't been so distracted by the hand. By now, though, it too has had time to heal. You're going to be just fine, Glenn. Another few days and I think you can—"

Glenn never did find out what Wiseman thought he could do after another few days. The conversation was cut short by the arrival of a worried-looking Joshua Hood.

"Yes, Mr. Hood?" Wiseman asked.

"Best drag out your needles an' whatever, Doc, for there's some wounded comin' in."

"What happened? An accident?"

"Worse. Sioux raiders. The trouble's started, I reckon. They hit a survey crew. Some o' my boys heard the shootin' an' hustled in t' lend a hand, but they wasn't quick enough to keep the Sioux from getting some licks in."

"Which crew?" Glenn blurted.

"Johnny Dumbrough's bunch," Joshua told him. "They were twenty-odd miles out shooting final lines."

"Dumbrough," Glenn said. "You're sure it was Dumbrough?" Young John Dumbrough was running the crew that had been Glenn's until he ran off and got himself wounded. If it hadn't been for another Sioux war party, he would have been leading those men when the Indians jumped them. "You say some of the boys were hurt?"

"Four hurt bad and a couple more with minor scrapes. One dead."

Glenn's stomach knotted, but he had to ask the question. "Who was killed?"

"I don't know his name. Some redhead mick a few months off the boat, somebody said. Just a boy."

"Oh, Lord. That would be Laddy Sullivan. I . . . knew him." Knew Laddy? Of course he had. Glenn knew every one of the fine young men in that crew. But Laddy. Such an eager, laughing, joyous boy he was. No, not was—had been. Glenn felt sick.

"Hair that color, them Injuns prob'ly thought they'd died an' gone to Heaven. Just think how handsome a trophy that must be on some red bastard's coup stick or bullhide shield," Joshua said.

"Gentlemen, please," Wiseman injected. "Can we talk about all this later? Tell me, Mr. Hood, these wounded you say are on the way in, how many are there and when will they arrive?"

"Like I said, Doc, there's four that are solid hit and a few scratches. Of the four I'd think two might could be real bad hurt. The other two oughta make out with some patching up. As for when they'll be here, I'd say they're half an hour, maybe forty-five minutes behind me."

"That gives me time to get things organized here," the doctor said. "Mr. Gilchrist, may I ask a favor?"

"Thaddeus, you know you can ask me anything you please. I'm in your debt, sir."

"We'll discuss that some other time. In the meanwhile I would like you to round up Miss O'Connell and her employees. They've all had some modicum of nursing experience thanks to you. More to the point, I know them and trust them to do as I instruct. You are mobile enough by now, sir, so I would like you to please find them and ask them to come assist me in the surgery. And, Mr. Hood, I may be needing some muscular assistance again to hold my patients down. Can I depend upon you and your scouts?"

"Reckon we'll be here if you need us, Doc."

"Very well then, gentlemen, and thank you."

Glenn slipped down off the operating table and went outside. It had been some time since he'd been outdoors by himself, and for a few seconds the sensation felt decidedly strange, as if he were doing something he should not. That passed, however, and he set off in the direction from which he'd seen Megan approach the infirmary day after day for the past week and more.

Oddly, or perhaps not so when he thought about it, he had no idea where Megan's saloon was situated in this camp. The last time he'd been out, she was not yet here. He had to ask directions from several passersby before he finally found her tent.

It was afternoon, and a good number of workmen were wandering hither and yon through the camp, but Megan's tent was virtually empty save for a handful of prosperous-looking gentlemen gathered around Henry Harrison Armbruster's poker table. Rachel Foreman was there as well, standing behind the plank-and-barrel bar in readiness should anyone wish something. And Victor Boyette sat in a corner whittling tiny face shapes into the bark of a willow twig.

Glenn tried Rachel first. "Where is Megan, Rachel?"

"She was gone when I got here a little while ago, Mr. Gilchrist. Victor? Have you seen Megan?"

"Not this afternoon."

"Damn."

"Is something wrong?"

Glenn told her. Rachel immediately pulled her apron off and dropped it onto the bar. "We'll help. Count on it. Victor."

"Yes'm?"

"Did you hear Mr. Gilchrist?"

"No, I reckon I didn't."

"Dr. Wiseman needs help at the surgery."

"But Mr. Gilchrist, he's standing right there. Besides, his hand don't need washing no more."

"I know, Victor, but the doctor needs our help with something else."

"Whyn't you say so right off then?" Victor grumbled. He folded his pocketknife closed with meticulous care and laid his twig aside, then stood and bobbed his head as if declaring himself ready. "Let's go." He was halfway to the door before Rachel could start in motion to join him.

"Is something wrong?" Henry Harrison asked without leaving his table.

Glenn went over and explained the problem.

"I believe you will find Miss O'Connell at the telegraph office, Mr. Gilchrist."

"Oh?"

"I am only guessing . . . and please understand that I do not mean to pry into Miss O'Connell's personal affairs; it is just that I owe the lady a debt at least as great as yours and am concerned for her welfare . . . But if I were to hazard a guess, Mr. Gilchrist, I would say she may be wiring her sister, Mrs. Fox, to stop the shipment of goods she'd asked for."

"Stop the shipment? Why would she want to do a thing like that, Mr. Armbruster?"

Henry Harrison looked slowly around the empty saloon. "Obviously the lady has not been complaining about her current state, but her business has disappeared. The price of beer and whiskey in this camp has declined practically to nothing thanks to her competitor, Mr. Norman."

This was the first Glenn had heard about Megan's perilous financial state, and it worried him.

"The only income the lady has at the moment is what these gents and I provide." The diminutive gambler looked at the fellows seated around him and winked broadly. "Knowing that," he said, "should make their inevitable losses more palatable, eh, gentlemen?" He grinned. "After all, it is easier to accept the notion of charity than the bitter truth, which is that you are all sheep set for my shearing."

"That will be the day, HH," one of the players said with good humor.

"See, Gilchrist? Even when I point it out to them, they refuse to believe me. What shall I do?" The sparkle in his eyes diminished, and he became serious again. "I tell you what, Gilchrist. I will stay here and keep an eye on the place. If any of us requires anything, we'll help ourselves and leave our money on the counter. You find Miss O'Connell. When you do, tell her she needn't worry herself about the saloon. I will accept full responsibility."

Glenn nodded and excused himself. Just as Henry Harrison had said, Megan was among those gathered at the telegraph station. She was just completing her transaction when Glenn arrived.

"Glenn. How nice to see you here."

"I wish it were, Megan, but I have bad news." He explained briefly. "Dr. Wiseman was hoping you would lend a hand. Rachel and Victor have already volunteered."

"Of course I'll do whatever I can."

"Henry Harrison is watching the saloon. He said you needn't worry about that."

"I'll go to the infirmary right now then."

"I'll only be a minute behind you," Glenn said.

Megan hurried out, but Glenn lingered inside the telegraph office.

Once Megan was out of sight, he leaned forward and beckoned the telegraph operator closer. "Jimmy," he whispered in a conspiratorial tone of voice.

"Yes, Mr. Gilchrist?"

"The message Miss O'Connell gave you. Have you sent it yet?"

"No, sir, Mr. Gilchrist, but I'll get on it right away."

"Uh, before you do, Jimmy, would you mind showing it to me?"

"Mr. Gilchrist, that would be entirely beyond the rules. You know that."

"Yes, I certainly do, Jimmy. Now, may I see it, please?"

The telegrapher looked around to make sure no one was watching them, then winked and pushed the pale yellow telegraph form across the counter so that Glenn could see.

It read: "AILEEN STOP MUST DELAY SHIPMENT COMMA AM WITHOUT FUNDS STOP MORE LATER STOP BEST TO LIAM AND KIDS STOP LOVE MEGAN END"

"I'll get that off right away, Mr. Gilchrist," Jimmy offered.

"No, what I think you'd best do is lose this message form."

"Sir?"

"I think what's going to happen, Jimmy, is that this form is going onto the top of your pile of messages to send. But a breeze is going to come up, and this paper right here is going to be blown to the floor behind that desk over in the corner. Do you see what I mean, Jimmy?"

The telegrapher swallowed hard and looked nervously around. He only hesitated for a few moments, though. Then he nodded. "If you say so, Mr. Gilchrist."

"I accept full responsibility, Jimmy. And I thank you."

"Yes, sir. Whatever you say, Mr. Gilchrist."

Glenn nodded at him and left the telegraph office. He was only a hundred yards or so from Dr. Wiseman's surgery, but instead of heading directly there, he went off at a tangent, detouring far out of his way. It was some twenty minutes later that he finally arrived at the surgery, barely ahead of the wagons bearing the survivors of his old survey crew.

Laddy, he thought, poor Laddy. But by then the wagons were rolling to a halt and there was work to be done. There would be time enough for grieving—what little of it that would be done for the young Irishman, alone on this continent and bereft of family here—sometime later on.

CHAPTER

35

General Dodge was boiling mad. He marched into Jack Casement's railcar and slammed his hat onto the table. Everyone, Joshua Hood included, recoiled and held their tongues. Such a display was most unlike the usually composed and clear-thinking general.

"Do you know what happened today?" he demanded of no one in particular.

"You've come up to see about that survey crew?" someone asked nervously.

"That's what brought me here, yes, but it's worse than that. Do you know what happened as I was on my way up here?"

"No, sir."

"We were making good time, nice and steady, when the engineer received an emergency stop order at the Crawford Station. Do you know why?"

The question, no matter how forcefully stated, was clearly rhetorical. No one ventured a response.

"The damned Indians were attacking again. *Behind* us. Can you believe that? Forty-odd miles *east* from here. One of the work trains was stopped for lack of steam, and a bunch of damned Indians rode down on them and captured the train, for God's sake. The whole train. Set fire to the cars and took the crew captive. Fortunately the wire operator at Buford Creek spotted the smoke in the distance and was able to see enough with his spyglass to recognize what was happening. He knew from when we passed through that I had a score of guards with me, so he wired ahead to Crawford Station and stopped our special. We backed down the track hard as we could go and managed to reach the scene before the blackguards could get away. My men dashed out and deployed as skirmishers, and the Sioux, damn them, gave up their prisoners and spoil in favor of a fast escape. But damn them anyway. Imagine! Attacking a stalled train in broad daylight, pillaging, burning—who knows what else they might have done if we hadn't been available to change their minds by force of arms." Dodge scowled and paced the floor, marching back and forth and gesturing with his hands while he grumbled about the attack. His mood was far from his usual equanimity.

Later, after he'd had time to calm himself and to receive a report of the Sioux attack on John Dumbrough's survey party, General Dodge motioned Joshua near. "We need to have a word in private, Hood. After dinner?"

"Whatever you say, sir."

Dinner, as befitted a meal served to the chief engineer and de facto leader of the entire Union Pacific construction project, was a full and formal affair, the table offerings almost as rich as the diners. With a few exceptions. When the other gentlemen were enjoying their cigars, Dodge asked to be excused and withdrew to the platform at the back of the car, motioning for Joshua to join him.

"I don't mean to take you away from the brandy, Hood. If you want to get a snifter and bring it out with you . . ."

"No, sir, I didn't want none anyhow. What is it I can do for you, General?"

"I thought you might have been wondering why I brought twenty volunteer riflemen with me on this little visit, eh, Hood?"

"Actually, sir, I just figured they was along t' guard you. That's what you said, wasn't it?"

"I said they were guards, but I do not believe I specified who or what it was intended they should guard."

"Reckon I don't follow your meaning, sir."

"I didn't want those men along to guard my person, Hood. I managed that for myself through the long years of war. I don't see any need for personal security now. No, what I had in mind, Hood, was what we discussed before. An effort to renew the peace treaty with Spotted Bull and his people."

"Yes, sir?"

"But, ahem, what I had thought . . . what I had intended after giving consideration to your recommendations . . . was an expedition on a smaller and less bellicose scale."

"You, me an' twenty volunteers?" Joshua guessed.

"Um, yes, actually."

"General, you're a fine gentleman an' smarter than I'll ever be, but—"

Dodge held up a hand to stop him. "I know. A party of twenty-some civilians would be asking for annihilation if we were to venture into the Sioux strongholds. Is that what you were about to tell me?"

"Yes, sir. Somethin' like that."

"After this morning, Hood, I fear that I must concur with your judgment. Sad to say. After this morning's experience . . . seeing those savages in person, their looting and burning, their disregard for life and property . . . They truly are savages, aren't they?"

"Kinda depends on what you mean by that, General. Truth is, they got their own ways. Good ways, some of 'em. But different from our ways. That's the thing. That's what we don't gen'rally see about our way an' what we don't gen'rally see about theirs. We're different, General. Different as night an' day. We don't live alike an' we don't think alike. But to say they're savages . . . Hell, sir, ask a Sioux an' he'll tell you that *we're* the ones as don't follow custom an' do the right thing; he'll tell you we're the ones as don't play fair."

"Is that right, Hood?"

"Yes, sir, it surely is."

"Don't these Indians realize that they must live in our world now and . . . play, as you put it . . . by our rules?"

"No, sir, they sure as hell don't. They ain't no more willing t' do that than we'd be willing t' change over t' their ways."

"If they don't adapt to our ways, you know, they will be exterminated. Not by design, not by desire, but sooner or later it will inevitably happen."

"I reckon there's a few of them that have that figured out already, General, but even so, they won't change. You see, sir, they believe they're right."

Dodge frowned and stared out across the prairie for long moments before he turned back to look Joshua in the eyes once again. "That is a sad assessment, Hood."

"Yes, sir, but I reckon you're paying me t' be straight with you. If that ain't so, then I expect you'd best tell me what it is that you want instead."

"The truth, Hood. Always the truth."

"Yes, sir. That's what I been tryin' to give you right along."

Dodge sighed. "After this morning, Hood, I am abandoning my hope that we few men of goodwill can settle this privately. After this morning, I've come round to your view that in all probability there is nothing we can do to forestall warfare and bloodshed. But in the name of humanity, Hood, we still must try. Before we give in to failure, we yet must try again."

"With soldiers an' bright shiny sabers an' a white flag overhead?" Joshua asked hopefully.

"Yes, Hood. With all of that. I have decided to forget my plan and adopt your ideas. Enough soldiers to make us safe but not so many as to send the Sioux packing unseen and unspoken to. Two troops of cavalry, you suggested?"

"Yes, sir, I reckon that'd be about right. Never mind what's supposed t' be the official count, out here all the outfits is understrength. Out here a troop o' yella-leg soldiers runs to thirty, forty men. Two horseback troops, a whole lotta flags and guidons in the air an' the two of us, General; the way I see it that oughta be just about right."

"I shall get my wire off to Bill Sherman this afternoon," Dodge said softly. "Plan to leave as soon as Captain Taney and his people present themselves ready for field duty."

"Yes, sir. I'll be ready."

CHAPTER

36

It took Captain Medgar Taney, commanding officer of the United States Army garrison at Fort Kearney, Nebraska, five days to comply with the orders issued by the commanding general of the army's vast Department of the Missouri, a command which encompassed tens of thousands of square miles and a majority of the uninhabited lands in possession of the United States of America.

General William Tecumseh Sherman had sent General Dodge a copy of the order, which specified clearly that action was to be undertaken immediately upon receipt of the message. And by the morning of the fifth day after, General Dodge was seething over the delay.

"The man is deliberately dragging his heels," Dodge complained to Joshua. "Is that orderly still outside, the one Taney sent to say he wouldn't be along just yet?"

"Yes, sir."

"Send the man in to me, if you please."

"You bet, General."

The corporal, whose kepi badge indicated he was attached to a supply unit rather than a field troop, seemed nervous when he reported. But then Grenville Dodge was a major general, albeit a retired major general. Even though Dodge was wearing civilian riding clothes, the messenger from Fort

Kearney came stiffly to attention and threw the best salute he knew how. "Y-yes, sir?"

"I want you to carry a message from me to Captain Taney, soldier."

"Yes, sir."

Dodge stepped in close to the corporal and gave him a critical looking over. The soldier seemed to wilt under the general's close inspection.

"I want you to tell your commander that I look forward to seeing him, along with two troops of cavalry, in full field marching order, at this railroad station, no later than noon today. Do I make myself clear on that point, soldier? What is your name, by the way?"

"T-T-Tupper, sir. Corporal Anthony Tupper, Quarter-master Corps, at-t-tached to Fort Kearney. Sir."

"Very well, Corporal Tupper. You are clear that I mean to say he must be here ready to march at noon on this date?"

"Y-yes, sir. Noon today, sir."

"That is correct, Tupper. That is in . . ." Dodge drew a bulbous watch from his vest pocket and consulted it for the time. "I make it now approximately half past seven. That gives the captain four and a half hours, including your travel time, to report to me ready to march."

"Y-yes, sir."

"You might also tell Captain Taney that if he fails to comply with this request—for after all I am only a civilian and cannot issue binding orders to any member of the United States Army—but do tell him, Tupper, that if he chooses not to comply with my request, I will this afternoon, no later than twelve-oh-five post meridian, send telegraphic messages to both General W. T. Sherman and General Philip Sheridan requesting explanations and redress. In other words, Corporal, you can tell your commander that I will see him comply with his orders on this date or I shall have him removed from the rolls of the United States Army and see his commission revoked. And if he believes I am only bluffing or that I haven't the ability to follow through with what I say . . . well . . . he can call me simply by failing to appear here in four-and-a-half hours' time."

"Sir?"

"Yes, Tupper?"

"D'you really expect me to tell Cap'n Taney all that, sir?"

"Indeed I do, Tupper. Do you have a problem with that?"

The corporal grinned. "No, sir, not at all. I just wanted t' get it straight that you was ordering me to do it, that's all."

"Good man, Tupper. Now be off with you. It's a half hour's ride back to the post. I wouldn't want Taney to have any excuses like not receiving my message in a timely fashion."

"I'll ride fast as ever I can, sir. That's a promise." Tupper saluted again right smartly, took a step backward and executed a tidy left face, then took off at a run for his waiting horse.

When Dodge turned around again, Joshua thought the general was having a certain small amount of difficulty keeping his face straight. Corporal Tupper had been remarkably eager to deliver dire warnings to his commanding officer. Damned popular fellow that Taney, Joshua suspected. You bet.

When Taney and his column arrived, well before noon, he made a point of yawning, stretching and in a bored and languid tone saying, "We passed my courier between here and the fort, General, but we were well off the road trying out our horses in squadron drill, and I don't believe he saw us. Was there any message for me, or was the man simply returning to duty?"

Dodge's expression did not change a whit, for which
Joshua greatly admired him. "Nothing important," the retired
general said.

"Very well. Shall we discuss the campaign then? I'd like
to get on with this as quickly as possible."

"There is little enough to discuss," Dodge said. "This is
to be a mission of peace, Captain. Your orders are clear
enough. While we are in the field, you will take strategic
direction from me. We will travel in full view and will
display a conspicuously mounted white flag of truce along
with appropriate ensigns and guidons at all times, so that any
native observers will become aware of the peaceful nature
of our mission. Our line of march will be determined by
the Union Pacific's chief scout, Mr. Hood . . . I believe you
know Mr. Hood already . . . and the civilian scouts he has
chosen to accompany the mission. We will proceed into
Sioux territory without any rattling of arms, Captain, or
beating of shields. We will not fire our rifles even to take
game. We will display no hostility, nor will we react if young
Sioux warriors seeking their first boasting rights whoop and
charge close to our column. Which Mr. Hood persuades
me is a distinct likelihood. Their young bloods will test
our forbearance, Captain. They will make noise. They will
bluster and wave their lances and ride literally close enough
to touch with a coup stick. But so long as the flag of truce
remains over us, the Sioux can be expected to honor it. They
will try it, yes, but they will honor it, and we must keep our
carbines slung and our sabers in their scabbards."

Taney was glowering. "That brings up a small point, Mr.
Dodge." The choice of "Mr." as opposed to "General" was
obvious and deliberate.

Dodge displayed no reaction. "And what would that be,
Captain?"

"Sabers. I instructed my men to leave their sabers behind. You don't know what these Indians are like, of course, but one does not campaign against them with sabers. The weapons are noisy to carry and awkward to handle and get in one's way in a campaign against these savages."

"Which is precisely the point, Captain. We are not campaigning against the Sioux; we are treating with them. And I wish the sabers to be worn for purposes of ceremony."

"My sabers are back at Kearney, I'm afraid. Of course I could send a detail back for them. It wouldn't take long. And in any event I propose that we remain here overnight and get a start early tomorrow morning. There are still some things that must be done, you see. My farrier says some of the horses still need shoeing, and my armorer has work yet to do. It really would be better if we were to make a fresh start tomorrow."

It didn't take any military genius to see that Taney had just trapped himself in a lie. He'd said earlier that they were already on their way and hadn't been dragged out by Corporal Tupper. But now he was admitting that neither the horses nor the men had been properly prepared for a field campaign before they pulled out of Kearney a little while ago. How any commander of horse soldiers could allow some of his horses to be maintained without adequate shoes, even for as much as a single day, was beyond Joshua's comprehension. But then he wasn't no brass-bound officer and gentleman, neither. All he was was a hired hand. But a hired hand that had spent considerable time among the Indians and still had his hair. To Joshua's mind that counted for something.

Joshua watched the general appear to accept all this booshwa without a flicker of expression.

"Very well, Captain. You may have the remainder of the afternoon in which to prepare. We will march at half past dawn tomorrow. Will that be satisfactory?"

"Whatever you say, Mr. Dodge."

"Dis-missed," the general barked without warning.

Taney snapped to attention and had his arm halfway to his forehead in automatic reaction to the authority in Grenville Dodge's voice before he realized what he was doing and stopped the salute in mid-motion.

The man colored a rich, bright hue with embarrassment before he spun on his heels and stalked away.

Behind him it was all Joshua could do to keep himself from breaking into guffaws, and he was certain sure that the general was having difficulty containing himself as well. Either that or he was suffering some sort of gastric spasms.

"I like your spirit, Gilchrist, but I cannot accept your offer." General Dodge clapped a hand onto Glenn's shoulder. The injured shoulder, in fact. Fortunately the healing process was well enough along that it did not hurt too terribly badly. "Too many of us and the Sioux will turn tail. Or so Mr. Hood informs me. Anyway, Gilchrist, my answer has to be no. I can't allow you to come with us."

After his last foray into the wilderness, Glenn was not so disappointed by the rejection as he might have been. But he'd felt it was an offer he should make. At least now he need harbor no guilt feelings about hanging back while others went out to undertake a mission he had come to feel was his own.

The members of the expedition were gathered for a sort of alfresco supper courtesy of the Union Pacific Railroad. Plank tables had been erected and hay bales set out in place of chairs or benches. The soldiers—officers stayed carefully apart—were enjoying the efforts of the U.P.'s cooks. Mountains of potatoes and hillocks of roast buffalo were disappearing with remarkable speed. Lanterns hung on poles, and General Dodge had given orders that the cooks were to keep the food coming as long as the soldiers cared to continue eating. The blue-clad men, who earned in a month less than a common railroad laborer could make in a week, acted as if they were in the midst of a grand gala. In the morning, though, the party would be ended. In the morning they would march toward the Sioux villages to make a peace, or possibly to die.

"I tell you what, Gilchrist. Why don't you join us at the officers table."

"That's very kind of you, sir."

"Good." The general led the way, taking his place at what passed for the head of the table. Captain Medgar Taney was at the foot. Although perhaps he considered that far end the head because he was the ranking serving officer present while Dodge was the ranking retired officer. Glenn understood that such things were of importance to military men. Little of it made much sense to him. And in any event, it was probably just as well that the two men were so widely separated. Neither seemed to have great regard for the other.

Glenn helped himself to a seat as unobtrusively as possible and reached for the platters of food. The officers, he noted, were packing the food away with every bit as much alacrity as the enlisted men.

Informal introductions were made round the table. On one side were Dan Casement seated at General Dodge's left, Joshua Hood, a second lieutenant named Howard— Glenn was unclear whether that was the man's first name or last—and Glenn's immediate boss, railroad chief surveyor Ben Goss. Goss seemed pleased to see Glenn up and around again. To the general's right were General Jack Casement, Glenn, First Lieutenant George Powell and a civilian named Reggie White. During the course of the dinner conversation, Glenn gathered that White was a correspondent for one of the larger eastern newspapers, although precisely which newspaper remained uncertain.

He suspected it was no accident that White had been invited to sit beside Captain Taney. Or if it were, then Taney was bent upon taking advantage of the newspaper-man's presence to gain mention of himself in print.

"The pity of it all," Glenn overhead Taney say at one point, "is that those gray-headed old men are tying my hands."

That remark occurred during a lull in the general buzz of noise that had come from several different conversations going on simultaneously. Apparently more than just Glenn and the journalist to whom it was directed caught the biting tone in Medgar Taney's voice, for there was a pause in the table talk while the Fort Kearney commander sailed blithely onward, either unaware or uncaring of the reactions by those around him.

"They don't understand what's needed with these red bastards, Mr. White."

"And I take it you do, Captain?"

"Harrumph! Damned right I do. If they'd give me free rein, I'd have this problem licked in no time. In no time at all, I tell you."

"And how would you do that, Captain?"

"Lick the savages and you lick the problem, Mr. White. It is as simple as that."

"I've heard the Sioux may not be so simple to lick, however."

"Nonsense. Proved it myself just a few weeks past, didn't I? Sent a single troop out and bested a horde of the filthy creatures, did I not? One troop of good Yankee cavalry, and a hundred or more Sioux were licked. One troop, sir."

Glenn frowned. The way he remembered it, the Sioux that day had numbered fifteen. Not approximately. Precisely. Fifteen. He had counted them himself. And there had been no battle involved. It was a slashing ambush and quick slaughter. Which certainly was not to say that the U.S. cavalry could not acquit itself well. Just to say that no demonstration of ability had been made that day, either way.

"Now the fine young officer whose mettle was battle-tested and battle-hardened that day is not even allowed to lead his troop. Howard there," he pointed to the now blushing second lieutenant across the table, "is no Ed Wollins, I can tell you, Mr. White, but those gray-headed old men instruct me to leave poor Wollins in temporary command at the fort while I assume personal command of my field force. Can you believe that senior officers would be so nit-picking in their orders as all that? Can you?"

Glenn glanced down the table at Dodge, but the general was calmly taking it all in. Glenn suspected—hoped too, for that matter—that this conversation would be related to those same gray-haired old men Taney seemed so incensed about.

In his excitement Taney pounded on the table beside the newsman's plate. "They are fools," he declared. "All of them. Timid old fools. Lost their guts, they have, and don't want to make way for better, more daring men. Why, I tell you, White, with two troops of United States cavalry and the leadership of men like myself and Ed Wollins, I could subdue the entire Sioux nation. Spotted Bull and that Red Cloud fellow and all the rest of them too. Indians can't stand up to disciplined fire, you know. They put on a brave show, but show is all it is. Stand firm before them and they'll break every time. Wollins proved it right enough in the Battle of Wollins Gulch. Did I mention we've named the site in honor of Ed's achievement? It seems only appropriate, of course. Anyway . . . where was I? . . . Oh, yes. Lo, the Poor Savage is nothing but bluster. My men, acting under my orders, carried the field without the loss of a single man that day. Not one man, I tell you. Those vaunted warriors of Spotted Bull's band broke in the face of their gallant charge."

Glenn could scarcely believe what he was hearing. Charge? The soldiers fired from ambush. Half the unsuspecting Sioux were dead before they even knew they were being fired on. There never had been a charge, just a wild melee as the soldiers chased down fleeing Indians like so many dogs coursing after so many rabbits. Surely Wollins—he'd seemed a decent enough young man, actually—surely he hadn't reported this sort of grand but spurious battle to his superior.

"With these men right here," Taney tossed a gesture in the general direction of the enlisted men he had been ignoring thus far, "I could lick Spotted Bull and every warrior in his band. I could solve this problem myself, Mr. White, if only those gray-headed old men would permit it."

Taney did not look or act drunk, but Glenn had to wonder if perhaps the captain were in his cups.

White, however, seemed to be eating it all up. And the newspaperman's interest, of course, only stirred Taney to greater and greater pronouncements.

The man's talk became acutely uncomfortable to overhear, and apparently Glenn was not the only one experiencing that reaction. After little more of it, the other conversations around the table were resumed, hesitantly and in some instances overloudly, and after a while it was actually possible for the other gentlemen to sweep Medgar Taney and his self-aggrandizing pontifications out of mind.

Poor White, however, seemed stuck for the night, because the only way it would have been possible to rescue him would be for the rescuer to take Taney's diatribe onto himself. And no one—certainly not Glenn—seemed willing to sacrifice himself like that for the newsman's sake.

CHAPTER
38

"Joshua, wait a moment, please." The party was breaking up, the soldiers marching off toward their half tents—Glenn suspected a good many of them would sneak back to enjoy a drink or several, but officially they were on their way to their blankets now—and the officers moving in the direction of Jack Casement's private railcar, where brandy and cigars were available.

Joshua Hood stopped and waited for Glenn to catch up with him.

"You said something about going back to your camp now?"

"That's right."

"Would you mind if I walk along?"

"Reckon not. You know the way, though, don't you? You been there before as I recall."

Glenn smiled. "I've been there, it's true, but I am afraid that I do *not* recall the occasion."

"Oh, yeah. You was, uh, not yourself that night."

"Something like that, right. Say, that man of yours that guided me . . . Short, was it? Silas Short?"

"Yeah, what about him?"

"I noticed you aren't taking him with you tomorrow. He's still with your scouts, isn't he?"

"Sure, but he ain't one o' my best. Silas, he looks the part real good. An' I got to admit he smells like a buffalo more'n any other white man I ever knowed. But there's other of the boys that I'd rather have at my back if it comes to a tight. If you know what I mean."

"Yes, I think I do."

"Want t' have you a word with Silas, do you?"

"Yes."

"Want t' tell me what about?"

Glenn only grinned and shook his head.

"Suit yourself."

They walked on in silence for a ways, then Glenn asked, "Did Henry Harrison Armbruster find you this afternoon?"

"Ayuh, he did."

"And I take it he had a talk with you?"

"You take that right."

"Might I ask what you told him?"

"You know damn good an' well what I told him, Gilchrist."

"All right then."

"This's our camp t' the right here. You can always tell. Look for the worst mess in sight. That's my bunch." Joshua raised his voice and called out, "Silas Short. Wake up. You got you a visitor."

Joshua stopped in the middle of the circle of bedrolls and low brush arbors. He picked up a couple chunks of split wood and tossed them onto the fire, raising a fountain of golden sparks into the night air. And quite a bit of acrid smoke as well. The smoke found Glenn's eyes with uncanny accuracy, and he began to cough and blink.

"Silas?" Joshua repeated. "Where the hell are you?"

"Right here, damn it, tryin' to sleep."

"You can sleep tomorra when you're supposed t' be hunting. That's what you do anyhow, isn't it? Right now you got comp'ny."

"Yeah? I'll be damn. I—" Silas came halfway out of a knee-high lean-to when he saw who the visitor was. "Listen, little fella, if you think you got money due you or somethin'—"

"I don't want my money back, Silas." Glenn grinned. "I hired you to guide me to the Sioux. You certainly did that, all right."

"Ha! Reckon I did at that, didn' I?" Silas wiped his mouth with the back of his hand and stood upright. He pulled a plug of tobacco from his hip pocket and bit a chew from it without bothering with such niceties as wiping away whatever filth might have accumulated on it. Glenn was not surprised to see that Silas slept in his clothes even while in his own camp. The man was no dandy. "So," Silas said. "If it ain't your money back that you're after, what is it you want with me in the middle o' the night?"

"Why, Silas, I wanted to let you know that I'm on my feet again and pretty well healed. My shoulder is doing just fine, and the hand feels good again."

"Yeah? Well I'm just real glad t' hear that, little fella. I was surely worried 'bout you all this time."

"Yes, I could tell that by the number of times you came to visit," Glenn said lightly.

"Yeah, well, I been busy."

"I understand. Believe me. And anyway I wouldn't have wanted to have this talk with you until I was recovered enough to make it interesting."

"Talk? What talk would that be, little man?"

Glenn grinned at him. "Mr. Short, you ran away and left me to the Indians at the first blink of trouble. There were only about a dozen of them, and you never once fired a shot in their direction, just turned tail and ran like the coward you are—"

"Say now," Silas protested, his expression turning dark.

"You played the coward then, Silas, and you lied about it afterward."

"You can't say that about me, damn you. I'll bust you half in two if you—"

"Fine. If you're man enough."

"What?"

"I already said you are a coward, Silas Short. And a liar. And it is no great threat if you tell me you want to take umbrage with the truth."

"Take what?"

"Offense, Silas. If you want to stop me from telling the truth about you."

"I warned you, mister."

"So you did, Silas, but what you don't seem to understand is that I've come here tonight to administer a sound thrashing to you."

Silas looked around at Joshua and the other scouts, all of whom were fully awake and interested in the conversation by now. "A little dude like you is gonna give me a thrashing? Is that what you said, mister?"

"Clean the buffalo shit out of your ears, Short, and maybe you can hear me better. What I said is that, yes, I intend to thrash you tonight."

Silas threw his head back and roared out his laughter. "Mister, that's one o' the funniest things I ever did hear. An' one o' the dumbest. Now, go away, little man, afore I get mad an' whup all over you."

"Silas Short, I challenge you to a bout of fisticuffs. That is to say, prepare to defend yourself."

Glenn removed his coat and shirt and stood bare-chested

in the night. He raised his left fist and held it chin-high and well out in front of him. He held the right fist equally high but only a few inches before his chin. Both hands were turned inward, and his wrists were cocked. His weight was evenly balanced on the balls of both feet, and he stood with his left foot extended. His head was erect. He breathed deep and began bouncing lightly on the balls of his feet.

Joshua gave him a quizzical look and said, "Are you sure you wanta do this, college boy? Y'know, Silas don't just smell like a bear, he's 'bout as strong as one too. An' quick."

"I assure you, Hood, I know what I am doing." Glenn continued to bounce and dance lightly.

"Yeah, I can see that you know somethin' about this Marquis o' Queensbury stuff. I bet you done some fighting when you was in college, didn't you?"

"As a matter of fact I did, yes."

"Gilchrist, this ain't college. An' out here fightin' ain't done to no rules, like you was dancin' la-de-da. This here is for real, an' Silas is damn sure likely t' knock out what little brains you seem t' have left. Now, forget this whole stupid thing an' go back t' your tent, Gilchrist, while I convince Silas he oughta go back t' sleep. Did he really run out on you like that?"

Glenn gave him a dirty look.

"You shoulda said somethin' about it before now."

"It wasn't yours to take care of, Hood. Still isn't. Now would you please stand aside."

"Hardheaded sonuvabitch, ain't you?"

"I have my moments."

"Can't talk you outa this?"

"Nope."

"All right then. Boys, we're gonna have us a fight. Drag in

some more wood an' build the fire up good so's everybody can see. An' Silas, you take off them pistols an' knives. This here is a fistfight, not a shootin' match."

"I ain't fighting to no pansy rules, Joshua."

"Nobody is asking you to," Glenn put in. "I know better than to think you would honor rules even if you agreed to them. After all, a man who would turn tail and run away at the first—"

"I already done told you t' quit sayin' that, mister."

"You know how to shut me up, Silas. But I say you aren't only a coward, you aren't even man enough to make me stop telling the truth about you."

"Damn you!" With a roar and a great swelling of his muscles, Silas balled his hands into huge fists and charged hard and fast.

He was four inches taller than Glenn and weighed at least half a hundredweight more than the wiry engineer.

And Silas was mad.

He bore down on Glenn with all the awesome force and speed of an enraged bull going after a matador's scarlet cape.

Glenn Gilchrist, his fists still cocked in the awkward and seemingly absurd style of the amateur pugilist, stood calmly awaiting the charge.

CHAPTER

39

As he charged, Silas Short launched a haymaker that started waist-high and slashed toward Glenn Gilchrist's face with all the force and nastiness of a Missouri mule's corn-fed kick. If it had landed, the fight would have ended then and there. If it had landed.

Glenn's light, skipping dance carried him out of the way of Short's punch by a scant inch or so.

And as Silas rushed past behind his failed blow, Glenn's left jab impacted smartly on his ear. The blow was not particularly heavy. In fact it barely stung. It was the insult of the thing that infuriated Silas so that he stopped, spun and rushed again.

Once more he charged blindly past while Glenn annoyed him with a pair of stinging jabs to the ear, to the other ear this time.

Amid the howls and yammering of his fellow scouts, Silas pulled up short and snorted.

"The little fella draws first blood," one of the scouts shouted.

"What's the matter, Silas? He too big for ya?" another added.

As much puzzled as angry, Silas swiped at a light, tickling sensation on the side of his neck. His hand came back streaked with red. One of those seemingly ineffectual jabs had opened a small cut on Silas's ear, and this first show of blood had led to the laughter of his peers.

Truly furious now, but made the wiser by experience, Silas quelled an impulse to wildly charge again and forced himself to slow down and think. He held his fists up in a guard of sorts and moved in closer to Gilchrist.

"Aw, you're wanting to box now," Glenn said. "Very sensible."

Silas scowled and, measuring his man, took aim and threw a hard right hand.

Glenn's awkward, high-cocked left flicked sideways, blocking Silas's blow on his forearm and diverting it harmlessly to the side. And while Short was unprotected, Glenn had time to jab, jab, jab again with his lightning left fist, each sharp jab smacking solidly onto the bridge of Silas's nose.

Silas sniffed, a runnel of blood seeping from his nose and into his mustache. He shook his head and, scowling, bore in again.

Silas moved doggedly forward, and Glenn danced lightly back and forth, in and out. With each bounce toward his massive opponent, Glenn scored another flickering jab or elusive hook. Lefts, lefts, then a right or two and back to the darting lefts.

Silas's face became a mask of bloody frustration. He wheezed and snarled, futilely punched air and swore, punched thin air and swore some more.

Glenn Gilchrist's fancy pugilism was cutting Silas to pieces bit by bit, and the catcalls and whistles of the scouts only served to add to the big man's humiliation.

The commotion was heard by men in the surrounding camps, and soon there was a solid ring of onlookers gathered tightly around the combatants.

Inevitably someone among the spectators expressed an opinion as to the outcome and someone else dissented. Immediately the opinions were backed with cash, most of the scouts choosing to bet against their companion Silas, while a majority of the Irish track gang put their money on size and strength over quick cleverness. Joshua Hood was drafted as judge and final arbiter of the betting.

While that was going on, Silas continued to wade into Glenn Gilchrist's snapping left jabs and jarring right hooks and uppercuts.

Silas was game even if he was not well versed in the fine art of fisticuffs, and he came back time and time again. And as often withdrew, usually with another cut or split somewhere about his face or head. His beard was as red with blood as if he were an Irishman himself.

Glenn continued to dance and punch, dance and punch, dart and pummel. "Drop, damn you," he hissed at one point. "You know you're whipped, so why don't you drop?"

Silas bowed his neck and covered his face with his left forearm while he shuffled in again with brutish resolve. The knuckles of Glenn's flying left hand connected with the cartilage in Silas's right ear, and the lobe of the ear split open, spilling more blood onto Silas's already soaked shirt collar.

But there was no quit in the big man. He hunched his shoulders and bore in again, this time ripping a low right hand that swept in beneath Glenn's high guard.

The punch buried itself wrist-deep in Glenn's belly, doubling him over and sending him staggering backward.

A roar of approval went up from the men in the crowd who had bet on Silas Short to win, and for that moment Glenn shared the feelings of the gladiators of old when the Roman masses turned their thumbs downward in their lust for blood.

With a shout of victory, Silas bulled in behind his success. He clamped his two fists together into one great, battering club and smashed Glenn over the head while Glenn was still bent over from the first numbing punch.

Glenn staggered and nearly fell but managed to right himself and backpedal away, gasping for breath and bleeding profusely from a split in his scalp.

Silas cried out again and bounded forward. His blood fully up, he abandoned the use of his fists and lifted one moccasin-clad foot into the pit of Glenn's stomach.

The sound of air being driven from Glenn's lungs was loud enough to be heard by the stunned crowd as the tide of the combat swiftly shifted to Silas's advantage.

Silas tried to kick Glenn in the belly again, but this time all his foot contacted was Glenn's arms as he clutched himself in agony.

Silas gave up his attack on Glenn's gut and this time kicked at Glenn's head. His foot struck Glenn on the forehead, snapping him upright and sending him tottering backward, his arms flailing in an effort to maintain his balance.

Grinning evilly now behind the bloody mask that was left of his face, Silas moved in for the kill. He aimed a kick at Glenn's groin.

Glenn stepped back and swept his right hand upward, grabbing Silas behind the ankle and lifting.

The unexpected counter took Silas by surprise, and with his own body weight moving in the same direction that Glenn was pulling him he lost his balance and crashed heavily onto his back, the force of the fall driving the breath from him. Silas lay on the ground, stunned and defenseless.

Glenn was in no condition to follow up on his brief advantage. He moved backward instead and bent over at the waist, sucking in great, strength-giving gulps of fresh air.

Silas's kick in the face had opened a gash over Glenn's right eyebrow, and he took a moment now to wipe the blood hastily out of his eyes.

Silas had rolled over and gotten to his knees. He remained there kneeling on the ground for long seconds, gathering his strength as he too took in great gulps of air. Then, shaking himself like a dog come ashore fresh from a swim, Silas stood upright.

As he did so, Glenn stepped in and, measuring his target, started a punch from his boot tops. Glenn put every ounce of weight and muscle he possessed into that one sweeping blow.

The flat of Glenn's fist landed flush on the tip of Silas Short's nose. Glenn could hear as well as feel the loud pop as cartilage gave way and snapped clean in two. A spray of blood made a red-gold halo effect in the firelight as Silas's nose was pulped, and the big man's head snapped sharply backward.

Silas's eyes lost focus and rolled back in his head even before the big scout had time to fall. His thick body swayed backward and then, muscle and balance coordinating by instinct even when there was no sentient intelligence left to direct them, came upright for a moment. Then, like a man shot dead while standing erect, Silas toppled forward. He fell facedown and hit the earth with no more resistance than a haunch of cooling meat. He didn't even bounce when he fell.

One of Silas's arms was flung to the side, his hand flopping into the circle of live coals at the edge of the fire. Glenn bent wearily over and took Silas by the sleeve, pulling his arm away from the fire. Glenn was so wobbly and weak from the exertion that he very nearly fell on top of Silas's inert form. But he did not. He wavered for a moment, then stood fully upright and took in a series of long, deep breaths.

"All right," he said to the stunned crowd. "Which of you guys were dumb enough to bet on him?"

There was a moment of silence, then the men began to laugh. There was considerable exchanging of funds for a few minutes there, then the crowd began to disperse.

Joshua Hood walked over and handed Glenn his shirt and coat. "You okay, Gilchrist?"

"Yeah." Glenn grinned. "More or less."

"You did better'n I expected you would."

"Better than he thought I would too."

"You know, of course, that you've cost me a man."

"He'll recover," Glenn said.

"From the fight, sure, but not from the humiliation. Come mornin', ol' Silas will be rolling his bed and riding outa here. Count on it."

"I hadn't thought of that, but if you are expecting me to apologize, you are going to be disappointed. I'd do it all over again if I had to." He smiled. "Assuming I could do it a second time, that is. Damn, but that man packs a wallop."

"You wanta know something, college boy? If you was t' get into it again, my money'd be on you t' beat him then just the same as you done now. You did all right."

"Which one of us did you bet on this time?"

Joshua laughed. But didn't answer the question. What he did say was "If it makes you feel any better, Gilchrist, Silas would be out o' a job tomorra whether you whipped him tonight or not."

"How's that?"

"My boys deserve better than bein' asked t' ride with somebody they can't trust if they get in a tight. If Silas don't quit—though I know he will—but if he don't quit on his own, then I'll fire him anyhow." Joshua looked pointedly down at Silas, who had begun to come around again and was sitting on the ground beside the fire now, listening to the conversation taking place a few feet away.

"Need some help gettin' back t' your tent?" Joshua offered Glenn.

"No, I'm fine now. Thanks."

"G'night then, college boy."

"Good night, Natty Bumpo."

"Who?"

Glenn smiled and shook his head. "You wouldn't know him. Good night."

Slowly and in some pain—but head high and with considerable pride—Glenn returned to the comforts of his own camp area and the cot that awaited him there.

CHAPTER

40

Megan poured water into the enameled basin and plunged her hands in. The clean water turned pink and then a pale shade of red as the blood that was caked on Megan's hands dissolved into solution.

She would have cried, she thought, except she was too tired for tears.

It was . . . She had no idea what time it was. The middle of the night, that was all she knew.

She glanced behind her at the mercifully unconscious form of Barney Martin, stickman—no, make that former survey crew stickman—for John Dumbrough.

Megan could fully appreciate now the horror that Glenn Gilchrist had so narrowly escaped, for Barney Martin had been among those wounded in the Sioux attack on Dumbrough's surveyors. That had been a matter of days earlier—Megan was too weary to think back for an exact number of days, and the time did not matter anyway, not now—time enough in any event for sepsis to set into the poor man's wounds.

Dr. Wiseman had sent for Megan just a little earlier, when Barney's anguished, pain-wracked writhing woke him and called his attention to the sudden, virulent onset of the gangrene. It was an ugly task Thaddeus asked her to help with, but Megan had become the closest thing to a nurse available at end-of-track. And she would not have been able to bear the thought of refusing whatever small measure of comfort she had to offer to the suffering patient.

Nevertheless it sickened her to see the cruel efficiency of Thaddeus's healing measures.

While Megan held a thick pad of gauze over Barney's nose and mouth and let some vile-smelling liquid drip onto it, the fumes of which rendered the patient unconscious, Thaddeus deftly and without expression used his tray of knives and clamps and cotton sewing thread to separate Barney's lower leg from the knee joint and cut the infected part away.

Thaddeus, of course, had taken the whole thing in stride, even describing to her each measure that he was undertaking, his voice an emotionless monotone.

"The patient is stable and in no great discomfort," he'd said, "so we can take our time and make his stump nice and pretty, eh? Hand me that clamp there, please, Megan. Yes, that one. Now the scalpel. No, the one with the curved blade. Thank you. Let me get the tendon out of the way . . . there! . . . and I can tie off the artery . . . That's right. Now cut it below the knot . . . and there. Now tie this off and this and . . . cut. Very nice, if I do say so."

Megan tried not to watch, and yet she felt compelled to see everything she could. She was fascinated and repulsed at one and the same time.

The most amazing thing to her was that, because the leg was being taken at a joint, there was no need for the ugly bone saws to be used. Thaddeus severed the joint with a few dexterous stabs of his knives and a little prying effort. In all, the operation was almost as simple as cutting a chicken leg away from the thigh for frying.

Toward the end, though, she had been so interested in watching that she neglected to drip ether onto the pad frequently enough, and Barney came out of the anesthesia before Thaddeus was done.

That was terrible, and only the thick straps that bound him to the table kept the patient from squirming out of Thaddeus's grasp.

"Careful, Megan," Thaddeus warned when Megan tried to amend her oversight by dumping a stream of liquid ether onto the gauze. "Too much of that will kill him, and I wouldn't want to save him from the gangrene just to lay him out with medications, eh?"

She flushed and dropped the tin of ether with a horrified cry. Thaddeus got everything back under control again and finished the job he was doing, arranging folds of living flesh and sewing them in place over the startlingly white knee joint as calmly and as competently as a good seamstress sewing a ruche into a piece of fine tulle.

"There," he said when he was done. "That should heal nicely, and I wager before long the only pain he'll feel from it will be ghost pains."

"Ghost pains?"

"It's a phenomenon all physicians know about but none understand. None that I've heard of anyway. For some reason patients often report feeling pain in limbs that are no longer attached. That is, there are pain sensations or sometimes prickling, tingling, even needles-and-pins feelings, that feel as if they are coming from where there used to be a foot or an arm or whatever. We can't explain it, but we can't deny it either. Too many patients report it for it all to be made up. So we call it ghost pain and try to avoid being trapped into explanations of the unexplainable."

"I see," Megan said, unsure that she did, but willing to accept Thaddeus's word.

All of that, however, had been some minutes ago. Now Megan was trying to make up for her lapse by taking over the rather messy chore of cleaning up the operating theater while Thaddeus stepped outside for a breath of air untainted by ether.

She tidied up as best she knew how and paused to check on Barney Martin. His color seemed good and his heartbeat strong and regular. Thaddeus had said the patient came through the operation in strong condition, and so it seemed he had. As usual Thaddeus had been right.

Megan made sure Barney was strapped firmly in place—it would not do for him to thrash about and break open the sutures holding his stump together—then went outside to join Thaddeus in the cool, refreshing night air.

"I want to thank you, Megan. I couldn't have done nearly so well with him if it hadn't been for your help."

She blushed. "I almost ruined it for you, Thaddeus. I know I did."

"Nonsense. You did just fine, whether you realize it or not, and I appreciate your help more than you can know." He hesitated. "Not just with this man tonight either, Megan. You've been a godsend to me all through this past week, indeed ever since Gilchrist was brought in. You've been wonderful."

Megan was still blushing.

"May I ask you something?"

"Of course, Thaddeus."

"Are you . . . That is to say, is there an understanding between you and young Gilchrist?"

It was a blunt question and most unexpected. But it was a fair question too, Megan admitted. And in truth it was a question to which she herself had to give some thought before she answered. "I . . . No, Thaddeus. Not really. I like Glenn. Very much. But . . . there is no understanding between us. I don't say that it couldn't happen someday or that it won't. But right now . . . no."

"Joshua Hood is courting you too, I believe?"

Megan nodded. "Yes, I suppose so, but I have no understanding, as you put it, with Joshua either. He and Glenn are both wonderful people, and I like them very much. I would even have to admit that I am attracted to both of them, different though they both are. But I am not committed to either of them. Why do you ask, Thaddeus? You are much too much the gentleman to ask something so personal without a very good reason."

Thaddeus coughed into his fist and stood motionless for a moment.

Then, awkwardly and suddenly shy but determined to play out this thing that he'd started, he stepped close to her and put his great arms about her.

Megan looked up in surprise, and Thaddeus bent his mouth to hers.

She felt the trembling in his lips and the gentleness in his arms, and she felt something within herself melt in response.

Big and powerful though he was, Thaddeus Wiseman was one of the most gentle of men, and Megan found herself responding to his embrace more avidly than she would ever have suspected.

She found herself returning his kiss with fervor, and she pressed her slim body tightly against him.

She could feel his response to her, and her heartbeat stirred and quickened.

The feel of Thaddeus's beard was soft and as gentle as the man who wore it.

He pulled her closer to him, and his tongue probed lightly into Megan's mouth.

Megan groaned and pressed herself to his body.

Thaddeus moaned low in his throat and sought her breast with one trembling hand.

The shock of that intimate touch brought Megan back to her senses, and she wrenched herself away from his embrace. "No!" she gasped.

Thaddeus released her at once. "I am . . . so sorry, Megan."

She tossed her head back to throw some straying wisps of bright red hair, hair as flaming red as Thaddeus's, out of her face. She looked at the huge, gentle physician, staring him straight in the eyes boldly and with pride. "Don't be sorry, Thaddeus. God knows I'm not."

"But . . ."

"Don't be sorry, Thaddeus. Don't you dare apologize to me. I wanted that every bit as much as you did. But I don't want all the baggage that goes with a love affair. I'll be no man's plaything, Thaddeus Wiseman. You should know that."

"I would never ask you to be, Megan O'Connell. Never."

"All right then." She nodded. "I . . . I like you, Thaddeus. I admire you. And I have to say that I shall be thinking of you in a new light in future. If you still want me to."

"Yes. Very much so." He reached for her again, and Megan allowed herself to be drawn into his arms once more. This time when he kissed her, it was slowly and with pleasure but without insistence. Thaddeus was willing to let her set the pace for this most pleasant exploration.

She returned his kiss, warming to the sensations of it. She felt a fluttering low in her belly and a slight weakness in her knees, but she was no mere girl to be swept past control.

When the moth threatened to be drawn too close to the flame, she backed away, and Thaddeus loosened his hold on her and let her withdraw as she wished.

"That," he whispered into the side of her neck, "was powerful."

"That," she whispered back at him, "most certainly was."

"I feel weak," he said.

"Don't . . . Please don't tempt me, Thaddeus. No more. Not right now. Please."

"I want you, Megan. I want to pick you up and carry you inside. I want to take you to my bed and undress you and make slow, quiet love to you. I want to taste every inch of your body and bathe you with my kisses. I want to take you to heights you've never known before and . . ."

Megan was trembling and weak now. His words, the thought of what he promised . . . "No. Thaddeus . . . Please."

"I want to do all those things, Megan, and a thousand times more." He reached out and took her gently by the shoulders.

"Before God, Thaddeus, please don't ask this of me. Not so soon. Not now. Give me time to think. Please."

Thaddeus stood over her in the moonlight. So close. So strong and masculine and powerful. And yet so gentle and kind and . . . She shivered. Megan wanted no entanglements right now. She had no time for such. But her body had no such reluctance. Her body made its own insistent demands. And those demands were on Thaddeus's side.

"Please?" she whispered, knowing that if he insisted, if he picked her up and carried her off, she would not resist. If he did that at this moment, she would most assuredly give in to him.

He hesitated, his hands warm on her.

And then, swallowing hard, he nodded and stepped backward, letting go his hold on her.

"I've fallen in love with you, Megan O'Connell. So much so that I would rather lose you than cause you hurt. Go home now, Megan. Go home and go to bed alone. But know this, Megan. I love you. I love you more than Glenn Gilchrist does or ever could do, and I love you infinitely more than Joshua Hood does or ever will. I love you and I'll not let you forget it. Do you hear me, Megan O'Connell? Do you know what I'm telling you?"

Megan felt like crying. With gratitude to this great and gentle man. And in frustrated disappointment as well. She nodded and, rising onto her tiptoes, once more kissed him tenderly on the mouth, but this time only briefly. Then she turned and ran swiftly into the night.

CHAPTER
41

"Tell me, gentlemen, what can we expect?"

Joshua looked up with some distaste at the newspaperman. Reggie White had been invited along on the expedition by Captain Taney, not by either Joshua or General Dodge, and as far as Joshua was concerned the man was not welcome.

The column was three days beyond the farthermost rails now, two days past the slough where the survey party was attacked. Joshua expected to reach Spotted Bull's village— or anyway the place where he expected Spotted Bull's village to be—sometime late tomorrow.

In fact he was counting on arriving in the vicinity late in the day. If they could once gain entry to the village, Indian protocol demanded that they be received as honored guests and allowed to remain overnight. Joshua was banking on his own reputation and General Dodge's integrity to win a peace if they could manage to stay overnight, because then there would be time enough to talk the thing through at the inevitable council fire.

If, that is, things worked out the way he hoped, and if Spotted Bull was where Joshua expected the Sioux leader to be.

Regardless, Joshua felt no inclination to share these hopes and plans with White. The newspaperman seemed as big a fool as Medgar Taney, and the two of them had become thick as the proverbial thieves since riding out from the rail end.

If anything, Joshua thought, White's presence fed fuel to Taney's bullheaded intransigence. The two of them seemed quite the pair, and where one was found, the other was generally close by.

"Reckon what we can expect," Joshua answered the cocky newsman, "is salt pork an' beans." The column was stopped for lunch. And Joshua's "guess" as to the menu could hardly be considered a daring one. Salt pork and beans was what they'd had every meal so far since leaving end-of-track. General Dodge hadn't complained about the fare or expressed any second thoughts about leaving the camp tenders behind, but Joshua certainly was having some regrets about the general's decision to rough it.

"I meant about the Indians," White said.

"What Indians?" Joshua squinted and peered around the horizon. "You been seein' Indians an' not telling us, mister?"

"You know what I meant," White accused.

Joshua scratched his chin and played dumb. "I do?"

"Oh . . . forget it," White snapped. He turned on his heel and stalked off.

"You really should quit goading the man like that, Hood. Lord knows what he'll write about you when we return to civilization," the general said. Dodge was squatting next to the fire Joshua had laid, waiting for their can of coffee water to boil.

Joshua looked at him and grinned. "It won't matter nohow, General. He'll most likely misspell m' name, an' nobody'll know it's me he's makin' fun of."

Dodge laughed.

"That coffee soon done?" Joshua asked.

"It hasn't even started to boil yet. Are you all right, Hood? You seem nervous."

"I'm all right, sir. It's just . . ." Joshua had no answer to give. No sensible one, anyway. It was just that he felt . . . nervous. No, not nervous so much as jittery. Antsy, some called it. He didn't know why. Didn't deny it either, at least not to himself.

"I think it's coming to a boil now," the general said, leaning forward and staring down into the can. "I'll put the beans in now. It won't be long."

"Yes, sir." Joshua didn't want the coffee so much as he wanted something to occupy himself with. He took another long, searching look around the horizon.

They were well out of sight of the Platte now, but it was somewhere off to the south, out beyond a line of low, rolling hills. To the east there was empty grassland and to the west the lightly wooded continuation of the hills that started somewhere south and ran in a north-by-northwest string. To their immediate north were more hills.

The land here was more heavily wooded than any Joshua had seen in months. The trees, cedar for the most part, were low and scrubby, but there were a good many of them. Joshua was sure that said something about the availability of water in the soil, but he didn't know what the message was. A farmer probably could have said, but Joshua was no farmer.

Joshua turned back to the general and said, "I think those soldier boys have the beans an' salt horse ready. If you give me your plate, I'll go over there an'—"

He was interrupted by the raucous blast of a bugle sounding boots and saddles.

"What the hell?"

"Mind your cinches, boys, mind your cinches," a sergeant called. "Damn it, Moncrief, don't you get on that horse without checking your cinch first, I told you. Weatherly,

Avery, Betz—as skirmishers. Flowers, Daughtery, Felix, Gertz—flankers, please."

General Dodge was standing, on his tiptoes and craning to see what it was that had prompted the army to go on alert like this.

"Over there," Joshua said, finally spotting the disturbance himself. "See in that line o' trees, sir? There's a band o' Indians over there."

"Sioux?"

"Yeah, I'd say they are. Hard to tell at this distance, though."

"Can you see if they are painted for war, Hood?"

Joshua smiled. Thanks to people like the newspaperman White, it seemed like every white man Joshua met believed Indians had to be painted ready for war before they could shoot an arrow at anybody. The truth, of course, was that the painting was a ritualistic thing that was deemed desirable and good. But it sure as hell wasn't necessary, and a Sioux warrior or any other could and darn sure would throw himself into a fight regardless of what clothes or decorations he happened to be wearing at the time.

"It's too far t' see, sir."

"They seem to be coming this way."

"Yes, sir, an' there's more of 'em than I thought. A couple dozen, anyhow."

"Do you think they intend to parlay?"

"More likely, sir, they're gonna test that white flag we're flyin'."

"You mean they will make a sham charge?"

"Yes, sir. Somethin' like that."

A private who looked too young to be shaving as yet came thundering over to them from the cluster of guidons and banners that marked Captain Taney's headquarters position.

"Begging the general's pardon, sir, but Cap'n Taney sends his compliments and a request that you civilians stay well back. There may be fighting, sir."

"Nicely said, Private. Please ask your captain to call upon me before he engages."

"As you say, sir." The private saluted and wheeled his horse away.

"Bright lad," Dodge said to Joshua. "You know good and well that imbecile he works for never said anything about compliments. Or requests either, for that matter." He smiled. "That private should be a diplomat. Better yet, he should be the officer in—No, forget I said that, please."

"Said what, General? I didn't hear nothin'." Joshua winked at Dodge. "Well, lookee there. I believe your friend Taney is comin' to call."

Taney, with the second lieutenant named Howard at his stirrup and the battalion colors bearer half a length behind and the newspaperman White bumping along in the rear, was loping toward them. The captain, whose field uniform was no less gaudy than his dress uniform, came to a sliding, dust-raising halt entirely too close to the unmounted civilians.

"Thank you, Captain. If you would be so good as to—"

"I've no time for this, mister," Taney interrupted, his voice cold and his manner brusque.

"I merely wanted to remind you—"

"I told you once, mister, I have no time for this. We are in imminent danger of attack by hostile forces."

"Nonsense, Captain. Mr. Hood here has already told you what to expect. Those Sioux will come close and make a lot of noise, but they are only testing us to see if we intend to honor the truce we've declared with that flag. Our orders are to hold our fire and maintain our position here. We'll not respond in a threatening manner, and they will go back and tell Spotted Bull that. It's what we've expected right along, Captain, and what we want to happen. Now please don't—"

"You don't get it, do you? You are just another of those washed up, gray-haired old men I was talking about the other night." Taney looked snotty and arrogant, and behind him, White was taking all this in. Joshua felt like hauling Taney down off his high horse—literally in this case—and trying to bash some sense into him. Except he knew General Dodge wouldn't approve, and so he kept his opinions to himself, except for whatever might show in his glare.

"For the record, Mr. Dodge—are you making note of all this, Reggie?—for the record, Mr. Civilian Dodge, my orders were to accede to your strategic command. And so I have done. But now my men are in danger of attack by hostiles. I therefore have the duty and the obligation to assume immediate tactical command. This supersedes your authority, Mr. Dodge, and does so entirely within the scope of my orders from departmental headquarters."

"That's all well and good, Captain. I'm glad to see you know your rules and regulations. So do I. I am not quarreling with your authority, man. I merely wanted to remind you that our mission here is peaceful. We are not to antagonize those Sioux. We will let them come as close as they like, and we will stand firm. Above all, though, we will not shoot. Not even if they fire first. Mr. Hood assures me that if they do any shooting, it will be into the air, just making noise and creating a fuss to see how we react. They will—"

"What they will be, mister, is dead. Because I will not risk the lives of my troops here. If those Indians maintain their assault on us—"

"What assault? They're riding in plain view across nearly a mile of open terrain. Why, they won't even reach us for a good five minutes. They aren't assaulting us, Captain. They are testing us. We must not be found wanting, sir."

"I'll tell you what's wanting, and that is your courage. Believe me, I can smash the entire Sioux nation if I ever get a crack at them. Then see if anyone wants your half-baked peace." Taney turned his head and spat. "You can't trust a stinking Indian to keep his word. It's about time people like you learned that."

"Taney, I'm warning you—"

"Very well, mister. I consider myself warned. Just see that you do too. Lieutenant."

"Yes, sir?"

"Prepare your men for battle, sir. Line abreast, carbine volley followed by a charge with sabers."

Joshua couldn't believe what he was hearing. Saber charge? Taney was abandoning the advantage of firepower for the glory of steel. The only reason Joshua could think anyone would do a thing so stupid was to make the illustrations that much more dramatic when Reginald White wrote about the engagement for his readers somewhere way the hell and gone back east.

Joshua wondered if Medgar Taney had any small idea just how good a Sioux warrior was when it came to fighting at close quarters. A stone war club, after all, might not look so glittering and fine when it was held side by side with a cavalry saber, but a war club could split a skull open— white or red, it made no difference—like a melon dropped onto an anvil. "Jesus," Joshua breathed.

"Captain!" General Dodge barked, his voice stern and commanding.

This time, though, Taney refused to respond. He turned haughtily away and spurred his mount back to the head of his men.

Joshua stood staring in disbelief as the orders were given. The two troops of yellow-leg cavalry wheeled prettily, horses curveting and sidestepping as the troopers guided them into a long, thin line.

Two troops. Taney said—hell, Taney no doubt believed— he could take his two troops and ride through the whole of the Sioux nation.

Lucky for him there wasn't the whole of the Sioux nation, or even the whole of Spotted Bull's band, facing him now. There were not more than two dozen Sioux riding into the teeth of the cavalrymen.

This time, at least, each side knew the other was there. This time there would be no surprises.

"Well, General," Joshua said, "the Sioux have come t' see do we mean that white flag. I reckon the good captain there is tellin' them. Soon as he's done making an ass of himself, we'll turn an' head back. No sense going any further."

"The good captain, as you choose to put it, is soon to find himself a civilian, I suspect," Dodge said, his voice thick with closely held fury.

"It couldn't happen to a nicer fella," Joshua said.

"They are coming close now. When do you think the Indians will begin demonstrating against Taney's position?"

" 'Bout a hundred yards. Closer if the soldiers don't do nothing. They'll start their hollering within seventy-five yards at the very latest an' ride within fifteen, ten yards in front o' the line if the soldiers aren't shooting. They'll make two, three passes like that, then head back."

"And when the soldiers open up?"

"When they do, if they do, the Sioux will know everything they come here t' learn. If that happens, they'll turn tail an' skedaddle right off. They won't hang around t' let the soldier boys kill 'em, an' I doubt they'll fight back. They'll just take their lesson an' carry it home like any sensible soul should."

The Sioux—they were close enough now that Joshua could see them better; they were Sioux all right and painted as if for war, or ritual—rode inside a hundred yards, sitting boldly upright with lances and bows and a few muzzle-loading rifles held in upraised fists.

Taney stood firm in front of them, his chin held high and defiant. Of course he was sitting at the head of a body of skilled troopers who outnumbered the Sioux roughly four to one.

"Ready," Taney called. "At my command." He raised his saber, then sharply dropped the point. "Fire!"

Flame and smoke rolled out from the thin line of blue-clad troopers.

Ahead of the volley several horses stumbled and three or four warriors fell. All but one of the Sioux, Joshua saw, were able to regain their feet and swing onto the back of another warrior's wheeling mount.

"That tears it, General. We're goin' home for sure now."

Exactly as Joshua had said they would, the Sioux offered no further resistance. But then that was not what they had come for. They turned their horses around and put the ponies into a hard run for the safety of the distant tree line.

"Dumb sonuvabitch," Joshua mumbled. He heard no disagreement from the general.

"Now what is he doing?" Dodge snapped.

Captain Taney had ridden his prancing mount ahead of the line of soldiers. He waved his saber wildly overhead and snatched back on his reins, spurring hard at the same time and causing his horse to rear with pain.

"With sabers, boys. Char-r-r-r-ge!"

And the whole blue line thundered off in pursuit of the handful of fleeing Sioux warriors.

"Jesus!" Joshua said, this time aloud.

"There's something . . . Damn it, General, I don't like this."

"What's wrong, Hood?"

"You see those Indian ponies, sir? How easy the soldiers is overtaking them? That ain't right, sir."

"Of course it is, Hood. It is only reasonable that grain-fed American horses will overtake grass-ranging ponies like those Indian mounts."

"In the long run that'll hold true, General, but in a sprint those short-coupled spotted horses oughta pull right away from the cavalry mounts. Look how much heavier loaded the big horses are. An' those ponies are built for short bursts o' speed anyhow. That's what's needed when you run buffalo, sir. Sprints, not long-distance running. There isn't no way the soldiers should be able t' get that close behind the Sioux, but it looks to me like the Indians are hanging just in front deliberate like." Joshua looked anxiously around, but there were no other Indians in sight.

"You know what I think, General? I think Captain Taney better be smart enough t' declare himself the winner an' not follow those Indians inta the trees."

"Really, Hood, I suspect your imagination is getting the better of you. I mean, I am no admirer of the captain there, but he does have two troops of well-armed and thoroughly disciplined soldiers at his back."

"He also has a bunch o' real mad Sioux warriors in front of him, sir. The question I'm asking myself at this point is just how *many* Sioux."

"I can't believe his command is in any danger. I mean, the Indians may turn and fight, certainly. But surely you don't believe—"

"I ain't saying I believe anything in particular, General. It's just that from what I know about Indians, well, if it was me, I'd as leave not ride inta them trees. That's all I'm saying, General."

Dodge stood with his arms folded and watched the soldiers press their charge not fifty, now closer to forty, yards behind the fleeing Sioux.

Between the general's camp fire and the scene of the brief skirmish, there burned the lunch fires so recently abandoned by the soldiers, with coffee cans boiling dry and untended beans scorching by the bucketful.

None of that mattered, but just beyond the cluster of dying fires stood, alone and useless, the limp white banner that had been a last hope for peace.

"They're almost to the trees now," Dodge said, as if Joshua weren't watching too. "If the captain feels as you do, Mr. Hood, this is his last chance to turn back."

"Yes, sir."

The Sioux disappeared into the screen of low, dense scrub cedar, and the bluecoat soldiers thundered after them with Medgar Taney waving his saber in the fore. The captain made an admittedly grand and glorious sight as he led his men in a charge with sabers drawn.

Joshua could see that much despite the distance. He frowned and shook his head. "I wish they hadn't done that."

"I just noticed something," Dodge said.

"Yes, sir?"

"That journalist. White. He seems to have gone with them."

"I figure his nose got trapped in Taney's backside, an' he couldn't get loose in time t' avoid bein' dragged along, sir."

Dodge tried to maintain a look of disapproval at the vulgarity, but he couldn't quite bring it off. "I suspect Mr. Durant would not approve of your attitude toward the press, Mr. Hood. You might keep that in mind in the future."

"Yes, sir," Joshua said with a grin that acknowledged he didn't mean a lick of it. Dodge was referring to Thomas Durant, vice president and chief driving force behind the Union Pacific, Credit Mobilier and all the other related companies and corporations involved in the great continent-spanning construction effort. Durant was as eager to court the press as Medgar Taney ever thought of being, the primary difference being that Durant was slicker, smoother and simply much, much better at it than Medgar Taney.

"Did you hear something, Hood?"

Joshua shook his head. Then he listened more closely.

And turned suddenly pale.

"Oh, Jesus," he muttered.

For somewhere far off in the distance there was a soft, rattling crackle like that of innumerable twigs being broken.

"Would the Indians be well armed with rifles, Hood?"

"No, sir, they'll mostly be using bows. Clubs and spears for close in."

The general looked grim. "I don't like the sound of it. That isn't volley fire. It's entirely undisciplined."

"I don't understand, General."

"If Taney had his men under control, their fire would

be coordinated. We would hear a contained burst, then a pause and another burst. This way, with this constant, ragged crackle, what it tells me, Hood, is that those men are acting as individuals, not as closely coordinated squads or troop formations."

"That don't sound good, General."

"Indeed it does not."

The firing continued, but slowly, inexorably, the battle sounds began to diminish.

"How many warriors would you say the Sioux have, Mr. Hood?"

"All together or just Spotted Bull?"

Dodge shrugged. His entire concentration seemed to be on the faint noises coming across the grass from afar, but Joshua knew he was paying attention.

"If I had to guess, sir, I'd say five, maybe six hundred warriors willing t' follow Spotted Bull. He don't command them, mind, but I'd say there's about that many that'd rally to him if he called. Then there'd be allied bands—other Sioux an' some northern Cheyenne, whatever. Put 'em all together, General, I reckon Spotted Bull might be able t' raise over a thousand men. Could be as much as twelve, fourteen hundred." Joshua thought on the question a moment longer, then nodded. "Yeah, call it about that. I wouldn't think no more'n that many."

"At least six hundred, though," Dodge said.

"Yes, sir."

The general looked grim. And sad, Joshua thought.

"Y'know who I feel bad for?"

"Yes, Mr. Hood. The same men I feel badly about. Those poor, gallant, criminally poorly led young men whose lives are being wasted on Medgar Taney's arrogant quest for glory and promotion."

Joshua nodded.

In less than twenty minutes the rattle of gunfire faded away, and after that there was no more sound from the distant trees.

Still Joshua and General Dodge waited. And after a time, five minutes—it might have been less, but it seemed a very long time indeed—after a time, a small group of Indians appeared at the edge of the trees.

"See 'em, General?"

"Yes. What do you think they want?"

"I'd say they know we're here. They prob'ly even know who we are."

"If they come this way . . . ?"

"We run like hell, General. They ain't our friends an' they ain't our allies. They might regret what all has happened just like we do, but there wouldn't be no quarter given if they was to catch us. That's just their way, General. They wouldn't mean nothing personal about it."

"Like being bitten by a half-tamed coyote? It isn't his fault, just his nature."

"Yes, sir. Very much like that."

"What do we do now, Mr. Hood?"

"Stay where you are, sir. I'll be right back."

Joshua walked at a deliberate pace to the area where Medgar Taney's headquarters had been. The hickory flagstaff holding the white truce flag had been planted firm in the hard Nebraska soil. Joshua took hold of it and twisted, pulling the shaft free. He looked long and hard at the Sioux who were observing him from afar. Then, his movements still deliberate and almost ceremonial, he furled the white cloth and laid it onto the ground.

Then he walked back to join General Dodge.

"Come on, sir. Reckon we'd best mount up an' move

along before those boys out there change their minds 'bout lettin' us."

"What about . . . you know?"

"We'll tell the army where t' find them, sir."

"Don't you think we should make sure . . . I mean . . ."

"General, the fact that them Sioux are setting their horses over there where we can see 'em, an' be seen by them, that's all we need to know. Now, please, sir. Let's mount up nice an' slow an' ride outa here without making any sudden moves or showing any fear."

Joshua lifted his near stirrup and hung it over his saddle horn while he carefully tightened his cinches. Then he mounted and waited while General Dodge did the same.

"What about all this equipment, Hood? We can't just abandon it to the Indians, can we?"

"General, you can do whatever you like, but there ain't a damn thing here that I need more'n my hair. So with all due respect, sir, I suggest we get the hell outa here."

Dodge reined his horse back toward the railroad, and a moment later Joshua did the same.

Joshua never looked back to see what the Sioux were doing.

"Are you Miss...um...," the man consulted a slip of paper in his hand, "Miss Megan Gallagher?"

"Close enough," Megan said. Probably a message from Aileen, she guessed. Aileen often forgot that Megan had dropped Keith's name and returned to their maiden name of O'Connell. Probably, Megan assumed further, Aileen was responding to Megan's wire asking her to halt the shipment of supplies until Megan could find the money to pay for it all.

"Delivery for you, Miz Gallagher," the man went on.

"Oh, that can't be right. I'm not expecting any packages."

"It isn't a package, ma'am. It's a whole wagon load of stuff."

"But that can't...I mean, I haven't ordered...That is to say I did order some things, but I canceled that order. Really I did."

"Miz Gallagher, all I know is that I got a wagon full of stuff out here and it's all shipped to you."

"But I haven't any money to pay for—"

"Ma'am, it wasn't shipped COD. This stuff is all paid for," the drayman said.

"I don't understand."

"Look, lady, it's late and I'm hot and tired and a week away from home. I don't want to argue with you. Honest,

I don't. All I want to do is make my delivery and buy a drink somewhere. Here, if you'll just let me unload so I can make my turnaround. I got a wife at home who's in the family way, and I'd sure like to be there before the kid is born. She says it's to be sometime this November. You know what I mean?"

Megan smiled. "I really don't mean to be a fussbudget, sir, but I really don't understand. You say you have a delivery, a large delivery, and it is addressed to me but it is all prepaid?"

"Yes, ma'am. The goods are prepaid, so is the freight. I have it all written down right here."

"I still don't understand."

"Lady, there isn't all that much *to* understand. If you are Miz Gallagher, then me and my helper will unload it. Just please tell me where you want the stuff piled."

"May I ask what freight you have out there for me?"

"Now that, lady, I can answer. It's all written down on my bill of lading here." He handed the paper to her.

Megan's eyes bulged. Pickled sausages. Pickled eggs. Hams. Cases upon cases of soda crackers. Beer. Grain alcohol. More beer. More raw alcohol. Everything she had asked Aileen to send and many, many times more. There was enough on this list to completely restock and resupply the saloon three times over.

"You said this is all already paid for?"

"Lady, for the last time, yes. It's all paid for."

"And it is all addressed to me?"

"You see it right there at the top there, don't you? That's you, isn't it?"

"Yes, that is me, all right."

"Then, lady, there isn't anything for you and me to argue about except where you want us to put your stuff."

"I suppose . . . I mean . . . back there, I think. Behind that canvas?" She pointed to the kitchen/storage area that had been largely unused since she set up business here.

"Fine, lady. Thank you." Shaking his head, the drayman walked out.

Megan watched as box after box and crate after crate was brought in and piled high. By the time the unloading was complete, there was barely room enough behind the canvas partition for kitchen purposes.

Also by the time the unloading was complete, Megan found herself surrounded by the people who loved her the most. By Rachel and Victor, by Glenn Gilchrist and Joshua Hood, by Henry Harrison Armbruster and Thaddeus Wiseman. Somehow word of the mystery seemed to have spread, and they'd all come to see.

"Would you have had anything to do with all this?" she demanded of the bunch of them.

"Whatever do you mean, Megan?" Glenn asked innocently.

"I mean . . . all of this. It's paid for. The man tells me it has all been paid for."

"How nice for you," Thaddeus said.

"Coulda been worse," Joshua added.

"But I don't understand," Megan complained.

"What is there to understand, dear lady?" Henry Harrison asked in a voice of sweet reason. "Just think what it means."

"What it means?"

"But of course," Henry Harrison said. "Think about it, Megan. You have all this stock on hand and no investment to speak of. If you were to sell it at a penny a glass, you would be making a profit, wouldn't you?"

"I suppose I would be, but whoever paid for this spent more than a penny a glass for it."

"Is that person or persons, whoever he or they may be, are he or they seeking a profit?"

"N-n-no, I don't suppose they are. Or he is. Or . . . whatever."

"The point, Megan, is that with this stock you can afford to compete with Ike Norman's prices. You can undercut *him* if you want. He's charging two cents, you can advertise a penny. And still deliver a quality product to your customers. How long do you think it will be, Megan, before Ike Norman caves in and asks you to call off the price war? A week? Two?"

"I don't know about this," Megan said. "I mean . . . where did all this come from? Who does it belong to?"

"Obviously it belongs to you," Glenn said. "It says so right on that invoice, doesn't it?"

"How would you know what it says on this invoice?"

"Isn't that what you told us it says?" he countered.

"I can't remember what I told you," Megan complained. She was feeling more and more confused. "This . . . Did you all band together and do this? Well did you?"

No one answered. She had a good idea, judging by the expressions on some of the faces before her, that yes indeed they had.

But none of them wanted to take the credit, or the blame, for it.

Megan gave them each the good, sound glare that they so richly deserved.

And then she began to cry.

Henry Harrison Armbruster was wrong about one thing, though. It took Ike Norman just three days to seek Megan out and ask her to terminate the price war and allow both parties to go back to a sensible sort of business.

And off to the west, farther and farther westward with each passing day, the shining rails of the great Union Pacific Railroad rolled across the vast, untrammeled continent.

||||||||||||||||||||||||||||||||||||||||||||||||||||||||||||||||||||||||||||||

SPECIAL PREVIEW!
If you enjoyed *NEBRASKA CROSSING,* here's
an exciting look at the third
book in the *RAILS WEST!* series,

WYOMING TERRITORY
. . . continuing the stirring epic of the courageous
men and women who built the Union Pacific
Railroad across the plains—to make America
one nation from shore to shore.

*Turn the page for an excerpt from
this bold new series from Franklin Carter.
Available in January 1994 from Jove Books . . .*

||||||||||||||||||||||||||||||||||||||||||||||||||||||||||||||||||||||||||||||

"You see anything yet?" William Thomas demanded, his breath driving steamy clouds from his mouth.

The repairman raised the feeble kerosene lamp a little higher. "I can't see more'n ten feet ahead. Darker than the bottom of a well tonight."

Thomas looked up at the slice of thin moon that kept dipping in and out of the low ceiling of clouds. There wasn't even any starlight. For the past hour, their little repair crew had been pumping and bumping along on the Union Pacific's new rails, stopping at every telegraph pole and carefully inspecting it before climbing back onto the pump-cart and continuing westward. Thomas estimated that they were now at least five miles from Plumb Creek.

"Mr. Thomas?"

"Yes?"

"How far are we going to go tonight?" Milt asked.

It was the question Thomas had anticipated and yet could not satisfactorily answer. "I don't exactly know. A little farther. If we don't find the break in the next mile or two, we'll turn around and head back out at first light. At least this way, I can tell management that we tried to find the break and get it repaired."

"That's all anybody could do," one of the repairmen

285

offered. "I think we've already given it a real honest try, Mr. Thomas."

It was true. They weren't all that far from the next telegraph office at Willow Island and Thomas knew that each foot they traveled diminished the chances that the break would be his repair crew's responsibility.

Over the clackety-click of the rails, Thomas heard a coyote's mournful howl. Off to the north he could see a glittering splinter of lightning reach down out of the heavy cloud cover and stab the dark plains. The wind was picking up and the temperature was dropping. Thomas thought that he could smell the approach of a storm. Snow would be more tolerable than a bone-chilling rain. And even this late in the year, it could still rain buckets on these open plains. Men could be killed by lightning. It had already happened to three unlucky Irishmen on Dodge's surveying crew in the Wyoming Territory.

For the next quarter of an hour, the men were silent, perhaps awed by the fury of the approaching storm. Occasionally, a huge lightning bolt would pierce the heavens and strike the earth then, a moment later, thunder would resound across the flat plains.

It was awesome and frightening.

William Thomas could feel the repairmen growing anxious. You couldn't shoot and kill a lightning bolt. Not like you could an Indian. He was about to say that it was time to turn back when suddenly the man holding the lantern cried out a warning. An instant later, Thomas heard a sharp, whirring sound like a pheasant launching into a hard wind. Only it wasn't a pheasant and when the man screamed and staggered, Thomas experienced a moment of sheer terror. The lantern and the man pitched off the hand-pump cart an instant before it struck a barricade and overturned.

Thomas lost his rifle in midair. He hit the rails and felt his ribs snap. A scream erupted from his throat and he struggled to get up and fight, or—God forgive him—run for his life.

But something was wrong with his knee. It betrayed him as he tried to rise and before he could quite gain his senses, he saw a shadow and heard the scream of a Sioux warrior. He twisted around and looked up to see a silhouette blacker than the angry sky.

"No, please!" he cried.

He punched upward and struck the Sioux warrior in the throat. The Indian's upraised war club chopped downward into his shoulder causing it to go completely numb. Thomas heard other men howling in pain and terror. There were two gunshots . . . or was it the thunder of the storm?

Thomas broke away from the gagging warrior and tried to run but his knee folded like paper and he fell from the roadbed into the deep prairie grass. He began to scramble away on his hands and knees, his mind threatening to unravel like a spool of twine. Maybe he could escape into the grass, somehow reach the Platte River and . . .

But the Indian was on him again. Thomas heard the Sioux's war club whistle as lightning flashed behind his eyes. He felt his long blonde hair being pulled violently upward until a moccasin pushed on the back of his neck and drove his face into the dirt, muffling his screams. He lost consciousness as the Sioux warrior took his scalp.

Thomas awoke bathed in a halo of fire. He did not want to awaken and was sure that he was dead. For a long, agonizing minute he lay still, feeling the wind freshen with the approaching storm. Over the roll of thunder, he could hear the ring of hammer striking steel. He raised his head as a bolt of lightning speared into the cottonwood trees clogging the banks of the Platte. One of the naked cottonwoods ignited like a pitch torch and Thomas witnessed the Sioux using the repairmen's tools to uncouple the rails and then twist them apart.

Dear Lord! These blood-thirsty savages knew that a west-bound supply train was coming and were determined that it should be derailed! Thomas rolled onto his stomach and wiggled deeper into the grass. His heart was pounding and his face was a mask of caked blood. All that he knew for certain was that he had to somehow warn the onrushing train's engineer that the tracks were separated. Otherwise, the train would derail and any survivors would be slaughtered just like his own repair crew.

Thomas reached the trees. He grabbed one and used it to pull himself to his feet. His knee was either broken or dislocated. He didn't know which and it didn't matter. He was afraid to touch what had been his scalp and could not even imagine what he must look like as he clung to the tree fighting the whipping wind and a deep belly sickness.

He tried to leave the tree with the idea of finding a stick to use as a crutch, or a cane. But the moment he began to leave, another bolt of lightning illuminated the surrealistic scene of the Sioux warriors dancing and howling in the storm. Thomas felt his body flood with paralyzing fear. This fear crystallized and shattered when he heard the lonesome whistle of the approaching train. Mindless of all else, he tried to intercept the train but fell. Pushing himself to his feet, he began to hop toward the blossoming oil-fired headlamp, bellowing a warning that could not possibly be heard by the engineer.

Somehow, Thomas reached the tracks. With the onrushing locomotive bearing down on him, he began to wave and hop up and down on one leg. The engineer saw him but only a moment before he could apply the brakes and Thomas was

struck by the cowcatcher, which spun his broken body high
into the air. The tortured screech of iron on iron overrode
the rumble of the summer storm and did not end until the
train slid off the twisted rails and crashed over sideways like
a team of lung-shot horses.

Six cars back in the only passenger coach on the Union
Pacific freight train, Aileen heard the terrible protesting
screech of the iron wheels as they smoked and burned against
the rails. At the same instant, she was hurled forward from her
bench seat and slammed hard against the sidewall. A moment
later, the world seemed to tilt crazily and a scream filled
Aileen's mouth as the coach yawed to the right. Balanced
on one set of wheels, the coach shuddered and rolled into
a nightmarish darkness.

"Jenny!" Aileen cried as she felt herself being lifted high
into the air and then hurled downward. A crushing weight
landed on her chest and Aileen struggled to breath as she
reached blindly for her daughter. "Jenny!"

Jenny began to cry somewhere. Her thin howl infused
Aileen with new life and she managed to throw off whatever
had pinned her to the side of the coach. Clawing her way
through the twisted benches and baggage, she found Jenny.
Pulling the terrified child to her bosom, she rocked Jenny.
Outside, they could both hear the triumphant howls of the
Sioux and the pitiful death cries of the supply train's crew.

"Oh my God!" Aileen prayed. "Jenny! Liam! God, help
us!"

In the darkness and chaos of the overturned caboose, Liam
found the money he had just lost at poker as well as a good
deal of the winners' money. All around him frenzied railroad
men were shouting and smashing at the windows and jammed

doors. Liam had no doubt that they would escape the caboose only to be cut down by the Sioux. His own plan, as soon as he'd groped around and was sure that there was no more loose money lying about, was to reach Aileen and Jenny, then try and hold out against the savages as long as there was any hope of rescue.

Glass shattered. Liam's fist closed on a few last dollars. He stuffed them into his pockets along with two pints of liquor. The men in the caboose broke through the jammed door and poured outside. Liam crouched and listened to the pounding hooves of the Indian ponies.

With one coat pocket full of money and the other filled with whiskey, he crawled to the door and watched as Indians on foot and on horseback raced up and down the overturned train. Several of the coaches were already engulfed in flames. The thought that Aileen and Jenny might be trapped by a raging inferno brought Liam to his feet. Taking a deep breath and drawing his six-gun, he jumped outside and ducked in close to the smoking wheels. When there was an opening, he raced forward like a rat sprinting for its hole. A Sioux noticed him, yipped in joyous anticipation and unleashed an arrow. Missing, he yelped in rage and his heels pelted his pony as he raced at Liam, intent on running him down.

Liam ducked under a smoking train wheel. The Indian jumped off his pony, drew a knife, and charged. Liam waited until the Indian was almost on top of him before driving the heel of his boot into the Indian's gut and stopping the attacker in his tracks. An instant later, Liam's fist smashed into the warrior's face. The Sioux collapsed and Liam grabbed the Indian's hair and used his knee twice with a bone-crushing effect. The Indian flopped over onto his back, twitching.

Moments later, Liam burst into the overturned passenger

coach. Fire and smoke filled his nostrils and burned his lungs. "Aileen! Jenny!"

He staggered forward, beating at the smoke and coughing violently. Over and over he called their names. Reacting with fear, he staggered backward knowing that Aileen and Jenny were gone.

Liam escaped through a window and threw himself up against the underside of the passenger coach. A sound close by sent his hand flashing for his gun.

"Don't kill us!" Aileen exclaimed out of the darkness.

Liam blinked with surprise. "Where are you!"

"Liam? Liam, we're back here under the coach. You got to help us. We're both hurt."

Liam pushed up hard under the coach and groped for the pair. No wonder they had not been found and scalped.

"How badly are you hurt?"

"I don't know!" Aileen whispered, throwing her arms around his neck and beginning to weep.

"Aileen! You've got to get ahold of yourself!"

She drew back. Liam could not see her face but he could imagine how frightened his sister must be as the Indians raced up and down the length of the train, killing the last of the white trainmen and smashing out windows with their stone war clubs.

"What on earth are we going to do?" Aileen asked in a trembling voice.

"I'm not sure yet." Liam reached out and his hand touched Jenny's skin which was cold. "Is she alive?"

"Yes, but she's hurt. I don't feel any bleeding but . . ."

"Shhh!"

Two warriors ran past, their legs flashing less than a yard from where Liam, Aileen, and Jenny crouched in hiding. Liam mopped a sheen of sweat from his brow. "We've got to get away from this train. If we can reach the river, we've got a chance."

A huge bolt of lightning flashed across the sky and the thunder that followed boomed so hard that even the iron horse trembled.

"Can you do that, Aileen? Can you run for the river?"

"My ribs are broken!"

Liam's hand locked on Aileen's shoulder and his fingers bit into her flesh until she whimpered. "Listen to me, damn it! If we don't get out of here before daybreak, we'll be slaughtered like everyone else. Is that what you want?"

"No, of course not!"

"Then broken ribs or not, you're going to run for those distant trees like you've never run before. I'll carry Jenny."

Aileen fell silent. Finally, Liam released his grip on her shoulder and said in a low, encouraging voice, "You escaped that burning coach and you're still alive. You can also get to the river, Aileen. We can do it together."

She nodded woodenly, but somehow found the courage to say, "Yes. Yes we can!"

"Good." Liam stood. "Hand Jenny to me."

"We're going to go now?"

Liam stuck his head out as far as he dared. Most of the Indians appeared to be gathered by the overturned locomotive tender around a huge bonfire. They were dancing around the fire, but a few were still on horseback, racing up and down the tracks looking for one last white man to kill.

Well, Liam thought, *it won't be me.*

"Give Jenny to me," he ordered, stretching out his arms for the child.

Liam threw Jenny over his left shoulder and drew his gun. His knees felt weak and he wanted to vomit from fear and whiskey but he couldn't afford that luxury.

"Let's go!"

He didn't wait to see if Aileen was following him but ran as hard as he could for the distant trees. His lungs were on fire and his leg muscles burned. Liam was sure that the Sioux would see him and Aileen but there was no time to even throw a quick glance toward the overturned locomotive. It seemed as if he ran a thousand miles before he threw himself headlong into the trees. Rolling Jenny off his shoulder, he crabbed around to see Aileen about forty yards behind. She was bent over and staggering.

"Come on! Come on!"

But Aileen couldn't move any faster. Even at a distance and over the sounds of the Indians and the storm, Liam could hear her ragged breathing. He stood up and began to move toward his sister but something caused him to turn his head. A lone warrior had spotted Aileen. Unnoticed by the other Sioux, this man had ranged out farther from the train tracks just in case someone had crawled off to die or to hide.

And now he saw Aileen and was rewarded.

Liam watched the Sioux's heels drum against his pony's ribs. Saw him raise a feathered war lance and come racing at Aileen who seemed oblivious to everything except reaching the cottonwood trees.

Liam swore in helpless fury. He didn't dare use his gun. That would certainly attract the entire war party and then there would not be enough trees in the entire territory to save his scalp.

Liam fumbled around in the dark forest until his hands found a heavy broken limb. He picked it up and as the mounted Indian bore down on Aileen, he rushed out of the trees and attacked.

The warrior was so intent on skewering Aileen that he did not see Liam until the last instant. The Indian tried to rein his horse at Liam but it was too late. The heavy limb caught him a glancing blow across the side of the head and the pony ran out from under him and into the Platte River.

Liam never gave the dazed warrior a second chance. He jumped onto the man's chest and beat his face until the Indian went limp. Jumping up, Liam ran back into the trees.

"We've got to get that pony!" he cried.

The Indian pony was spooked. It was standing knee deep in the slow but freezing current and when Liam rushed to the edge of the riverbank, the pony snorted with fear and edged deeper into the water.

"Whoa!" Liam said. "Whoa."

The horse snorted again. It did not want to go deeper into the river but neither did it seem to want to have anything to do with the white man who looked and smelled strange.

"Easy," Liam crooned, remembering how the Union Pacific's Joshua Hood had shown him how to calm a spooked horse.

He waded into the river, gritting his teeth against the cold. The thought entered his mind that he should retrieve Aileen and Jenny and wade downriver, being careful not to leave any tracks on the shoreline. But the Plumb Creek station was at least six or seven miles away and Liam did not think that he could carry Jenny that far or that Aileen could bear up to this bone-chilling water that long.

They needed the horse. Besides, after all they'd just been through, Liam was of the opinion that he richly deserved the glory of capturing a Sioux pony. It would be a fine thing to ride the animal all the way to Cheyenne wearing its Indian saddle. A fine thing that would turn heads and not be soon forgotten.

"Easy, horse," he crooned, slowly moving out into the swift, icy water.

Moments later, he had the animal by its horsehair bridle. The glow from the inferno now rapidly consuming the supply train was enough to reveal that the pony was a chestnut, one of Liam's favorite colors. Liam rubbed the animal's neck and spoke softly to it. After a minute, the pony nuzzled him and sighed. It dipped its head and drank deeply from the river.

Liam led the Indian pony back to the shallows noting with satisfaction that the Indian saddle had stirrups and a pad.

"Aileen, have you ever ridden a horse before?"

"You know that I haven't. And certainly not a wild animal like that one! Anyway, I can't . . ."

Liam reached out and grabbed his sister. She was thin and worrisome and it was easy to swing her up onto the pony's back. Aileen clutched at the animal's mane. It snorted and danced.

"Easy!" Liam said to his sister. "You're scarin' this horse and we need him."

Aileen bowed her head and took deep breaths. "What about Jenny? We're not leaving her."

"Of course not!"

Liam picked up the child and eased Jenny up onto the pony's sharp withers. "You hold her and I'll lead the horse downriver so that we leave no tracks."

"But they'll find its owner in the morning! They'll know that we escaped."

"You're right," Liam said. He led the pony over to a half submerged tree and tied it. Then, ignoring Aileen's protestations, he sneaked back out to where the unconscious Indian lay. Grabbing up the man's war lance, he buried it into the Sioux's chest, then grabbed the dead Indian by the hair with one hand and returned to the river.

When Aileen saw the body and realized what her brother had done, she turned away and began to retch. Ignoring her,

Liam dragged the Sioux's corpse out into the strong current and let it float away.

"Hang on just as tight as you can to Jenny," Liam advised before he started leading the pony downriver.

Liam knew that he had left tracks on the riverbank and that the Sioux would pick up those tracks at first light. That's why they had to reach safety before morning.

A bolt of lightning struck and ignited another cottonwood. The pony tried to pull away. Aileen whimpered in fear until Liam got the pony back under control. He was so cold that his teeth were chattering as he watched the burning tree. The heavens opened up and sleet began to sweep across the Platte River.

It was miserable. Worse than miserable. The cottonwood branches overhead began to whip at the driving sleet as the wind moaned.

Good, Liam thought as he led the frightened pony out of the river. It will drive the Sioux to shelter and maybe even cover our tracks.

*A STIRRING NEW SERIES OF THE BRAVE PIONEERS WHO
BUILT THE MIGHTY RAILROADS OF A NEW FRONTIER*

RAILS WEST!

Franklin Carter

When the Civil War ended, America turned West, and so the
race began to build a railroad across the Plains to the
Pacific. *Rails West!* is the magnificent saga of the courageous Americans who made the Union Pacific, the Great
Northern, the Atchison, Topeka and Santa Fe a reality. From
wealthy magnates who gambled their fortunes on the grand
enterprise to hard-living laborers who drove the spikes,
here are the dramatic novels of the men and women who met
the challenge, and opened the door to a new continent.

__RAILS WEST!   0-515-11099-X/$4.99
__NEBRASKA CROSSING   0-515-11205-4/$4.99
Look for the next novel in the series, Wyoming
Territory, *coming in January 1994.*

For Visa, MasterCard and American Express ($15 minimum) orders call: 1-800-631-8571

FOR MAIL ORDERS: CHECK BOOK(S). FILL OUT COUPON. SEND TO:	POSTAGE AND HANDLING: $1.75 for one book, 75¢ for each additional. Do not exceed $5.50.
BERKLEY PUBLISHING GROUP 390 Murray Hill Pkwy., Dept. B East Rutherford, NJ 07073	BOOK TOTAL $ _____
	POSTAGE & HANDLING $ _____
NAME_____	APPLICABLE SALES TAX $ _____
ADDRESS_____	(CA, NJ, NY, PA)
CITY_____	TOTAL AMOUNT DUE $ _____
STATE_____ ZIP_____	PAYABLE IN US FUNDS.
PLEASE ALLOW 6 WEEKS FOR DELIVERY. PRICES ARE SUBJECT TO CHANGE WITHOUT NOTICE.	(No cash orders accepted.)

431

FROM THE AWARD-WINNING AUTHOR OF
RIVERS WEST: THE COLORADO, HERE IS THE SPRAWLING
EPIC STORY OF ONE FAMILY'S BRAVE STRUGGLE
FOR THE AMERICAN DREAM.

THE HORSEMEN

Gary McCarthy

The Ballous were the finest horsemen in the South, a
Tennessee family famous for the training and breeding of
thoroughbreds. When the Civil War devastated their home
and their lives, they headed West—into the heart of Indian
territory. As a family, they endured. As horsemen, they
triumphed. But as pioneers in a new land, they faced
unimaginable hardship, danger, and ruthless enemies...

__THE HORSEMEN 1-55773-733-9/$3.99
__CHEROKEE LIGHTHORSE 1-55773-797-5/$3.99
__TEXAS MUSTANGERS 1-55773-857-2/$3.99
__BLUE BULLET 1-55773-944-7/$3.99

For Visa, MasterCard and American Express ($15 minimum) orders call: 1-800-631-8571

FOR MAIL ORDERS: CHECK BOOK(S). FILL
OUT COUPON. SEND TO:

BERKLEY PUBLISHING GROUP
390 Murray Hill Pkwy., Dept. B
East Rutherford, NJ 07073

NAME————————————

ADDRESS————————————

CITY————————————

STATE——————— ZIP—————

PLEASE ALLOW 6 WEEKS FOR DELIVERY.
PRICES ARE SUBJECT TO CHANGE WITHOUT NOTICE.

POSTAGE AND HANDLING:
$1.75 for one book, 75¢ for each
additional. Do not exceed $5.50.

BOOK TOTAL	$ _____
POSTAGE & HANDLING	$ _____
APPLICABLE SALES TAX	$ _____
(CA, NJ, NY, PA)	
TOTAL AMOUNT DUE	$ _____
PAYABLE IN US FUNDS.	

(No cash orders accepted.)

440